"*The Arcanum*: Harry Potter meets *Sea Hunt* in this delightful tale of families, friendships, and fiends who struggle to keep a dark secret from the young brothers whose childhood is swept away by hidden forces. L. J. Litton's debut novel delivers on all levels and is sure to delight young and old with its well-drawn characters, plot twists, and mix of science and sorcery."

> —S. W. O'Connell, award-winning author of Yankee Doodle Spies historical fiction series, retired United States Army officer

"This is much more than a young adult book. This is a multi-generational book written at the level of Cussler and Clancy that challenges and excites the reader along a winding path of adventure."

> —Tom Lintner, renowned international aviation expert, licensed airline transport pilot, former USCG-licensed captain–international waters, certified PADI dive master, author and entrepreneur

"A complex fantasy set in an indeterminate time with medieval, contemporary, and futuristic elements, *The Arcanum* is a good read that challenges readers to appreciate the intricacies of the story. Separated from a powerful ancestral family with a troubled and complicated history, the Gordons' youngest generation navigates a treacherous world of family and foe—as they seek their own identities and come to understand their own special abilities.

"The author's knowledge of such disparate settings as large meetings of global leaders and deep-sea diving and exploration adds authenticity and grounds the story—effectively spanning reality and fantasy."

> —Jan Umphrey, editor, adjunct university professor of literature and composition, and former associate publications director at a national education association

The Arcanum:
Bradley Gordon's First Adventure

by L.J. Litton

Published by

3705 Shore Drive
Virginia Beach, VA 23455
800-435-4811
www.koehlerbooks.com

THE
ARCANUM

BRADLEY GORDON'S FIRST ADVENTURE

L.J. LITTON

VIRGINIA BEACH
CAPE CHARLES

I dedicate The Arcanum *to my soulmate and life partner, Michael Robert Litton, whose support and encouragement fueled my inspiration and creativity.*

TABLE OF
CONTENTS

Chapter One: Venere. 11

Chapter Two: Amazon 26

Chapter Three: Precaveros 33

Chapter Four: Solana 38

Chapter Five: Aftermath. 44

Chapter Six: Nopar 57

Chapter Seven: The Choosing. 67

Chapter Eight: Michael 73

Chapter Nine: Adventure Begins 82

Chapter Ten: Spurt of Energy 97

Chapter Eleven: Jay. 103

Chapter Twelve: Strangers. 109

Chapter Thirteen: The Arrangement 120

Chapter Fourteen: Long John. 130

Chapter Fifteen: Quentin 148

Chapter Sixteen: Treasure Revealed 154

Chapter Seventeen: Seth 162

Chapter Eighteen: Entrapment. 170

Chapter Nineteen: Celtston Elders. 181

Chapter Twenty: Tristen 197

Chapter Twenty-One: The Pursuit 206

Chapter Twenty-Two: Peter 211

Chapter Twenty-Three: Foregone Conclusion 230

Chapter Twenty-Four: Night Dive 236

Chapter Twenty-Five: Thwarted 244

Acknowledgments. 250

Glossary of Terms 251

PROLOGUE

On a cool autumn night, Lord Veldor Gordon emerged from the fog on the bogs of a dark Scottish moor with no witness to question from where he came or to where he was bound. Anyone present would have been relieved to see Veldor on his way—grateful they were passed unnoticed.

Veldor stood six feet five inches, with a broad brow set off by blond hair and steel-blue eyes. He had an air of strength bolstered by his imposing stature. A tightly groomed beard framed his face and fit well with his chain mail and leather.

He walked rapidly, with a long stride and familiarity with this place and its peril. His sword hung close to a sapphire-adorned, sheathed dagger, his crossbow slung over his left shoulder. A man came running behind him, smaller than Veldor, but with the same Gordon clan facial features and dress—but armed with only a sword. Veldor's youngest brother, Andrew, did not fear approaching but dreaded the encounter.

Veldor sensed a presence before he heard footsteps, and turned to confront his intruder, relieved it was only Andrew.

"Veldor, don't take the side of an outsider! Robert would never do that to you. *Please . . .* please, reconsider."

"I'm sworn to this duty. You should be helping me. Robert must turn Tristen over to the Veneré to undergo the *Kupellation*. We both know he'll fail the test and will be returned to his parents. Only then, can we put this nasty business aside, and get Robert back in the good graces of our fellowship."

"You're brothers, you've fought together in battle, protected each other. Protect him now, as he protected you!" Andrew pleaded. "You ignore the reasons that should sway you from your course. This task is based in folly; to continue is to put the Gordon dynasty at risk."

Veldor stood silent, ignoring his younger brother. Undaunted, Andrew persisted. "Robert has a duty to protect his only son. What would you do if he were yours?"

Andrew grabbed Veldor's arm, forcing eye contact. "Let the child be. If all is as you say, time will reveal the falsity of these accusations. If you bring Tristen in like a suspected Arcanum, he may not live to manhood. Think about what you're doing."

"You should be ashamed of yourself. Our heritage means more than the machinations of a few pawns. The Veneré's responsibilities are much greater than yours, Robert's or mine," Veldor scolded, pushing Andrew aside as he continued on his way, not bothering to look back and Andrew knowing well enough not to follow.

Within minutes Veldor arrived at a lone rowboat beached on the shore. He swiftly boarded and started rowing across the calm narrow river tributary. The surface of the water, a large unbound mirror, reflected the pale-yellow full moon filling the western horizon of the night sky. He was lost in thought, blinded to the beauty of his surroundings as he neared the Gordon castle lands.

"I pray I'm not too late," he muttered to himself, pulling heavily at the oars.

I must be more successful with Michele than I've been with Robert. After all, she is the mother to the only male Gordon heir in our bloodline. The idea that Tristen could be an Arcanum, a reputed great mystery of nature—much less the True Knowing One and possessing abilities beyond all others—is absurd.

Veldor was aware that recorded history showed only one *True Knowing One* existing at any given time, once a millennium. Hence his name, *The Millenarian,* could choose to bring peace and tranquility, where all could enjoy prosperity and justice with his great powers.

The official written chronicles documented the potential for pain, suffering, world dominance and destruction should the Millenarian pursue power over benevolence. It's for this reason the Veneré came into being—to locate and to shepherd the Millenarian towards the pursuit of man's enlightenment and enrichment, and to steer him away from gaining a lust for power over all else. There existed much concern among the ranks because this millennium was closing and he had not yet been found, causing some to doubt his coming.

Veldor dug the oars into the silt bottom to get the boat as close to dry land as possible. *If the Millenarian is to bring forth such a wondrous state,* he thought, *why should anyone fear the unlikely chance Tristen is found to be him? Something is amiss here. I will press the issue with the Veneré at our next encounter.*

Tristin's fate is certain if the Veneré consider him dangerous or unwilling to protect the secrets they hold so dear.

The bow crunched into the broken shells and pebbles on the small beach leading up to the peak on which sat the magnificent Gordon castle. Veldor set aside troublesome thoughts, confident that his godson would work well with the Veneré. It was why he could betray the trust of his own brother. To think otherwise would prevent him carrying out his duty as leader of the Gordon Chivalran, one of the elite Chivalran regiments located strategically throughout the globe, charged with the responsibility of finding and dealing with the reprobate Arcanums at the behest of the Veneré. Veldor wasn't going to be the first to fail.

His own father ended the life of their local vicar's son, who could manipulate material. The Veneré had deemed him a threat, so Veldor hunted him down and slew the boy with a dagger to the heart, leaving the child lifeless upon his father's church steps.

Veldor laid the oars down and glared at the castle atop the steep cliff overlooking the bay, sitting a thousand feet above sea level. He had lived there his entire life, yet still he marveled at the fortress that made castles of lore and legend appear lesser by comparison.

He disembarked and started the mile-long trek up the precipitous hillside to the castle, grabbing onto rocks to pull him up and over sections where the vertical climb steepened. At the top, he planned to enter the fortification by way of a perilous cliff-side hidden entrance.

Upon arrival, he glanced at the waves violently crashing against the rocks two-hundred feet below, realizing he had never attempted this feat carrying weaponry. He knew his next maneuver would be challenging. He carefully felt along the backside of the L-shaped stone wall until he found the rusty steel rung that tore at his bare hands as he swung himself around the corner, landing on a stone ledge, where he reached up and tightly grabbed the next rung, and climbed to the concealed entrance. His fingers and palms bled where rusty edges had ripped into them.

Veldor reflected for a moment, stirred by the salty air and cool breeze, happy to be alive. He thought back to when he had discovered this entrance as a boy while playing with Robert and Andrew. Only they knew of the entrance, a tightly held secret, as he hoped this messy affair would stay.

Veldor exhaled and tucked in his stomach as he squeezed into the narrow passage. In no time, he came upon the backside of the heavy tapestry concealing the clandestine entryway. With some effort, he carefully pushed the weighty tapestry out far enough to look both ways down the dimly lit stone corridor void of any other décor. Seeing and hearing no one, he strode towards the light of what he knew to be multiple oil lamps illuminating the servants' main space, the hub that allowed the domestics to move unnoticed about the castle while performing their chores.

This hub was a twenty- by thirty-foot oval-shaped, gray stone-walled room with a twelve-foot-high polished stone overhead. The walls were made visible by slender glass chimney-adorned oil lamps, sitting atop two-foot-wide stone shelves recessed into the walls and spread throughout the room. Seven passageways intersected the space.

As Veldor stepped into the hub, Robert and Michele emerged from the far-right corridor.

"Where would you be going with little Tristen in your arms, burdened with bags and cloaked for travel?" scoffed Veldor as he slowly walked towards the fugitives.

At the sight of Veldor, Robert, feeling the threat of his brother's advance, quickly positioned himself in front of his family. Michele crouched low behind her husband, slowly retreated into the passageway.

"I was hoping to convince Michele to comply with the wishes of the Veneré this night, and then I wouldn't need to discuss the issue with you again. After all, how could a mere toddler be dangerous?" Veldor reasoned. "Neither of us possess any of these special gifts the Veneré speak of, but we've definitely witnessed them on several occasions in council chambers. We both know the Veneré's concerns about Tristen have merit, but I never observed him doing anything remotely like what I witnessed. They're able to make people pass out with their minds being the only weapon deployed . . . definitely cause for concern. I've not seen Tristen express such abilities, have you?"

Veldor received only a blank stare and continued.

"You were heading straight to the underground marina stairwell. The sea is your chosen path to freedom? You know we would come after you."

"I'd hoped to be gone by now, and my son's whereabouts would no longer be yours or anyone else's concern," Robert replied.

"Robert, you've always been unwilling to bow to authority, the reason you were denied your birthright to be a commanding officer of the Gordon Chivalran. You're fortunate to have been allowed in the regiment at all. You never stop questioning the logic of the traditions that make us who we are. Your constant attack on centuries-old Veneré practices has done nothing to better your standing. The world's continued existence without a full-scale global war is *proof* that the Veneré's ways and means are sound, and that yours are not. Yet, once again you mean to defy them. You have to know that if you flee, Rosen wins. The Veneré will side with their leader over you." Veldor paused to allow his brother one last rebuttal.

Robert, aware of the courtesy being extended chose his words carefully. "How can you consider turning Tristen, your nephew, over to the Veneré after what we've seen happens to the young boys found to possess abilities? They either become one of the Veneré's special abilities cadre or disappear. Few live beyond adolescence. He'll be lost to us forever! It's ludicrous to think that a Chivalran's off-spring could be an Arcanum. It is contrary to our written history. Have you never questioned the motives behind what's being asked of us? *None* of this makes any sense."

Veldor countered. "It's my fortune to have fathered two daughters, so I don't have to worry about either of them being the Arcanum. They're not male heirs of parents with only one child, like Tristen. I agree with one thing you've said brother: your attempt to flee makes no sense."

"Are you willing to pay the price of losing our dynasty to one of our Gordon surnamed cousins with the required male lineage if Tristen is lost to the Veneré? You're gambling that one of us gives birth to another male heir. When did you become so reckless?" rebuked Robert. "You are either with me, or against me. Are you nothing more than a lemming who cares not for his family? Please brother, step aside . . . or die."

Both men took a step back, slowly drawing their swords, their eyes locked. Robert moved slowly, shifting the fight away from his wife and child. The clashing swords reverberated off the walls, echoing throughout the underground stone passageways.

Veldor's superior swordsmanship dominated as the two men tired from the onslaught. He gained the offensive, sweat pouring from their brows, his younger brother forced to slowly retreat to the far side of the chamber.

Michele looked on in horror and disbelief, unable to speak, unable to move as she witnessed Robert fall against the wall. He was barely able to stay up on one knee, the result of a deep slice to his unshielded right calf. He grimaced in pain.

"Had enough?" demanded Veldor as he briefly stepped back.

"Can we leave?" gasped Robert.

"No."

Robert forced himself up from his knee to stand one legged against the wall, his watery eyes barely able to focus from the searing pain of his wound. He lifted his sword as Veldor charged.

"Veldor, stop! Don't *murder* your own flesh and blood," pleaded Michele.

Robert's situation worsened with each blow, sword still in hand, still determined to protect his loved ones, but with little hope he could overcome his older brother. The loss of blood sapped his strength as Veldor pressed his advantage.

Unbeknownst to Robert, Veldor didn't want to kill him. He only wanted to incapacitate him so he could take the child to the Veneré to undergo the Kupellation. He believed that given time, Robert would understand, and everything would be as it had been between them.

"Our family legacy is what makes us who we are," Veldor said. "I will see to it that Rosen and the others treat Tristen honorably."

Veldor felt a sharp pain in the back of his head. He had only a moment of astonishment before his eyes went blurry and he felt himself falling, unable to move a muscle, as if in a dream. As he fell, his sword went awry, striking Robert's midsection, slicing through his abdomen and spilling out his entrails. Veldor fell atop his brother's ravaged, bloody body as the two of them hit the stone floor with a *thud*.

"Robert!" screamed Michele, running over to where the two men fell, frantically laying her blanketed son down on the cold stone floor. She grabbed Robert's face. "Robert, look at me!"

His bright steel blue eyes opened momentarily. He smiled lovingly at her while simultaneously his lungs expelled their last breath.

"Robert . . . no, no, this can't be happening. Please say something, anything."

Out of the corner of her eye, she spied Andrew standing there, holding a cudgel in his right hand and looking utterly dismayed.

"What did you do?" she sobbed.

"I only wanted to knock him out to give Robert the time he needed to get the two of you to safety . . . not this!"

Michele pleaded. "Robert, please don't leave me." But he just lay there, his face ashen, his body already starting to lose its warmth. She wept as her body convulsed.

"Look at what you've done! You caused Veldor to disembowel him!" screamed Michele.

"I didn't mean to," exclaimed Andrew as he began pacing. "This is not what I set out to do. I've only made things worse for everyone! They're dead, and you and the child are in serious trouble."

Andrew stopped pacing to look at Michele. "I must take Robert's place and accompany you. I have to save Tristen to honor my brother's wishes. His son must live to become the hereditary ruler of the Gordon dynasty. I'm the only one who can make sure this happens, now."

He walked over and gently pulled the weeping Michele from Robert's lifeless body. He helped her gather up her son and their few personal belongings, leading them out of the chamber through a passageway, where they found the spiral stone stairwell leading to the marina.

Halfway down the steps, Michele attempted to pull herself away from Andrew. "I can't leave him."

Andrew reached up and grabbed her hand, pulling it firmly against his chest to get her attention, "We have to get out of here. No one knows you three were leaving. Robert told me the plan was that they wouldn't find out you had gone until the morning. Dawn's light will shine within the hour. The domestics will rise to start their chores, and it will become known you are not in your beds. Stop resisting the inevitable. Come with me. I cannot protect you from the Chivalran *and* the Veneré. Once the bodies are found, they will turn the countryside inside-out hunting down their assailants. We must be long gone before then. What is done is done. Tristen's fate is all that matters now. I will care for you and him in Robert's stead to atone for my misdeed. I will bring Tristen back to rule the Gordon dynasty when the time is right, but now we *must* flee."

The fugitives arrived at the mooring place of their skiff to freedom within minutes. Michele was awestruck by the sparkling quartz overhead that rose to a height of one hundred feet, accompanied by a glistening, stone, horseshoe-shaped walkway that overlooked the brightly lit marina, illuminated by too many oil lamps to count.

"I didn't know this place was down here. What else has been kept from me? There's so much I don't know . . . don't understand."

During their careful descent down the forty-two stone steps to the wooden docks, Andrew explained.

"The Gordon Chivalran built this boat launch centuries ago for their exclusive usage. It has never been used by the Gordon household so there hasn't been a need for you to know it existed. The Chivalran have a special cadre of servants who ensure the lamps are illuminated and tend to the boats and the marina."

"Tristin is all I have left. Will you be able to place his needs over yours? I must know your answer before I leave this place with you."

"My nephew's survival and wellbeing is now my life's *only* pursuit. I'm sworn to right the wrong I've caused you this night."

They walked down to the uncomfortably quiet dock area, absent of any human presence, the silence intermittently interrupted by the soft splash of an errant wave tunneling into the enclosure.

They soon arrived at the larger of several rowboats moored nearest to the sea egress. Once on board, they quickly shoved their belongings below the back seat. Michele sat while Andrew freed the mooring lines. With one strong shove, he pushed the boat away from its berthing and took a seat.

One long hard stroke on the oars, followed by another, advanced the boat out into the bay to meet up with the schooner Robert had scheduled to take him and his family to a safe haven—a mysterious destination located somewhere in the Americas.

CHAPTER ONE

VENERÉ

Thirty-five years had passed since the *Gordon incident*, as it became known, and things had quieted down in Scotland. However, in other parts of the world, not so much.

A special meeting of the Veneré had been called to take place in the high hall of the Rosen estate, a fortress rising 800 feet at its tallest turret. It was built with seven-by-five-foot grey granite stone block walls that were four feet deep, now shielded with modern-day impregnable glass windows that disallowed the unsanctioned transfer of information in and out of the castle.

The estate had been erected centuries earlier in the thick grasslands and forested terrain of the lush Scottish meadowlands, and was located at the foot of the mountains at Inverness. Inverness, known as the *Capital of the Highlands*, offered a gateway to the sea, the same gateway Andrew, Michele and Tristen Gordon used to seek their freedom.

The Rosen estate was an integral part of Scotland's destiny. No one was privy to its part in all that had come to pass, nor could they know its influence on the future. The Rosen castle was not just absent from tourist maps, but all maps, due to the surreptitious influence of the Veneré. Only a select few people in the world were aware of its existence, and fewer still were ever asked to visit.

The height of the mountainous terrain and vastness of the grounds and surrounding forest lands veiled the castle in the secluded valley, allowing the occupants the privacy they desired.

Seth McLeod was the leader of the estate's team of security experts, who were all former members of the special forces of the armies they had served. He stood five feet, eleven inches tall, often wearing black pants, black shoes, a grey-black long-sleeved turtleneck shirt, and a black leather jacket that complemented his dark brown eyes and hair laced with gray. A walking cliché, but still his attire flattered him, a deliberate choice to emphasize his youthful countenance for a man of forty-five years.

He trusted no one else to make the last security check of the room where the Veneré would meet this day, because of the supreme importance of the event and those attending. As Seth entered the square-shaped meeting hall, he glanced up at the ceiling of the immense room, as if looking at it for the first time, done purposefully to ensure he missed no inconsistencies. He marveled at the ceiling's vaulted thirty-seven foot height, with its ornate ceramic floral patterns, boxed in by an intricate braided rope border. A centrally located chandelier, five-feet in diameter and made of pure gold, rubies and opals, illuminated the contents of the room, a reminder of the excesses of the past. The Rosen family colors of gold, red, and white decorated the entire room, and along with the smell of silver birch ablaze in the sofa-sized fireplace, established a flamboyant yet peaceful ambiance.

Seth watched manor-owner Elias Rosen's house staff and personal assistant finishing up the final touches of the table settings as they situated the utensils and porcelain to accommodate the food and drink to come and set down the reading and writing materials.

Seth made his way to the exit, slowly walking around the hall, looking up and down the walls. He admired the solid mahogany panels that were interrupted by a massive interlocking bookshelf system hosting an enormous collection of limited-edition, leather-bound books. The topics covered advanced mathematics, Newtonian and quantum physics, material sciences, geology, biology, a myriad of languages, global history of war and international law—the laws of the land and the sea. Elias Rosen, known to all simply as Rosen, had an insatiable appetite for knowledge.

Seth's thoughts were interrupted by a long and loud *bong... bong* announcing that the first of the Veneré had arrived. His final check completed, he gave a quick nod signifying everything was good-to-go to Rosen, who entered on the other side of the room. Seth slid the great hall's twelve-foot-high and three-inches-thick, steel-cored wooden doors into their opposing recesses, and slipped away, leaving Rosen to greet his associates.

The Veneré arrived one at a time, five men and one woman, dressed in exquisite, tailored silk suits, shirts and ties. They wore gold and silver cufflinks and tie pins accentuated with an array of jewels, and the finest handmade leather shoes and belts. They hailed from around the globe—Korea, Australia, Italy, France, Austria, Scotland, and the United States. All with unique and distinct ties to all the Chivalran regiments located in their individual regions of responsibility. Each was a descendent of their respective houses and so named, each with responsibilities and duties so great only they could attend this special session.

Once all members were present and it appeared everyone had a chance to exchange greetings, Rosen called the room to order in a raised but congenial voice.

"Good afternoon, everyone. I want to thank you for coming on such short notice and with so little information provided to convey the need for this special in-person session. I think it's time we get started. Could everyone please take your seats?"

The attendees assumed their places at the massive hand-carved solid mahogany table that could easily accommodate twenty people. They were seated comfortably in tall wooden high-backed chairs with over-stuffed velvet cushioning, each chair its own throne. The distance separating the participants allowed each enough room to comfortably take notes, while effectively discouraging side conversations, thus affording the venue chair control over discussions. This arrangement worked well over the ages, as Rosen hoped it would today.

He glanced around the table observing the mannerisms of his associates.

When the members were settled into their seats and had what they needed, the last of the domestics left the room, quietly opening and shutting the doors behind them. Rosen started the proceedings.

"I called you here today because we may have a rebel or a traitor in our midst—potentially more than one. I'm not sure how to refer to them. Of course, I'm confident that the traitor or traitors are not one of *us*, but they are ones we thought to be trustworthy within our ranks."

All motion at the table ceased as everyone turned their heads toward Rosen.

"We've been concerned for some time with the variations in our mission success rates. We have too much to do with the scarce resources we currently have deployed. We are responsible to manage things beyond that which we have read or heard about from disparate news sources. I believe none of you would disagree that global affairs have become *too* chaotic, and it's almost impossible for us to positively influence the outcomes of events that, in years past, would be of little or no consequence. Marginally successful missions, or even worse, failed missions, are unacceptable in these times. The lesser behaviors of mankind are prevailing at unprecedented levels never documented in our history, save during events such as the rise and fall of empires and dynasties, horrific natural disasters or other global catastrophes."

A few of the attendees started flipping through the stack of papers in front of them when they began to lose interest in Rosen's diatribe. Rosen noticed and quickly honed-in on the pertinent conversation.

"My concern is closer to home. While intricately related to the ever-increasing global turmoil, I think you'll find my news disturbs you on a more personal level. I believe we have missed an Arcanum who could very well be the True Knowing One—the Millenarian. There could be no better time for us to unveil such a person. While this *someone* eludes us, their abilities grow, yet they've been hidden from us. We must ask ourselves why? Who could hide such an occurrence?"

The members sat upright and stiffened as they looked around the room at their contemporaries with inquisitive expressions.

"The *who* is one of our trusted lieutenants. I expect that at first, you'll have trouble believing, as did I. You'll want what I'm telling you to be untrue."

Rosen paused as he glanced around the room, while allowing his words to sink in.

"The undocumented Arcanum is the daughter of Chief Solano Misticato of the Misticato Chivalran, his oldest child and heir to the vast mineral-rich Precaveros tribal lands, Solana Jeju Misticato-Gordon. We missed finding her as a child because we were looking for a boy and an only child. This situation is an enigma, one we cannot ignore. These unique circumstances are why we hadn't found her, and why she's been able to grow so old and her abilities so advanced. She's twenty-nine years old and we don't yet understand the total scope of her talents.

"She has parented two male children. We've yet to discern if they possess any special abilities. But even more disconcerting, these boys are the sons of Tristen Gordon, making them the grandchildren of Lord Robert and Lady Michele Gordon, as well as Chief Solano, himself."

All the participants cast looks of disbelief, some gasping.

"I know this is a lot to take in. I also realize the Gordon family aspect of the information brings into question the genesis of my concerns about Solana. It could make you wonder if my motives for bringing any of this to light are pure. Am I attempting to cover up the sins of my father? Or am I afraid the Gordon family's rightful heirs will be returned to power, and unseat my kin so nicely positioned in the Gordon Chivalran regiment?"

Rosen could tell from his associates' expressions that he had succinctly summarized their thoughts.

"I know this brings into question anything else I have to say and may make you feel uncomfortable about supporting any actions I propose. You will ask yourselves how you can trust what I'm saying when my family has much to lose. I tell you now, if I had wanted to handle this without your knowledge, I have the resources to have done so. Instead," he said, as he stretched out his arms, "here I am, letting you know what I found out, to allow *us* to figure out the best courses of action."

Within seconds of Rosen's conclusion, accusations among the attendants started to fly, the first from Melensen Glomar. Glomar was a direct descendent of one of the lesser known families that established North America, the youngest of the Veneré.

"How can we be sure this isn't personal?" he said to Rosen. "Your father was known to act rashly at times, and to make accusations that weren't supported out of personal vendettas. We've seen the documents. It's hard for me to trust your motives when it comes to the Gordons."

Rosen stood, pounded his hands on the table as he addressed Glomar with a stare that rattled even the bravest amongst the Veneré.

"What are you implying? Are you accusing me of attempting to defame the innocent for personal gain or to save my own reputation? Do you believe I would falsely accuse one of our own colleagues with no basis to support my findings? You really think so little of me?" he emphatically replied.

Glomar relented. "I'm not meaning to *imply* anything. My questions are legitimate. The fact is, I don't want your claim to be true. Your announcement is damning and makes for a treacherous situation that could unravel the fabric of our entire dominion."

André Angelic Puritité of France leaned forward in his chair, placing his elbows on the table as he interlaced his fingers, capturing the attention of those sitting around the table. In a low, mildly-accentuated voice, he cautioned the attendees.

"I'd like us to be careful that we don't unwittingly do anything to cause an uncontrolled panic. While panic can be a useful tool, I think it prudent we don't take actions we may regret later."

Rosen looked at André, who had only been allowed to join the Veneré because his older brother, Felipe, died carrying out a dangerous assignment levied upon him by the Veneré. He died a hero and the Veneré got André. Rosen didn't feel the need to respond and give André's advice any credence. Silent contempt served him better.

Seated to the right of André, a man partially rose from his chair and leaned his outstretched hands on the table. Bentley Helleon of Austria was an imposing man of European aristocracy and the longest-serving Veneré member.

Bentley addressed the room while staring down Rosen.

"I must admit I'm entertaining a fear that this is all about your family retaining the unrightfully gained positions assumed on the Gordon Chivalran High Council. It's inconceivable a member of the Veneré also has a highly placed family in a Chivalran regiment. This incident only goes to show us all why we must correct the imbalance—*this* impropriety. It should've been rectified long ago."

Bentley, lowering his tone, continued.

"The appearance that any decision we make could actually personally benefit one of us bodes poorly for us all. It calls into question the basis for the outcome of any decisions being made. Surely you must understand this, Elias."

Rosen's face flushed pink. Bentley angered him, but Rosen could ill afford to respond like he felt. He drew a long breath, waiting to calm himself and gain some modicum of composure. Speaking almost in a whisper, Rosen responded.

"You muddy these discussions by talking of things long past, things that require *no* remedy."

Bentley countered. "All you've offered thus far is your dire concern. I don't think you can blame us for stating we need more. We need facts from a reliable independent source. Whether you like it or not, your family's intrusion into the upper echelon of the Gordon Chivalran has never been accepted; it's barely tolerated. What happens next could cause great turmoil in our ranks if we don't act prudently, and from an integrity-based position that no one can challenge. If not, more than a threat of a non-identified Arcanum will plague us. You have made unfounded accusations against Chief Solano, who has shown us no ill intent and who has our respect.

"What's more, when the Chivalran find out Tristen Gordon is alive, and if he's found to be free of special abilities, it will present its own challenges. Pursuing his wife may not be the most prudent thing for us to do right now. We need to first conduct a comprehensive investigation."

André jumped back into the fray.

"I'm gravely concerned that the next words out of your mouth will be a proposal for us to act against Chief Solano. It could result in turning the Chivalran regiments against us. The Veneré have acted in the past based upon mere supposition, and the incidents didn't sit well with the Chivalran. If it turns out Tristen is a normal man, possessing no special ability that would've warranted past actions, there's no telling how this will affect our rank and file."

"André is on to something," Glomar added, directing his remarks at Rosen. "Whether you like it or not, your father's reputation for acting on personal vendettas is earned. We need to tread lightly so that you, too don't become so-known. People will look to see if the son is like the father."

The participants murmured in agreement.

"It has been many years since the Gordon incident occurred and *yes*, it is of issue, but Solana's abilities are real and appropriate actions must be taken forthwith," insisted Rosen.

"Another concern I have is that Chief Solano won't take these accusations lightly," Glomar said. "His daughter is slated to take over the leadership of the Misticato Chivalran regiment when he steps down within the next few years. Are we willing to risk hindering this change of command? Chief Solano is held in high regard by the other Chivalran, and we'll be openly questioning his honor. Let's be clear here. You're accusing him of sheltering an Arcanum and providing sanctuary to refugees from the Veneré. If what you're espousing is true, the consequences for him and Solana would be dire."

Bentley's face, now a deep red with beads of sweat, challenged Rosen.

"Do you have any tangible facts that support these outrageous charges against Chief Solano and his daughter? We need something substantial before I'll agree to any pursuit."

Rosen, feeling the heat of intense emotions, replied in a courtroom-like fashion.

"I sent a Gordon family emissary you all know and respect, Michael Patrick Gordon. His loyalties run deep, as you are well aware. He witnessed Solana using her special abilities while on an assignment. I'm certain none of you will have any problem believing the independent accounting of what he saw. He witnessed Solana manipulating matter, and he saw her conducting an out-of-body experience where she remotely spied on one of her targets to gain intel prior to carrying out an operation. He also videotaped her picking flowers without using her hands. She merely concentrated on a section of wildflowers that parted at their lower extremities, as if cut with shears, and then flew to her awaiting hands, where she smelled the fresh bouquet. All of this is documented in Michael Patrick's written report sitting in front of you, including copies of the frames taken from the video he shot of both events. These two actions are nonthreatening in and of themselves, but I believe we need to know to what extent her talents have matured, and if she possesses any others. Are these facts tangible enough?"

The facial expressions of each of the Veneré changed from

disbelief to ones of grave concern as they picked up their copies of the report.

Cheju Hallason of South Korea motioned to Rosen that he wished to speak. Cheju, the quintessential gentleman, was small with thin, black, greying hair and dark brownish-black eyes—a quiet and noble man, and the oldest living member of the Veneré.

Rosen nodded his consent. Every one of the attendees stopped flipping through the pages of the report to listen.

"I want you all to know that I share each and every one of your concerns, including yours Elias," he said, giving Rosen a look of reassurance.

"Thank you," said Rosen, as he relaxed his shoulders and settled into the velvet cushioning of his chair.

"Any actions taken must be well thought out, all things considered," Cheju continued. "This situation holds the potential to become calamitous if not properly managed. We've already entertained reasons enough for us to tread lightly. Once it's known that Tristen lives, Robert has the potential of becoming a martyr to many of the Chivalran."

"Cheju, I agree with you and Rosen," proffered Keaton "Keats" Madley of Australia, a strawberry blond with congenial smiling, hazel-green eyes. Keats, while opposite of Rosen in demeanor and disposition, found himself Rosen's friend and confidante. "It's imperative we discover to what extent Solana's talents have grown *and* if her children have any notable abilities of their own."

"Thank you both for comprehending the gravity of the situation," Rosen said. "It's very reason I took the time to obtain the crucial evidence prior to this engagement. I knew we'd need to act quickly and an unconventional approach to the resolution of this matter would be warranted. I think a surprise visit to the Precaveros tribal lands is in order. We'll announce intentions of bringing Solana to Europe to undergo the Kupellation upon our retrieval team's arrival, thus denying Chief Solano the opportunity to stall our efforts and to build a justification for his transgressions. It's important that he understands we're doing him a favor by not making all of this known to the rest of our associates . . . at least for now. Only through our benevolence and his willingness to cooperate can his family and the Misticato Chivalran be saved from some of the negative consequences that could befall them.

"I'm certain Chief Solano will appreciate the special consideration being extended. He'll be told that he's more than welcome to accompany his daughter. After all, she'll be our guest—not our prisoner. Solana is a valued member and a leader in our ranks, one held in high regard, as is her father."

"We should allow her to undergo the Kupellation in the Precaveros village to at least give the impression she's being treated with some level of decorum," lobbied André.

"Solana must come here, where we can be certain no external influences bias her results. If there aren't any noteworthy findings, she'll be allowed to return to her tribe. My suspicion is that Solana will be remaining here, in country, based upon what I've shared with you today. She'll either be one of our new and prized Special Abilities Task Force members or found to be more, and her future uncertain. I recommend we figure out our next steps once the evaluation is completed," Rosen said.

"Rosen, it's safe to say that you have won the majority of us over to your way of thinking, but I sense there's another reason for you to have gathered us here, versus holding this discussion remotely," said Hellion.

Rosen responded. "I took some liberties that some of you might take issue with at first glance. I feel it prudent to disclose them to you now, to allow me to allay any misgivings you may have."

Next to Helleon sat the Lady Lamenta Skagelé of Italy. Lamenta, hailing from one of the Veneré's founding families, was tall and slender, with sleek black hair and dark green eyes. She had a nearly flawless olive complexion, but for the almost invisible scar located on the lower side of her chin that added just the right touch of mystery to her visage.

"After hearing your pronouncements, I'll admit I'm curious about Solana myself—but not curious enough to take rash actions that could potentially break apart long standing relationships with the people who do our bidding *without* question," Lamenta said. "I, like the others, believe we need to move with extreme caution. I'm afraid you've already done something that won't allow us any flexibility."

André provided Lamenta unsought support.

"I think we should call a meeting of the Chivalran leadership to solicit their input before we proceed. Let's engage them and get their *buy-in* so they'll willingly support whatever measures we collectively judge to be appropriate."

"It seems you once again prefer the path of least resistance, and you have the audacity to propose we gain consensus from our underlings?" Rosen challenged. "We've seen throughout the world what attempting to gain consensus reaps—*chaos*. No one is in charge. This is not a precedent I'm willing to set. Who within our ranks will fault us once they learn the facts?"

André sat back in his chair after feeling the slap of Rosen's rebuke.

"We can't be sure Chief Solano will deal with us openly and honestly in this matter, because he's hiding his daughter's talents from us; shirking his Chivalran duties as a result of his love for her," Rosen concluded. "While noble, his fatherly connection to our target of interest has clouded his judgment, making him untrustworthy."

"I agree," said Lamenta.

"I believe we've had enough discussion. It's time to vote," Rosen said, glancing slowly around the table, taking care to have a moment of eye contact with each of the Veneré.

"Should we pursue bringing Solana Jeju Misticato-Gordon to my estate to undergo the Kupellation?"

One-by-one the Veneré voted,

Helleon, "Aye."

Glomar, "Aye."

André, "Nay."

Cheju, "Aye."

Lamenta, "Aye."

Keats, "Aye."

Rosen voted "Aye." Then with a bit of smugness in his voice, he announced, "The *ayes* have it. I want to thank all of you for your support in this matter."

Rosen sighed with relief. "Knowing there could be no other outcome once the evidence was presented, I took the liberty of setting the wheels in motion. Solana should be in our custody by nightfall. I sent my personal guard to accomplish this vital task, because they are well equipped to handle this delicate situation."

A look of incredulity crossed the visage of each of the Veneré.

"I'm asking every one of you to remain here overnight as my guest. Furthermore, I'm requesting that each of you agree not to pursue any outside contact with the world at large until we receive confirmation that my team has successfully completed the mission *and* is heading home with the package."

Everyone attempted to express their outrage at once, but Glomar's booming voice won out.

"How dare you show us such disrespect. I stood up for you and showed my support, while all along you were deceiving us!"

Lamenta uncharacteristically started talking before Glomar had finished.

"What you've done shows me that *you're* the one who's not to be trusted!"

André spouted, "Your disrespect for me is well known, but this is too much. You believe the Veneré to have turned into a dictatorship and you the dictator. You had no right and no authority to take these unsanctioned actions."

Keats, furrowing his eyebrows and shaking his head in disbelief, spoke. "I need you to explain yourself. Please help me to understand what's going on here. What were you thinking?"

"I knew you'd be upset until you faced a fact I've already accepted: we know something is amiss. As of late, we've experienced mission challenges where we've never experienced them in the past. It's as if, prior to our operations, word has been getting out about our intentions, resulting in many of them not executing to plan. *Someone* has to have been leaking information to our intended targets. Due to the serious nature of these circumstances, I couldn't take the chance that a leak might result in our not collecting Solana."

Rosen continued, "There you have it. In addition to Chief Solano's trust being of issue, I'm worried that another of our own may be of concern. I'd like to be able to exclude us and our closest associates from the list of potential traitors. I'm asking you to spend one night at my home without *any* outside contact until the mission is complete. What will it hurt if we spend tonight together? You were already planning for the potentiality, should our meeting go long. I'm talking *one* night. We could use this time very productively. Although technology allows us to communicate remotely, it doesn't allow for the intimate interactions that only being present in person can afford. The exchanges we had this afternoon re-emphasize our need to increase our in-person gatherings. I sense a loss of personal intimacy between us that has opened the door to mistrust. Since when do we question one another's motives?"

The pensive look on everyone's faces gave Rosen the confidence to continue.

"I propose we have a nice dinner and engage in casual conversation to start vanquishing the distance growing between us. We must retain our close relations if we're to be successful in carrying out our duties. There is no room for division amongst us."

Each member of the Veneré sat motionless, not uttering a word. Everyone knew if they fought this reasonable proposal, they would become suspect. Each provided curt head nods of agreement with his proposal.

Cheju raised his hand.

"Let me provide another succinct synopsis of where I believe we are and what must be accomplished. We must all espouse Rosen's concerns about Solana while we de-emphasize Chief Solano's role. This will require we collectively devise a sound communications strategy that includes relaying the existence of Tristen Gordon and his children to concerned parties. Each communiqué must be accomplished at the right time and in the appropriate setting. It's imperative we show a united front to retain the veneration of our global compatriots.

Rosen called for one last vote. "All in favor of working to devise a plan to accomplish Cheju's well summarized goals this evening?"

The Veneré unanimously, but reluctantly, voted, "Aye."

They worked throughout the evening, building their unified engagement stratagem, a large part devoted to maintaining the support, loyalty and obedience of their regional Chivalran regiments. Rosen had pushed them all unwillingly into a corner, one that only united they'd escape.

In another part of the world, Rosen's personal guard arrived on Chief Solano's doorstep.

CHAPTER TWO

AMAZON

The *Uno*, a sparkling white, three-hundred-and-fifty-foot luxury yacht cruised off the coast of the most northeastern shores of Brazil, carrying her crew, an interesting cadre of passengers, and a very intriguing payload. It was a beautiful day, with powdered blue, cloudless skies and a tropical eighty-five degrees. The white sands below the surface gave the translucent turquoise water the look of warmth and welcome, but those on board would not be partaking of the sites and scenery.

The *Uno* crew could see the otherworldly fringes of the Amazon River basin from the bridge of the ship. Here the mountainous Andes terrain fell into the dense forest-clad valleys bordering the region. The waters they were entering consisted of a myriad of brackish, murky channels, splashed with multi-colored flora as far as the eye could see.

The unpredictable weather and rumors of fierce predators inhabiting the area kept the place free of outsider intrusions. A privately funded exploration team once documented sightings of over a thousand crocodiles, many of them over fifteen feet long. Jaguars, ocelots, and massive snakes also lurked.

Not a person was in sight, affording the privacy desired for those on board the UNO and the solitude required to execute a covert mission. The ship had managed to transit up the river to the Precaveros tribe's unnamed tributary river's entrance in no time at all.

The loudspeaker system awakened the spec ops team slumbering serenely in their shipboard quarters by announcing, *"The Uno has arrived at the infil destination. The galley is open to serve breakfast from 0630 to 0730."*

Chris Cassara awoke because of the booming announcement, feeling as if he'd slept for ages, a very rare opportunity for a person in his line of work. As the leader of Rosen's personal guard, also known as the *Tranquility Team*, he usually awoke long before his compadres to strategize and reassess the various scenarios and potential plans to ensure he'd considered any plausible situation the team might encounter. In this case, he had two full weeks during the at sea transit from Scotland to Brazil to make his plans and to ensure his team's readiness for the upcoming mission. No more planning needed, only execution of the mission remained.

He jumped out of bed and quickly donned his jungle assault cammies that went well with his light brown hair and hazel eyes. He ducked his athletic six-foot frame in order to safely transit through the ship's passageways as he headed towards the yacht's mess deck to eat prior to going ashore, the timing of his next meal uncertain.

Arriving at the dining hall, he nodded to his team, all of whom were clad in similar attire. Chris quickly consumed his meal in almost perfect silence with the rest of the guys. The clanking of the utensils on the emptying food plates provided the only sound during the meal. With a clean plate, Chris rose and headed towards the bow of the ship to gain a vantage point to view the river that they would be embarking upon in order to stealthily transit up to the Precaveros tribal lands to obtain their objective.

Chris arrived at the bow of the ship and saw for the first time the boundless Amazon basin. From the twenty-foot height off the water, he observed an unending expanse of flat marshes and a multitude of rivers and tributaries fingering seemingly everywhere and nowhere. In stark contrast, barely visible, was the entrance to the unnamed river, located ten degrees starboard. Overhanging trees, vines and shrubbery hid the size of the opening and all of its occupants, who he knew existed because he could hear the loud shrieks of the monkeys, tree frogs, seriemas and other surface dwellers. All sounds faded as he walked to starboard to get a closer look, the creatures aware an uninvited presence had entered their territory.

Chris knew this operation would be challenging, since the team was entering wild, undulating country with no validated maps or charts. The Precaveros tribal lands bordered Venezuela, Guyana, Suriname, French Guiana and Brazil, and none of these countries took the responsibility to map or chart the region because no known economic value surpassed the inherent dangers required for entry. The terrain was impossible to access except by small boat. Even more disconcerting, the Precaveros tribespeople were descendants of the rare, pureblood Amerindians that were documented to inhabit this remote part of the Amazon basin. Rumors of their cannibalism persisted, even in modern times.

Chris, totally ignoring the harsher aspects of the environment he was entering, allowed himself a moment to ponder over the last two weeks. He couldn't believe how long it took them to arrive, the worst part being the slow and arduous passage across the vast Atlantic Ocean. He and his crew were raring to go and desperate to do something to break the monotony.

He welcomed the fresh smell of the salt air. The light humid breeze refreshed him as it gently blew across his exposed skin, making him feel alive and adding to the excitement he felt prior to every mission.

Blake Regalos surreptitiously snuck up on him. He was Chris' second in command, a dark-haired Chris look-alike who could easily be mistaken as his younger brother. Blake sidled into a position on

Chris' right, assuming the same spread-leg stance, crossing his arms in kind, looking the same direction as Chris, while commenting with a playful sneer on his face.

"It was so easy to sneak up on you. You must be feeling so old. Your instincts appear to have atrophied, your senses dulled. I feared this would come as we age, but ever since you turned thirty, you've really started to go downhill. You're certainly more mature and wiser, but has it been worth the loss in stealth and ability?"

"I see you enjoyed your breakfast. The tad bit of salsa on your collar obviously left over from the huevos rancheros you ate," Chris countered. "Your virile odor indicates you chose not to take advantage of the time we had this morning to shower. Should I go on? We both know you wouldn't be standing here if I hadn't determined, the moment I heard the latch open, that you were no threat to me."

Blake smiled.

"Blake, maybe two years from now, when you come of age, you'll have perfected the undetectable observation skills that I now possess. One can only hope that you'll be as gifted."

"You keep telling yourself that, and maybe it'll help ease your passage into old age," said Blake, nudging Chris in the arm with his elbow.

With a wink and a smile, Chris began going over the morning's mission plan with his second-in-command.

Both men stood on the deck of the *Uno* in silence once they completed their mission recap. The few moments of reflection allowed them to think about the importance of the unprecedented mission at hand—one arm of the Veneré acting against another.

As if on cue, both men hastened towards the stern. They slid down three sets of aluminum ladders by holding loosely onto the smooth metal railings. They arrived at the entrance of the small boats bay area where they met up with the rest of Tranquility Team. The two, four-man teams were all focused on getting their two rigid inflatable boats, also known as RIBs, ready and outfitted with the last few accoutrements—extra ammunitions and other weaponry they hoped would not be needed.

Upon seeing Chris and Blake, their teams encircled them, so that they could have their last-minute tag-up.

"This mission isn't one you'd call normal," Chris said. "We're going to *snatch-n-grab* a special abilities target with ESP and psychokinesis talents. We're not certain of her proficiency in these two areas. She may possess other abilities. There are known seers within the tribal elders, but we're not sure if we have a full accounting of the abilities the others in the tribe may possess. Chief Solano has kept much hidden from us. The *unknown* is our primary risk factor. Executing a mission contained within these parameters is as of yet unprecedented. We are truly in virgin territory."

Blake expanded. "Since none of us possess any special abilities to any great extent, we have developed a risk mitigation strategy. We have our own special abilities cadre on the boat to address this shortfall, a few of Rosen's favorites, whom I affectionately refer to as *spec abs*. They're providing us cover, literally blocking us from view or thought reception while we embark on this mission. They will be keeping our target from becoming aware of our existence until we're ready to reveal ourselves."

In unison, the team shuffled about, looking back and forth with apprehension.

"Okay now, let's settle down," Chris said. "You're used to working *with* the spec abs, but we've never been asked to pursue one of our own. Moving in on a fellow Chivalran's turf and taking the heir apparent—*man*."

Chris, usually full of confidence, felt something he rarely allowed himself to entertain—uncertainty. Not knowing about a very key aspect of his mission was disconcerting. He continued.

"What *do* we know? We all know that the Misticato Chivalran have *Intuitives* and *Empaths* in their ranks, and Solana may very well be one of them. That's why we'll need to be extra focused on clearing our minds, so we aren't detected too soon. We don't want to give any prior warning to her or *any* Misticato. You men have been trained in mental camouflage. I need you to fully employ those defenses now. Don't even think about the mission tactics until our quarry is in our sites and, ideally, under wraps! Don't think about who we are or where we hail from, understand?" pressed Chris.

All of the men responded in an ardent cacophony of, "Yes, sir," "Ooh Rah," and "Aye, Aye, Captain!"

"Fortune is smiling upon us. Overhead asset reports indicate the adult Precaveros tribespeople and their pledges are well on their way to the foothills for their annual Sabiduria Ceremony, in keeping with the intel we received from our source. By the time we reach the village, Chief Solano and most of the villagers will be more than two hours away on foot; only mothers, children and the infirmed will remain in the village," said Chris.

The guys all laughed.

"Simple? I think not," countered Blake.

Chris added, "The mothers are formidable members of the Misticato Chivalran, as are the others; Solana is one of these mothers. You must assume that all are able to protect and defend themselves. The Precaveros are infamous for beginning combat training the day they're weaned from their mother's bosom."

Chris added one cautionary note. "No one gets hurt. We're here to *snatch-n-grab-n-go*, not to engage."

In unison, Chris received nods of affirmation.

"We're to be back on the boat before the eighteen hundred dinner bell. Rosen is expecting a status report by then. Any comebacks? . . . None? . . . Let's get out of here."

With that, Tranquility Team unlatched the two RIBs and positioned themselves for the opening of the boat bay doors. Chris stood by the prow of one with his three-man team, and Blake stood at the prow of the other with his.

The boat bay doors opened without making a sound. The teams laid the RIBs in the water, while simultaneously boarding, as they took their pre-appointed spots and got underway.

The clouds and fog, so common for this area, had moved in within the past hour, helping to blanket their exodus. Not that it was needed; there wasn't a soul in the vicinity to bear witness to their departure.

Luckily for the team, the severe flooding season had slipped a few weeks, which would have made transiting upriver to the tribal grounds nearly impossible from torrents of a rain-swollen river. As it was, the unnamed river's water level was only three feet deep in some areas, just deep enough for the boats afloat, making for a somewhat unremarkable transit.

Chris left two men behind to operate the rescue helicopter sitting on the *Uno's* helipad. The pilot and his spotter readied the helicopter as an integral part of Plan D, *D* for Damn—things didn't go as planned.

CHAPTER THREE

PRECAVEROS

In the heart of the secluded Precaveros village, the tribe gathered in the community center. These proud individuals possessed knowledge, skills, and abilities antithetical to what would be expected of a person living in an isolated and nearly uninhabitable region of the world.

The well-educated Precaveros tribespeople spoke many languages and were competent in the sciences, geography, astrology, anthropology, and history of the world. Their knowledge had been passed down from generation to generation. They possessed physical prowess well beyond the average human, which included an unparalleled understanding of nature. They were a powerful people—mentally, spiritually, and metaphysically—and were treated as a sovereign nation by neighboring territories. Tribal lands rich in untapped natural resources made the Precaveros people wealthy beyond measure.

All the villagers of age thirteen and older gathered around, readying themselves to make the long walk up to the Montaña ceremonial grounds for the annual transit of youth to adulthood ceremony—the *Sabiduria Ceremonia*—the Ceremony of Wisdom.

Many of the younger children, not yet of age, watched the older children prepping for their adventure, all hoping and waiting for their time to make this most auspicious journey. The very young ran around and underfoot, annoying those readying themselves for the journey. The remaining members, mostly mothers, attempted to corral their young ones and worked to redirect their energies toward less disruptive activities.

One such mother was the chieftain's oldest daughter, the beautiful Solana Jeju Misticato-Gordon, wife to Tristen Gordon, and mother to Bradley and Quentin Gordon. The word *Solana* was synonymous with the *sunny spot* or *the illumination*, and the bearer of the name lived up to her namesake. Everyone loved being in her welcoming and cheerful presence. She was beautiful and statuesque, standing nearly six feet tall, muscular and with a sun-kissed light brown complexion, hazel-green eyes, and long brownish-black sleek, straight hair. Solana was also a Misticato Chivalran warrior and leader, and the heir to the Precaveros tribal chieftainship.

"Bradley . . . Quentin . . . please come here."

Both boys stopped what they were doing and ran into their mother's loving embrace.

"You two seem to have a lot of energy," she said smiling down on their expectant, happy faces. "I need someone I can trust to do me a great, big favor. Are you two available?"

The two boys eagerly nodded.

"Will you please go to the butterfly clearing to catch me a special white-winged butterfly? The wing decoration will include small, circular, turquoise and yellow, overlapping markings. I want to use its likeness in the mural I'm painting. I hope to finish it by day's end."

Just then she spotted Lucas, chasing another boy who was running all around the celebrants.

"Bradley, please go grab Lucas and invite him to accompany you. He looks to be in need of something more productive to do."

Solana felt a special maternal instinct when it came to Lucas.

His mother had died a few years before from a venomous snake bite. Lucas had become Solana's informally adopted third son; Lucas and Bradley spent most of their waking hours with one another.

Right when Bradley, Quentin and Lucas started to head into the forest, they saw their grandfather, Chief Solano, moving to the center of the tribespeople to make an announcement. They stopped at the forest's edge to listen to what he had to say.

Solana looked on with a sense of peace and serenity as her father, Solano Misticato, motioned for his people to gather around. He was chieftain of the Precaveros tribe, and the high chair and leader of the Misticato Chivalran, who were the guardians against the evils of this world. They protected the innocent from malevolent forces that usually came in the forms of nefarious or ill-natured people, threatening circumstances, and all manner of potential hazards or dangers.

Chief Solano called out, "It's time for us to leave for the Montaña."

The crowd immediately ceased talking and moving about. Even the rambunctious children stopped to listen to Chief Solano's announcement.

"This journey will allow us who have made the transition into adulthood, time to reflect on how well we've been performing our duties and living our lives. The initiates will learn the secrets of how to gain your *sabiduria*—your wisdom. We'll be gone for three days and three nights. We will return with the new moon, when those new to adulthood begin your lives as novice leaders of the Precaveros tribe and become Misticato Chivalran new recruits. The ceremony has now officially begun. Silence is a key aspect of our journey, and from this moment forward, not a word is to be spoken."

Chief Solano then turned around and waved his arm in the direction of their sacred site, signifying the ritual's commencement.

The tribespeople followed in single file behind their benevolent leader and reverently walked in silence out of the village and into the dense forest, heading to the Montaña.

Soon thereafter, Bradley, Quentin, and Lucas arrived at the near perfectly ellipse-shaped butterfly clearing in the forest. It was a tree-lined, grassy meadow that contained a multitude of wildflowers in colors spanning the visual spectrum—white, pink, red, orange, yellow, lime, turquoise, blue, and purple. The brilliance of the flowers contrasted with the greens and yellows of the trees bordering natures' botanical garden, which played host to hundreds of beautiful butterflies of all sizes and shapes. Also enjoying the floral bounty was an abundance of bees, hummingbirds, and other such creatures, also flying about and relishing the different attributes of the flowering plant life.

The boys were hypnotized by the many different and intoxicating smells emanating from the plethora of flowers, too many diverse sweet and lovely fragrances to tell which was coming from where. The only real quandary that beset the boys was deciding which butterflies to capture for their mother. She only asked for one specific kind, but there were others that were just as—or even more— beautiful.

They immediately started chasing the butterflies with reckless abandon. Lucas stopped to catch his breath and watched Bradley and Quentin scurrying around happily. The two sandy-blond-haired and blue-green-eyed boys of Scottish decent were a noticeable contrast to the bronze skin, dark brown hair and black-brown eyes typical of the Precaveros tribesmen, and of Lucas himself, but who were his chosen brothers.

Lucas and Bradley were both seven years old but Bradley stood a good three inches taller. Bradley protected his adoptive brother and possessed skills at games and tribal prep activities that bested the other children his age in almost all areas. He didn't enjoy the hand-to-hand combat drills as much as he was expected to by the elders. He also balked when it came to overcoming his opponent, if he thought he might hurt them. Lucas admired this about Bradley.

Bradley and Quentin were the sons of Tristin and Solana of the Precaveros tribe. They lived an exciting and fulfilling life, where their only jobs were to grow up, learn their ancestral teachings and history, and become proficient in skills that allowed them to be valued members of the tribe.

CHAPTER FOUR

SOLANA

The two hours seemed to pass in an instant, as the boats carrying the Tranquility Team barely struggled against the mild current to reach the shoreline of the Precaveros tribal land. They stealthily disembarked and donned their face masks, with no need for Chris and Blake to tell them any last-minute intel. The team members were focused on the beautiful landscape and mountainous terrain—no op details. They trusted the spec abs to do the rest.

To a person, they felt the op would go off without a hitch. No sign of crocodiles or other fearsome predators, to include the pre-warned Misticato Chivalran.

Blake signaled to his men by pointing at his watch, instructing them to mark the time—ten hundred hours. Then they surreptitiously entered the thick primordial forest in pursuit of their quarry.

They soon found themselves in the heart of the Precaveros village proper, the center of the charming and unassuming adobe-constructed grouping of buildings and homes. It was quiet and only a few of the tribe were present upon their arrival, all occupied and busy executing their daily routines. Without any effort they immediately located Solana, who was standing at the far side of the village square, talking with an elderly woman in front of the largest building in the complex.

Solana couldn't believe her eyes when she first saw the spec ops team across the way; she was rarely, if ever surprised by anyone. Her gift afforded her with intuitive abilities that had served her well since before she could remember. Why hadn't she been warned of their coming long before she could see them? She looked away and back again to ensure she was not hallucinating.

"Oh no," she exclaimed, looking to the elder woman standing with her, "They've come for me."

"Run, Solana," spouted the elder. Solana didn't need to be told twice as she fled.

Chris realized she had seen them and motioned to his men and they started after her, but they were too late. She surprised them when she sprinted into the dense forest and the chase ensued.

Solana calmed herself as she sprinted. She knew she needed to be clearheaded to work her magic. Once she felt some level of calm, she was able to sense that her pursuers were sent by the Veneré. *No. No. That's not right . . . Rosen is who sent these men.* She quickened her pace. *I've no clue as to what I might've done to deserve this. Why can't I read their intentions? For some reason they're shielded . . .*

Regardless of her mental prowess, she received only garbled information. The intruders' thought patterns weren't clear. She hadn't been scared in such a long time that she'd forgotten how to calm herself. She needed to address the insidious nature of this emotion that was threatening to overtake her. She managed to snap out of it when a more terrifying thought occurred to her.

My boys . . . I have to make sure my boys are safe.

Bradley, Quentin, and Lucas were blissfully unaware of the goings on as they frolicked in the butterfly clearing. Lucas looked on as Bradley and Quentin attempted to catch a particular butterfly that matched their mother's description. Lucas admired their teamwork and was at a loss to figure out how they worked in tandem without speaking to one another. They seemed to know what the other was thinking and they effortlessly responded in kind, finally catching their prey.

How'd they do that?

Suddenly, they were interrupted by Solana running into the clearing yelling, "Boys, hide. Bradley, get your brother and do what we practiced. Don't come out until I tell you that it's safe! Hide now!" as she fled to the opposite side of the meadow.

The three boys, startled and frightened, quickly stopped playing and went to hide. Lucas jumped behind a large fallen tree by himself while Bradley and Quentin ran and hid behind a set of bushes and quickly employed their masking abilities, as practiced during drills with their parents. They thought of being sheltered in a cave that no one could find and repeated the words over and over in their heads, *we are safe, hidden, and sheltered.* They could see each other in their imagined cave but no one else was there with them. All Bradley could think was *Oh no . . . where's Lucas?* He knew not to go look for him as he and Quentin could hear strangers talking just outside of their cave.

"She was calling out to her sons. Spread out and look for them. We get them, we get her," ordered Chris. Soon thereafter, one of the men walked right past the two boys while yelling back that he couldn't find a trace of them.

They were thankful that they were small and that the task force overlooked their hiding place. Neither Bradley nor Quentin knew what the others saw and were unaware of what occurred when their masking abilities were employed. But to Lucas, the brothers had vanished from sight.

The two brothers were not found, but Lucas was.

Chris gently grabbed him by the arm while speaking to him kindly in his native tongue.

"Young man, please don't worry. We're not here to harm anyone. I want to talk with Solana, and I need your help to find her. I need you to answer a few questions for me. Understand?"

Lucas looked ashen. He didn't move nor speak.

"Have you seen Solana?"

Lucas barely nodded.

"Where did she go?"

Lucas hesitantly pointed a finger in the direction Solana ran, still unable to utter a word.

Chris's team went in the direction Lucas pointed, while he remained behind with the scared little guy who was shaking.

"Are you Solana's son?"

"No."

"What's your name?"

"Lucas."

"Have you seen either of her two sons? Do you know where they are right now?"

"No . . . they're not here." Lucas spoke the truth. He had no idea of Bradley and Quentin's whereabouts, and all he could think about was that he wished he'd gone with them.

The Tranquility Team hurriedly searched the area, looking around in the bushes, the forest, and all along the full length of the cliff face overlooking the river from a forty-foot height above, the swift flowing rapids emanating from a sixty-foot tall waterfall. They found no trace of Solana or her sons after searching the village and the surrounding area. The villagers rendered no assistance in their endeavors.

"Chris, our Plan D cohorts are underway, ETA forthwith," reported Blake.

"Good," responded Chris.

The Plan D team arrived in what seemed like hours but was only a twenty-minute flight. They scoured the area from the air, which was a near impossible task due to the thickness of the forest canopy. No body was found in the river, up or down stream. Even using the infrared radar that picked up the heat signatures of the materials and living entities all around yielded nothing. Solana had disappeared into thin air, and without a trace. Her tracks ended at the upper cliff face.

The tribespeople kept asking Chris and his team, "Why are you here? What has Solana done to deserve this? Surely her little boys have done nothing to you?"

Chris confided in Blake, "What if by chasing her, we caused her to fall off that cliff in her attempt to get away from us? From the top of the cliff, I could see something that looked like clothing floating on the water's surface. There's no way to discern if it belongs to her or not, and we still haven't found a body. She has simply disappeared, or worse."

Blake whispered back, "No one could've survived the fall. There's nowhere else for her to have gone. She must be dead; her body stuck in an underwater eddy. That's why our heat sensors haven't picked anything up. She couldn't be hidden from our spec abs *and* our multitude of sensors. Let's face facts. The water isn't deep enough for someone to have survived a fall on those rocks from that height."

"Retrieve Solana. That's all we were asked to do," Chris ordered. "What a mess we've made of this op."

"I know. The only thing that's worked out in our favor today is that Chief Solano and most of the tribespeople aren't anywhere near the village."

The spec ops team kept looking for another thirty minutes, when Chris finally decided to call it quits; they left no calling cards when they departed the village empty handed.

Once back on board the Uno, Chris gathered his team for a post op mission assessment.

"I'm not sure what happened today. I don't know how we're going to be able to explain to Rosen that she just vanished into thin air, without a trace, not a footprint to track, and no body found."

Standing erect, with his hands on his hips, his throat extended fully, and looking straight up at the overhead, Chris began to talk to his team with a forced calm.

"I think we all know I should've done more to account for Solana's special abilities. I won't make that mistake again. I don't want you feeling the brunt of my fiasco. As the team leader, I should've better prepared you for this mission. This is going to be a wakeup call for everyone. A member of a Chivalran regiment with special abilities like these is unprecedented. You all performed well. I couldn't have asked you to be any more professional. We operated in a realm outside our understanding today."

"Wrap up your mission assessments and get them to me by seventeen hundred so I can consolidate them into our after-action report. Chris will be sending it out by eighteen hundred this afternoon," directed Blake.

"You're dismissed."

CHAPTER FIVE

AFTERMATH

Back at the Precaveros village, chaos ensued. Chief Solano, Tristen, and the rest of the tribesmen were sent for immediately upon the intruders' arrival, in keeping with the village security plan. They returned within four hours of the incident to learn Solana was missing, and that no one had seen either of her two sons since the intruders' arrival and abrupt departure.

Lucas was the most reliable witness concerning the last known whereabouts of Solana, Bradley, and Quentin, but questioning him reaped little insight.

Just as search parties were planning to head out, the dazed Quentin and Bradley came walking into the village square. The villagers opened a pathway for the two boys to pass, and once they spotted their father and grandfather, they ran into their open arms, both boys in shock and close to tears, their faces etched with despair.

Once the boys relinquished their death grips on Chief Solano and Tristen, they helped the boys take a seat on a set of wooden benches. Quentin refused to loosen his hold on his grandfather's left arm. Thus, Chief Solano knelt on one knee, resting his right hand supportively on Bradleys' slumped shoulder, and asked his first question.

"Please tell us what happened? Do you know where your mother is?"

"She told us to hide in our cave until she came back for us, but she *never* did," said Bradley, crying and barely able to speak.

Chief Solano allowed Bradley a few moments to collect himself. Then, with the utmost patience, he continued.

"Did she say anything else?"

"We," said Bradley pointing to himself and Quentin. "We can't feel her presence. She isn't here. I know those men couldn't find her. They were so mad that she ran away. I heard them say that they thought she fell over the cliff, but we didn't hear her scream. Wouldn't she have screamed?"

Chief Solano gently wiped the tears from Bradley's cheeks, attempting to console him.

"We don't know what's happened, but with your help we hope to figure that out. We want to find her and to make sure she's okay."

Bradley continued. "We spoke the hidden words over and over in our heads and were hidden in our cave; we stayed quiet and didn't move a muscle. We could hear talking, but we couldn't see anyone. I don't know where she went."

Bradley's voice cracked and his eyes teared. "I should've helped her. I shouldn't have hidden!"

"Son, you did the right thing. *She* wouldn't have wanted you to put yourself in peril for her. It's her job to protect you, not the other way around. She would be very proud of you. Because of you, Quentin is safe. You're both safe," said Tristen.

As if on cue, two of the village mothers came forward from the crowd and reached for the hands of the two weeping and exhausted distraught brothers. They walked them to their dwelling so that they could get cleaned up and fed.

The rest of the tribe split up into search parties that headed out in the four prime compass directions with hopes of finding their missing Solana. They searched until darkness to no avail. The men who pursued her were well out of the area. They left no evidence beyond their footprints leading to and from the river's shoreline.

Chief Solano, Tristen, and a few of the chieftain's closest and most trusted elders stepped inside the tribal council chamber room for a private conversation. Once away from any prying eyes and ears, Chief Solano blurted out his thoughts and feelings with a very uncharacteristic level of frustration.

"I can't rest until we recover Solana and exact revenge on this unsolicited attack on our homeland and my family. They obviously possessed special abilities to remain masked before, during, and after the assault, or we surely would've had a different outcome. Even Solana was taken by surprise, but from what we've been told, once they were in our midst, she was able to detect that she was their target."

A murmur of agreement came from all present.

"The most disconcerting aspect surrounding this mystery is that only the Veneré or one of the other Chivalran regiments could have been bold enough to execute such an endeavor," surmised Chief Solano.

"Who would do such a thing? How did they know Solana had two sons, and what else do they know?" asked a tribal elder.

"Good questions. They certainly knew when to come to the village, when we would be most vulnerable," responded Chief Solano.

Tristin, listening respectfully to the discussion, found himself disappointed to learn the elders were as perplexed as he.

"We must move out quickly to gain the upper hand on these aggressors," Tristin said. "Who are they? What are they capable of? Is their mission considered complete or will they be back for more?"

"I agree. Please call the Misticato Chivalran to the pavilion. We need to prepare a battle strategy," bade Chief Solano.

Tristen departed immediately to gather the regiment.

The Misticatos assembled within minutes in the great pavilion. A heavy and solemn feeling blanketed the participants, as was visible in their exhausted and somber expressions. Their world had been intruded upon, and for the first time in centuries, they were the victims versus the aggressors.

Chief Solano entered the room, but something seemed amiss. He looked diminished by the absence of his confidante, Solana. It was known by all that Solana would assume leadership of the Misticato Chivalran when Chief Solano stepped down. She was a proven leader amongst the tribespeople, and an accomplished warrior. Chief Solano valued her wise counsel and her unconditional loyalty.

He sat down in his u-shaped mahogany seat, only slightly larger than the rest of the meeting room chairs. They were situated in an interlacing circular pattern four chairs deep, each row one foot higher than the row in front. His throne, of sorts, was located at the top of the outer circle. It was centrally located, between his personal advisor on his left and the second-in-command on his right, the chair noticeably empty.

"My first order of business is to temporarily fill my second-in-command position while Solana is away. Daniel Pagan, please assume the chair of my second-in-command." He motioned to his right. Daniel was the youngest of Chief Solano's two nephews, and the son he would've wanted should he have been blessed with a male child.

Daniel took the seat to the right of Chief Solano, but warily, and while watching for any reaction from Tristen or the others. All present observed Tristen giving a slight nod to Daniel to let him know he recognized him as the more fitting person. A sense of relief spread across the gathering, and Daniel was grateful to have one less distraction to deal with during this distressing time.

The assembly met until the wee hours of the night, while groups of tribespeople came and went. Some packed their belongings to travel to other places, with no indication as to where they were going or when they'd return.

By three o'clock in the morning, only the Misticato Chivalran leaders remained. One by one they received their marching orders and retired to their respective dwellings to get some much-needed sleep. Only Chief Solano and Tristen remained in place to discuss a very important matter—the boys' fate.

"It's bad enough they came for her, but how did they know she had two sons?" Tristen said. "These perpetrators must know that she possesses special abilities. I fear it won't take them long to figure out that the boys possess special abilities equal to their mother's, and they haven't reached puberty yet. I suspect since they asked Lucas if he was her son, they mustn't know what the boys look like. They may not know that they're Gordons."

"You and I think much alike. We know it is best that we relocate Bradley and Quentin to somewhere safe, where no one would think to look for them," declared Chief Solano.

"I want them safe, but I don't want us separated," Tristen said.

"We can no longer operate under the false assumption that everyone outside of the tribe believes you and your parents to have been lost at sea. We can no longer assume your secret has been kept. We've been betrayed by one of our own people."

"What are you talking about? My father told me that he and my mother came to Precaveros and liked it so much that they never left."

"In light of current circumstances, there are things that you should know. Things that your parents hoped to shield you from. Try not to judge us too harshly for keeping this a secret for so long, but the truth of the matter is that Andrew Gordon was not your real father. He's your uncle. Your birth father's name was Robert Clifton Gordon."

"Where has my so-called *birth* father been all my life?"

"He died many years ago by the hand of your uncle, Lord Veldor Gordon, the oldest of the three brothers. Veldor was the head of the Gordon dynasty and high chair of the Gordon Chivalran. He was attempting to turn you over to the Veneré, who suspected that you possessed special abilities, potentially at the level of an Arcanum. The Veneré went so far as to claim you had the potential to be the True Knowing One.

"We now know for sure this claim was politically motivated. We believe it happened because people were starting to feel a sense of desperation. The end of the millennium was nearing, and they hadn't seen any indication their savior would arrive. Many unorthodox things started happening. The pursuit of a Chivalran's son was one of them. My father stepped in to stop the madness; that's how you came to be here."

"My uncle betrayed his own brothers?"

"Veldor was blinded by his duties that mandated you be submitted for testing—the Kupellation. There's no question, he was duty bound as the head of the Gordon Chivalran. He did what was expected of him. The only thing in question, and which has been discussed for decades, is if the claim of your special abilities was founded in truth. We both know you have slight abilities, but nothing that would've warranted such an inquiry. Many Chivalran and their kin have *slight* abilities."

"Had you been honest with me—with us—we could have made better plans to address this potentiality. How can I protect my boys from forces such as these?"

"Tristen, your anger will not help us to protect them. You must listen to what I have to say. Can you do that?"

Tristen gave an almost undetectable nod.

"Your father and mother, Lord Robert Clifton and Lady Michele Gennette Gordon, were in process of fleeing their homeland when Veldor attempted to stop them. When they refused to turn you over, he engaged your father in a sword fight. Your uncle, Andrew, stepped in to stop them fighting because he could see Veldor was about to defeat your father. He snuck up on Veldor from behind and hit him on the back of his head, knocking him out. But as Veldor fell, his sword went awry, causing him to wound and kill your father accidently.

Andrew felt honor bound to assume your father's place. He swore an oath to your mother to fulfill Robert's vows to keep you safe from harm. Over time, he and your mother grew to love one another, and eventually married in a surreptitious ceremony, because the rest of the tribe believed them to already be husband and wife."

"This can't be true."

"But alas it is, and their hasty departure from Scotland, in the middle of the night, validated the claims about your powers. To dissuade pursuers, the escape vessel was reported lost at sea during a fearsome storm. Flotsam confirmed the report. Your deaths closed the matter nicely. It left all believing that the True Knowing One had died, thus all would have to wait until the next millennium to be saved. These misguided notions allowed you to grow to manhood safe and sound under the protection of the Misticato Chivalran. Andrew accepted a life of deprivation; exiled in a foreign country, but an oath kept."

"My dreams of castles are *actual* memories?" Tristen asked.

"Yes. The man you know to be your father had every intention of bringing you back to Scotland should the right circumstances present themselves, but they never did, until now. To protect your sons, you must return to your homeland to set the record straight, and to claim your rightful position in the Gordon dynasty and the Gordon Chivalran. You're the oldest living Gordon male in your generation and the rightful heir to the Gordon dynasty. The Gordon heir is chosen from the oldest Gordon of the next generation, not handed down within one family. This allows all families within the Gordon clan the opportunity to produce the heir."

"Go *back* to Scotland, when as far as I'm concerned, I've *never lived* there in the first place," exclaimed Tristen.

"We've trained you so that you possess the needed qualifications to assume the position of the high chair of the Gordon Chivalran regiment. It's time you claim your inheritance."

"I can understand as a child why you might not have told me, but why was this kept from me for so many years after I reached adulthood?"

"As time passed, Andrew felt it no longer seemed important to reveal the truth. There was no reason for you to return home. When he died, I made a deathbed promise to never reveal your history to you unless a dire situation presented itself."

"You mean like now?" Tristan snarled.

"I can see my decision was not the correct one to make. You've always had a right to know and to make your own choices in this regard. I can tell you, Andrew did what he did out of love, as misguided as it all seems at this moment."

"This is *too* much." Tristen said. "Why would I return to a place where I was feared in the first place? Wouldn't rivals within the Gordon dynasty want me killed? Wouldn't Solana be compromised as well? And the boys?"

"The Gordons were betrayed by their adversary within the Veneré, Alfred Rosen. The story is long, and you are deserving of the details, but now is not the time. It's imperative you be made aware that there will be those in the accuser's family, Rosen's family, who will not welcome your return. His son, Elias Rosen, is now *the* leader of the Veneré, and members of his immediate family have infiltrated the ranks of the Gordon Chivalran and the Gordon dynasty via marriage to your kin. They sit in positions they have never deserved and that many of us feel to be inappropriate. These men will be reticent to relinquish their ill-gotten gains upon your return."

"Is it safe for me to go to Scotland?"

"Your return will validate that the accuser made false accusations concerning you. You're living proof that the allegations were unfounded. Rosen and his heirs have much to lose when this all becomes known, making them very dangerous adversaries. But they're not your only threat. The overall ramifications to the relationship between the Veneré and the Chivalran will be of grave concern to all parties."

"I see."

"Blind faith and misguided judgment have landed us where we are today. I'm sorry for the part I played in this deception. Only you alone can right this wrong. This journey will not only reunite you with your kin, but it will afford you opportunities to make alliances with those in other Chivalran regiments that can help us find Solana. We need allies we can trust," implored Chief Solano.

"I'll do whatever's required to protect my family—*our* family."

"I would expect nothing less of you, my son."

Chief Solano continued.

"We both know Solana's abilities are strong and she's not limited to one special ability, as are most. I'll be accused of hiding a potential Arcanum just like your real father, but this time the claim is true. Their only problem is that they need evidence, and the evidence has vanished."

"That's another good reason why it's best we relocate the boys," Tristen said.

"Without the boys and Solana, there is no case. Like your father, I wanted to protect my child and my grandsons. Thus, when I became aware of the situation as an adult, I chose to maintain the secrecy. In retrospect, I'm not sure I've done the right thing; only time will tell."

"I understand why you did it."

"The Veneré and the other Chivalran Regiments will soon learn that I kept your whereabouts from them, in direct violation of the prime Chivalran Rule of Law: *to seek out and present to the Veneré all suspected special abilities persons so that the Veneré can learn the extent of their abilities, and to ensure they mean to protect, not harm this world.* This is no small mandate. It has been in place for thousands of years and for good reason. None of this will bode well for either of us, or the Misticato Chivalran."

"I'll gather my things and will be on my way at first light," proclaimed Tristen.

"Not so fast. We need to address this issue in its entirety, from more than one perspective. While it's true that we need the Northern European Chivalran regiments' support if we ever hope to gain a full understanding of what's happening, it's risky for us to engage them. Part of what has me worried is that from what we've been told by those who encountered the intruders, several of them spoke English with Northern European accents. Where exactly did they come from? Until we figure out who they are and where they're from, approaching your kin could be our greatest folly. If it turns out that the Gordon Chivalran were the perpetrators, all is lost," tendered Chief Solano.

"We both know that Solana wouldn't have vanished and continued to veil herself unless something serious was afoot," added Tristen. "I know that she's still alive. I have to believe she's protecting us from them—whoever *they* are. I must take the chance that my father's family will be on our side, once they learn what has actually transpired. I'm doing this for Solana and the boys."

"I was hoping to have heard from her by now, but knowing Solana as we do, she's too smart to reveal herself. She won't until she knows for sure what's going on, and who in our ranks betrayed us," said Chief Solano.

"Yeah, I know, but it doesn't stop me from wishing we knew what she learned that scared her so much and caused her to go into hiding," muttered Tristen.

"The older family Chivalran regiments have the resources needed to get to the bottom of this. Their support is essential. They're very loyal to kin. That's why you're making this journey instead of me. Your family ties go well beyond the Gordons. You're the only one who has experienced a loss equal to mine, and you're the only one I trust to build the needed coalitions. You'll be leaving via a transatlantic vessel scheduled to depart in forty-two hours."

"Understood."

"It won't be safe for Quentin and Bradley until you're able to make things right concerning the Gordon Chivalran. You must take your rightful leadership positions first. I think it best the boys not return to Scotland with you until then. In the meantime, I cannot ensure their safety if they remain here."

Tristen nodded his agreement.

"Whoever came for Solana knows the boys exist. We need to get them out of here as soon as possible."

Chief Solano gently grabbed hold of Tristen's arms as he looked into his eyes.

"Son, I agree with you. I don't believe they know what the boys look like, because none of our people gave them any information. Hiding them should be easy if we choose wisely. The safe haven must possess similar natural attributes to our tribal lands. Nature will aide us in masking their inherent frequency outputs transmitted whenever their special abilities are employed. They still have no control over them and are unwitting to all they possess. I've just the place in mind that will serve to shield their existence from prying eyes."

"My separation from the boys will be hard on them, especially after their mother's disappearance. I know this is the right thing to do, but they're so young."

"I feel as you do, but I know, *we* know, we have no other choice. I believe my daughter, Benitita, is the only one to be trusted to care for the boys. She loves her nephews and is best suited to comfort them during this very hard time in their lives."

"She lives so far away. Isn't there somewhere closer?"

"Her children are the only blood relatives who happen to have the same hair, skin, and eye coloring as Bradley and Quentin. Plus, the North American fishing village where they live is remotely located on a scarcely populated island. The island, Celtston, possesses unique magnetic anomalies that will provide the perfect natural cover, and it's a lot closer to Scotland, where you'll be."

"Okay."

"I had Daniel contact his cousin, Benitita, earlier this evening and she has already sent word back that she'd be honored to care for them, but *only* with your permission."

"Of course, she has my permission *and* my gratitude," confirmed Tristen.

"The islanders live similarly to how we do here in the village. They'll collectively watch out for the boys, under the oversight of the Celtston Island elders, who have confirmed the boys are welcome to stay while we sort this all out. They are aware of the risks involved."

With a heavy heart, Tristen asked what he most feared.

"When will they depart?"

"Within the hour. I've already made the necessary arrangements. They'll be taken to a night crawler, laying wait for them at the mouth of the river. This boat has a planned meet with a cargo freighter, scheduled to be anchored off the coast of Brazil at zero six hundred. The night crawler will depart zero four thirty."

"I'll be the one to take them," Tristen said.

"As it should be. This will allow you the time to say a proper goodbye. I don't have to tell you how important it is that no one be made aware of their departure. Your sons must not be told what's happening until they're already on their way. We can't take any chances with a traitor in our midst."

The boys were safely aboard the large cargo freighter, huddled in a small, colorless, and unadorned stateroom made of metal—a stark and unfriendly place. They sat atop a three-inch-thick mattress, covered with damp sheets and an itchy woolen blanket smelling of mildew, the only furnishings in the room. They could feel a chill through the thin, tan, cotton blanket they were given to warm themselves as they leaned against the cold metal bulkhead.

They could feel the ship's movement, but with no portal to allow them to look outside, they couldn't tell where they were or the time of day. All they knew was that they were going to their Aunt Benitita's house and they couldn't wait to get there.

As frightened as Bradley was, he still made an attempt to comfort his little brother.

"Quentin, don't worry. We'll be back home before you know it.

Quentin hadn't said a word since they left the village, and Bradley couldn't stand the quiet, so he kept on talking.

"I dreamt about Mother last night. If she were dead, she wouldn't be in my dreams."

Quentin let out a little sniffle then quietly admitted, "She was in mine too."

"See, everything's going to be okay," said Bradley, not realizing that he needed to hear it for himself.

"We're finally going to meet our cousins. Father said they're really nice and two of them are close to our ages."

"I'm scared, Bradley. What if Mother is really gone?"

"You'll always have me, no matter what. My one and only job is to care for you when she and father aren't around."

Bradley hugged his little brother and gave him a gentle kiss on his forehead, like he witnessed his mother do so often.

CHAPTER SIX

NOPAR

The boys left the sanctuary of the Precaveros tribal lands believing it to be temporary. Their father left for Scotland to reunite with his family, promising to return for them within a few months, over eight years earlier.

Bradley Gordon, now a strapping young man of fifteen years, and Quentin, a younger version of his older brother at age thirteen, had learned to adapt to their new surroundings.

The two brothers lived peacefully on Celtston, in the upper North Atlantic Ocean, off the outer northeastern region of the North American continent. The island was so small and remote that it appeared only on a few maps and charts that had been created by the inhabitants themselves. The islanders were all descendants of Northern European settlers who had discovered the island when seeking refuge from warring factions many generations before. While the island's whereabouts were known by a few who dabbled in seafood exports—due to the abundant fisheries and other rare and delectable marine species—nothing else of note existed on the island to attract outsiders.

The winter and fall seasons were cold and inhospitable, infamous for extremely rough seas, high winds, and frigid winter temperatures that were almost always below freezing. Locals named the winter winds *the Trepidations*. The seas surrounding the island exceeded twenty feet in height on most days, creating a natural fortress wall as if *Mother Nature* herself were protecting the island from unwelcome visitors.

The milder summer and spring months held no attraction, because temperatures rarely exceeded seventy-five degrees Fahrenheit, and there wasn't a sandy beach for the would-be sun worshippers. The one Celtston rock-free zone was fully dedicated to the port, every square foot used to maximize the output of the island's main income source—fishing.

Outside communications were scarce and unpredictable due to the effects of the northern magnetic anomalies. Few electronics existed, and those that did were satellite radios and the rare television set located in the harbor master's office and the town hall. There was little use for cell phones and other gadgetry. Marine radios were the main source of communication. The islanders were free of the electronic addictions that plagued most of the world's human inhabitants.

Despite their isolation, the islanders were not backwards by any measure. They were well read and loved all kinds of music. They were highly educated in history, math, sciences, geography, biology, chemistry, and earthly natural phenomenon pertinent to their region of the world. They were fluent in many languages, in keeping with their survival needs and desire to maintain the wisdom of their ancestors. This knowledge enabled them to communicate with foreign exporters, a few importers, and the rare visitor who came to the island from time to time.

Bradley and Quentin enjoyed life with the Northcutts—Aunt Benitita, Uncle Richard, and their children, Chance, Nicole, and Spencer.

They shared bunkbeds in a room within the three-story, wood framed, white clapboard, Victorian-style seaside home. No personal pictures or wall hangings adorned their bedroom walls, except for a single painting with the Northcutt's ancestors, all very stern looking and darkly clad, not typical of a young man's taste in artwork. Why should the boys bother to decorate when they were only supposed to be here temporarily?

Windows and porches ran around the expanse of the house's three levels, save where the two sets of double-wide stairs cut the front and back porches of the first level. The splendid home, known as the *Northcutt House* by the locals, sat on a very high cliff, with a spectacular view of the ocean from all four sides. On a clear day, one could spy on all transit of boats and their occupants in and out of the port and monitor the goings on almost everywhere.

At night, there were no streetlamps or other light-pollution sources, allowing for world class stargazing. At times, the full harvest moon almost filled the entire quarter of the sky, appearing so close one could reasonably fly a plane up to visit. The air itself felt charged with a positive energy that seemed to put smiles on all onlookers' faces.

While grateful his aunt and uncle were taking care of him and Quentin, and appreciative of all that Celtston had to offer, Bradley longed to be back in the loving arms of his parents. He intensely disliked Celtston's cold season that chilled him to his inner core, freezing his ears, fingers, toes, and any skin not covered in layers of wool and fleece. He longed to see and smell the flowers, to witness the life that teamed in the forests, and to partake in the mysteries and wonders unique to the Amazon basin, while wearing light cotton shorts and shirts, and open-toed sandals.

Bradley worked on board the fishing boat *Nelson* during his summer vacations from school. One day, while swabbing the deck, he took a few moments and looked around, enjoying the sunny and warm summer day. It had to be at least seventy-eight degrees Fahrenheit, and it felt good. He was part of the hustle and bustle of boat hands, fish cleaners, dock maintenance crews, and the myriad of customers busying themselves at the Celtston commerce center.

He could see the entire port from where he stood on the *Nelson*. The port provided refuge for the twelve Celtston fishing boats after they completed their workday. Each boat was forty to fifty feet in length and was accompanied by flocks of seagulls, pelicans, and countless other seagoing birds, encircling their food sources. Bradley could hear the cacophony of the birds as they loudly squawked, as if to warn the boat crews of their many attempts to steal one of the sea creatures that burdened the boats now moored with their ample catches of the day.

He and his cousin, Chance Northcutt, had almost finished with scrubbing the residue of smelly sea creatures from the main deck. Chance, a spitting image of his father, shared a strong familial likeness to Bradley. His sea-green eyes had just a hint of the Northcutt blue, as did Bradley's from the Gordons. Chance, a strapping young man with the curliest blond locks, stood an impressive six feet two inches tall, just like Bradley—tall for a fifteen-year-old boy. Chance carried himself as if he hailed from the royal family of his ancestral home, Austria—or was it Lithuania? He never could remember, and his father didn't like to discuss his family's history, pre-Celtston.

Chance looked up from his work and took notice of a very solemn Bradley looking out over the port.

"You look so serious and you're being so quiet. What's bothering you?"

"Nothing," said Bradley as he got back down on his knees and started scrubbing the deck with zeal.

"*Nothing.* I don't believe you. You can tell me. I won't tell anyone."

"You have to promise."

"I said I won't tell anyone, and I won't," replied Chance.

"I can't believe it has been eight years since my mother's disappearance and since my father left us to go to Scotland to meet and reconnect with his family. Where is he? Why hasn't he come to see us at least once in eight years?"

"My dad told me that what your father is doing is really complicated, and that if he doesn't do it right, he could really mess things up for you and your mother. He also said that he can't come to Celtston to see you, fearing that someone might follow and find you and Quentin. He wants to keep you two safe."

"I know, but as much as Quentin and I appreciate being able to live with you and getting to know you, your house has never felt like home. It's like I'm on an eternal vacation in a foreign land. I miss being at home."

Bradley stood and looked out over the port as his shoulders slumped forward and he let out a long and slow sigh.

"These days, particularly these days, I really miss my mother, my father, my grandfather, and the rest of the tribe, especially, the boys in the tribe. I had a best friend. His name was Lucas. I'm worried about what has become of him without my mother and I being there to care for and protect him."

"You'll be able to catch up with him one day. I'm sure he'll understand."

"I wasn't able to tell Lucas what was happening when we left, because we had to sneak away during the night. I'm still not allowed to contact him, because everyone's afraid that if I do, I'll tip off whoever it is that's trying to get to us. I hope that someone let Lucas know why I left so quickly. I've always wondered what, or if, Lucas ever thinks about me."

"Bradley, I know you care about your friend, but I think something else is really bothering you. What is it?"

"Okay. Your dad has made sure that I understand he has no intention of taking the place of my father. He has his family to care for and you're his priority. I totally understand this, and I don't want to seem ungrateful, because I'm not. No telling where we'd be if your parents hadn't taken us in."

"I know my dad told you that you're Quentin's only caretaker, and that you'll have to eventually assume total responsibility for him when you turn seventeen, because that's when you become a man on this island. But I know he won't just abandon you. And you'll always have me. I'll help you out when I can. There won't be much I can do at first, but you can always count on me. Heck, this will only come to pass if your parents don't come to retrieve you before your seventeenth birthday; there's plenty of time before then. My dad thinks your father will be coming to get you soon. He likes to always have a backup plan, so he wants to make sure you're prepared, just in case something goes wrong. Everything's going to be okay. You'll see."

"I don't know. I'm not aware of any contact being made with my mother. No one has reported to have seen her, or at least I haven't received any information about her whereabouts. So much time has passed. It's hard for me to believe she's still alive. Wouldn't she have been found by now? The only thing keeping me positive is that since I arrived in Celtston, I feel her presence now and again, but so little of my mother's being. She rarely enters my dreams anymore."

"That doesn't mean she's gone," countered Chance.

"There's another thing. My mother was teaching me about my abilities. No one here has any of them, as far as I can tell. In the village I could openly practice and learn how to use them. Here, everything is a secret. I'm told not to discuss it. I feel so different than everyone else. Quentin and I *are* different than everyone else."

"You're right," conceded Chance.

"To make matters worse, I rarely hear from my father and even more rarely from anyone back home. I receive cryptic letters telling me to be good. Take care of Quentin. It won't be long until your father will come and get you. Be patient until then. Every time I get a letter, it makes me unsettled and more impatient. I'm really starting to lose hope that he's ever going to come."

"Bradley, my parents are keeping your father and grandfather up to date on what's going on with you. I know you want to show them you can handle everything on your own, but I can tell you're scared. But you're not alone. My dad told me that your families are watching out for you, the Misticatos and the Gordons, plus your extended family, friends, and relatives here."

"Look, I have to be real. My father's intentions are fine, but I need to make sure Quentin and I can survive on our own. I can't afford to keep hoping he'll show up someday, not after all this time has passed . . . Oh shoot, look at what time it is! I have to hurry and finish up here and collect my pay, all thirty dollars of it," laughed Bradley. "I'm meeting up with my friends after work today and I promised them I wouldn't be late, for once."

Bradley talked of less serious matters as he picked up a mop and started swabbing the deck with Chance.

"Well at least we get paid more than Quentin. Look at the little guy, hard at work at the fish house down there. Remember when we were like poor Quentin? We got paid a whopping twenty-five cents per five pounds of degutted and beheaded fish. What a nasty, unrewarding job that was. Glad that job is held by little kids. I was so glad when I finally reached five and a half feet, so I could work as one of the boat crew candidates. I think we were both lucky to be tall. Quentin has our height, and he'll be off the docks sooner than the rest of them. . . Look at Quentin's face. Looks like he got sprayed by a skunk." The boys laughed.

"You know Quentin and I work hard. We know we're expected to carry our weight. I've had to work my butt off since I arrived on this island. I buy our clothes and everything else we need. We moved here when I was seven years old. I feel cheated. I never got to be a kid, because my folks decided to go do whatever it is they're doing."

"Bradley, my dad always tells me that everything happens for a reason. I'd like to think that's true, and that good things are coming your way."

"Well, in the meantime, the height of fishing season is almost over and we're of age to be promoted from swab to full deck hand. If I can only get a spot on one of the boats, then I'll feel better about everything. It's important to me. I can't believe the new crew selection is happening *this* Sunday, in *two* days."

"I hope we're both still on the *Nelson*," said Chance.

"That's *if* I'm chosen."

"Bradley, come off it. You and I both know that you, Nopar, and I are the best deckhands of our age on the island. It's not a question of *if* we'll be chosen, but which boat we'll be assigned to. Since we're both so good, I bet they split us up."

Bradley returned to swabbing the deck with enthusiasm. Then he spied his three best buddies, Skeeter, Kyle, and Ed Moe, walking down the long wooden dock towards him. It was Friday and they were looking forward to having some fun and adventure.

"Bradley, hurry up! You're on one of the smallest fishing boats in all of Celtston, but we beat you swabbing our decks! You slacker," yelled Skeeter, laughing at his taunt.

"It's easy to get done first when you don't have any fish to sort," yelled back Bradley, who quickly went to rinse his mop and hang it to dry. He grabbed his duffle bag and headed to the boat ramp. Right before departing, he turned to his cousin, who was rinsing his mop before doing the same.

"Chance, you want to come with?"

"Nah, you go ahead. I have plans of my own, but thanks for asking."

As soon as he met up with the other boys, rough housing and horseplay ensued as they hastily walked towards shore.

Once the boys finished complaining about the hardships of their labors, Bradley started to once again talk about what he'd been thinking about all day and every day for the last two months.

"I'm really worried about Sunday. You guys know that only the best of us are made permanent hands on the boats. These jobs are the only real jobs on the island, except for the harbor master. I'm only going to get *one* chance in my lifetime for consideration."

His three friends rolled their eyes as Bradley obsessed.

"If I don't get chosen, I don't know what I'd do. I wasn't born here. I'm not sure I'm going to be able to overcome the fact that I'm a *come here* and not a *from here*."

"Bradley everyone knows that you and Chance are the best, and Teddy Nopar a distant third. We all know Nopar wouldn't be considered even close to you in talent, if he wasn't the harbor master's son."

"Stop worrying," Skeeter admonished. "You're a shoe-in. Besides, there's nothing you can do about it anyway. How about you give it a rest? Give us all a break."

"You know, I wouldn't be so uptight if Uncle Richard wasn't so clear when he told me that once I was of age, I would no longer be his responsibility. I'm going to be seventeen in less than two years. I *have* to get one of the deckhand spots . . . but you're right. Nothin' I can do about it. Let's go have some fun!"

As if a gun were shot indicating the start of a race, they began running down the dock, neck-and-neck.

"Well look who it is, the four misfits," spouted Nopar. He pushed a fifty-gallon drum of smelly water tainted with rotting fish remnants over the side of the boat, hoping to soak the four friends as they raced towards the shore.

"Ooops. Sorry, I didn't *see* you coming. None of us knew you were down there."

Nopar and the other deckhands busted out laughing at the unsuspecting victims.

Fortunately, a strong breeze blew at just the right moment, causing Nopar's aim to be off a bit, and only Skeeter was hit with a few droplets of the refuse.

"I don't get why Nopar won't leave me—us—alone. I don't understand what I ever did to him." Bradley said. "I can't believe I was dumb enough to try to befriend him when I first got here. He seems dedicated to making my life miserable. I wish he'd give it a rest."

"Prior to your arrival, only Chance could beat Nopar at some things, but not even he was able to beat Nopar at *everything*. Your arrival changed that. So he hates you. No surprise to me," said Skeeter.

"You're everything he's not. You're tall, blond, and handsome," said Kyle. "And nobody knows why you moved to Celtston. There's lots of gossip about why you're here. My mother says it *adds to your mystique*. Nopar hates you getting all of his attention. It detracts from the one thing he loves most—himself. Nopar thinks he's something special because his daddy's the harbor master and the mayor . . . he hates you . . . so what?"

"Face it, Bradley," Skeeter chimed in. "The guy despises everything about you. To make matters worse, you're a nice guy. He's never going to like you or us because we hang out with you. Forget about him."

CHAPTER SEVEN

THE CHOOSING

Following the morning gathering on Sunday, the people of Celtston met in the town square to witness and participate in *The Choosing* celebration for the coveted fishing boat crew selections. It was a rare time when everyone on the island dressed in their Sunday best. The males wore collared, short-sleeved, thick cotton shirts, shorts, and untarnished canvas boat shoes; the ladies dressed in multi-colored cotton sundresses and flat leather sandals.

Bradley and Quentin arrived at the fairground with their uncle and cousins; their Aunt Benitita had left home hours earlier to help with the setup.

"You're in for a real treat," beamed Uncle Richard. "We couldn't have asked for a better day. No rain, a nice cool northerly breeze, and not a cloud in the deep blue sky—a perfect day."

A variety of minstrel bands, made up of the local artisans, played an assortment of music genres. The musicians were strategically located far enough apart to not spoil the effects of each other's music.

"And look at that wood planked dance floor. It's laid smack dab in the center of all the happenings. I guess someone is anticipating the festivities sure to follow," grinned Uncle Richard.

"This is *great*," Chance said. "There must be thirty tables setup. I've never seen so many different foods and crafts. This is so much better than last year."

"The food smells so good!" exclaimed Bradley, as his stomach grumbled. His brother Quentin and his cousins all shook their heads in agreement.

"I can smell the homemade sweet pies . . . *mmm* . . . *mmm*," rejoiced Bradley, his eyes shut as he swung his head from left to right, donning a broad grin.

"I can't believe what I'm hearing. You kids just ate breakfast. I can't fathom how you could be hungry already," laughed Uncle Richard. "I remember when in days past, I too would have been ravenous from the smells of sweetbreads and fried apple pies."

Spencer split out from the group and headed into the crowd as he called out, "I'm going to find Mom. She promised she'd save me a piece of Mrs. Nopar's homemade double-chocolate cream pie."

"See ya," said Nicole as she, too, took her leave. "I promised to meet up with Eileen Ann at the pop stage."

Chance, Bradley, and Quentin followed suit, leaving Uncle Richard to fend for himself.

Bradley headed towards the soothing sounds of the Scottish Highlanders' voices and bagpipes, knowing that was where the best fish and chips could be found. Skeeter, Ed, Moe, and Kyle followed. Quentin had decided to follow his cousin, Spencer, hoping for a free sample or two for himself.

Within an hour, Captain Nopar made his way to the lectern located at the center of the celebration. He lightly tapped on the microphone. Everyone stopped and all noise ceased. Bradley and his friends ran from the booths on the fringes of the festival grounds to where they could be front and center for the Choosing. Bradley grabbed Quentin along the way, "Quentin, come on . . . we need to hurry so we don't miss anything."

Upon arrival, Bradley could see the onlookers staring at the stage

with anticipation. He could hardly stand it as he listened to Captain
Nopar recount the reason the ceremony took place. It seemed like
an eternity until he finally proclaimed, "Without any further ado,
I will begin calling out the names of the chosen candidates along
with their boat assignments. When I call your name, I will ask that
each of you come forward and stand with your boat crew."

"Chance Donald Northcutt, assigned to the *Nelson*. Theodore
Sinclair Nopar, assigned to the *Parsons*."

The names kept being announced and boat assignments made,
but Bradley Gordon's name wasn't among them. He started to
lose focus on his surroundings, and he could hardly see distinct
features of anyone standing nearby, as the last name was called. He
immediately became despondent.

What am I going to do?

"Bradley, I can't believe what just happened," Skeeter said.
"You're a way better fisherman than . . ."

When it was all said and done, his friends left the immediate area
with their families to celebrate the fact that all of their names had been
called, and he found himself and Quentin standing alone. Quentin
looked on as Bradley slowly walked away, knowing it was best not to
follow. On his way out of the village, Quentin called to his brother.

"This isn't fair. You should've been chosen."

Bradley slunk away to be alone.

Lineage had won out over skill and ability. Family connections
won over talent and competence. Bradley fought the urge to
become resentful and negative, although those emotions were
surely understandable. If anyone on the island really cared for him,
wouldn't they be outraged, and wouldn't they support his justifiable
anger? He knew in his heart, they wouldn't.

*Anger and resentments are pure poison; there is no such thing as
justifiable bad behavior, and it will kill you from within.* This is what
his Uncle Richard and Aunt Benitita said to him over and over.
Curse them!

Bradley took in a long and deep breath of air as he attempted to slow his rapidly beating heart, and to stop his hands from shaking. He knew he needed to clear his head. He hated himself for being so self-absorbed and it made him feel worse, if that was even possible, because it wasn't in his nature to sit on a pity pot.

I have no idea what I'm supposed to do now.

The last remnants of his childhood innocence vanished when Captain Nopar had spoken his last words. "This concludes the ceremony."

I miss the time when my only job was to catch a butterfly to make my mother happy. How could she leave me . . . and where's my father? I just want to go home. . .

Bradley's fear and anxiety turned to anger as he started beating himself up for thinking he'd be accepted as a Celtston waterman. He knew the same fate—rejection—awaited his brother. They were visitors, only.

Bradley eventually tired of aimlessly walking about the island and slowly found his way back to his uncle's house. Not surprising, Uncle Richard was waiting up for him. He could see the lights burning brightly on the first floor of the house at this late hour and dreaded the discussion sure to come. There was no way to avoid the confrontation. Bracing himself for the encounter, he entered the house and, sure enough, his uncle was in the foyer waiting for him.

Uncle Richard motioned to Bradley to follow him into the kitchen. Bradley hurriedly sat on the comfy green and blue plaid cushion of the solid cherry wood kitchen nook. Uncle Richard placed two fresh, steaming cups of sweet cocoa, laden with whipped cream, on the table.

"Bradley, I want to know what you're thinking, and what your plans are, now that the Choosing ceremony is over."

"I don't have a clue. I can't believe I wasn't picked. Everyone knows I'm better than Smokey, Douglas, and pretty much everyone else. Why didn't anyone speak up on my behalf? Why didn't you?

I'm trying to make this okay in my head, but I'm really struggling to understand what happened."

Uncle Richard didn't say a word; his facial expression said it all. Bradley could tell that he wasn't surprised at the outcome.

"You think that I need to be real. I get it. I'm not one of you. What would make me ever think you'd take from one of your own, and give something so precious to me?"

With a shaky and quavering voice Bradley continued. "I don't hate anyone for it. I understand how it all worked, but I can't stop myself from feeling cheated and so utterly alone. I'm at a loss as to what I'm supposed to do."

Bradley, unable to control his emotions, blurted, "Where's my father? When will he come to get us? Are he and my mother even still alive? Why won't anyone tell me what's really going on? You and the rest of the Celtston elders have to know something more than what you've been telling me. What are you hiding from me? I have a *right* to know!"

He uncharacteristically lashed out at his uncle as he stood. "Back home, I felt loved, I felt so happy, but now I feel . . . empty. I feel like I lost my parents all over again."

Uncle Richard pointed his index finger to indicate he wanted Bradley to retake his seat, and then cleared his throat.

"I know you feel unloved, but you're mistaken. There are many who love you and care for you, including myself and your Aunt Benitita. In time you'll know what I say to be true. I know you don't like to hear it, but you're *not* yet old enough to handle the facts of the matter. I'm asking you to trust me when I tell you this will be over soon. I need you to hang in there."

"If you didn't hear, *there is no more time*! I have no future and I don't know what to do," cried Bradley.

"Bradley, you hail from royalty. Your families, both the Gordons and the Misticatos, are powerful and influential peoples. In time, you will reap the benefits of their collective wealth and heritage.

Don't lose faith in us now, especially since we're so close to coming to closure on all that has plagued us and you and your brother. In the meantime, you're nearing manhood. You can't afford to think like you are. Feeling sorry for yourself won't help. It certainly won't put a roof over your head, or Quentin's, nor food on the table. You have talents. You'll be able to make a good living."

"Yeah . . . right," feigned Bradley.

"I've been thinking about a few options for you. One came to mind that I consider perfect. Are you interested in hearing my idea?"

Bradley nodded.

"Ever since old man Celton passed, we've been without a dedicated oyster farmer. I think you're a natural replacement for him. If need be, I'll let you stay here while you get established following your high school graduation, but only if you start putting your energies towards that end. I expect you to go see Michael Robert Sidlau, Old Man Celton's grandson, first thing in the morning. I want you to ask his permission to dive the oyster beds that are easily accessed from his land. I have the scuba equipment you'll need. My boys have no interest in the pursuit, ever since Chance's best friend's older brother died scuba diving when he was a little boy. It happened about a month before you arrived in Celtston. Chance thinks it too dangerous and way too cold. He'd rather be on the water than in it, and Spencer won't do anything like that without his big brother. There you have it. If you want the equipment, it's yours."

Uncle Richard stood up and walked over to Bradley. He pulled him up and out of the nook and gave him a big bear hug.

"Good night, Bradley. Think it over."

Bradley quietly entered his bedroom, careful not to wake his sleeping brother.

CHAPTER EIGHT

MICHAEL

Bradley awoke with a more hopeful outlook on life. He jumped out of bed, quickly dressed, and headed down the stairs towards the kitchen, lured by the aromas of cooked bacon and freshly brewed coffee. His stomach grumbled as he entered the kitchen, where he found his aunt and uncle engaged in deep conversation while seated in the kitchen nook. Bradley stopped in his tracks, concerned that he might be intruding.

"Come on in, Bradley. Your aunt and I are talking about your situation; perfect timing," encouraged Uncle Richard.

"How'd you sleep? Your uncle and I slept like babies rocking in their mothers' arms," said Aunt Benitita.

"Sorry for getting up so late."

"You had a big day yesterday," Uncle Richard said. "We would've been surprised to see you any earlier."

Bradley took a seat next to Aunt Benitita as she slid further into the booth.

"I thought about my circumstances all day yesterday. I even dreamt that I talked it over with my mother, like our discussion when I got home last night. I realize that there are *plenty* of things I can do."

Uncle Richard jumped up from his seat to get Bradley a plate of fried eggs, bacon, buttered homemade sourdough toast, and a glass of freshly squeezed, extra pulp orange juice—Bradley's favorite breakfast.

"Bradley, I'm happy to hear that you're starting to realize you possess talents others don't have," said Uncle Richard. "Like we talked about last night, you're a natural born waterman. I believe you possess the intellectual prowess and the required intuitive nature needed for a successful oyster farmer, spear fisherman, and treasure hunter."

Bradley's eyebrows raised, "A treasure hunter?"

"Yes, you heard me correctly—*treasure hunter*. The oyster farm is adjacent to a system of unexplored underwater lava tubes that have hardly been touched. There is a long history of unsuccessful endeavors because those attempting the adventure rarely had the proper equipment, making it near impossible for them to do well. For the uninformed and unprepared explorer, the surrounding waters and the lava tube system, made up of a myriad of caves and tunnels, are way too dangerous. The unpredictable seas that continue to flood the cave system, seemingly without notice or warning, have caused many a loss of life, and people *presumed* dead, who have never been found."

"Uncle Richard, I'm finally starting to understand what you've been trying to tell me. I'm physically strong and able-bodied. I have a chance to create a real job out of this. I'm going to turn the negative thoughts and feelings I've been obsessing over into positive ones. Instead of finding fish from the top of the water, I'll find them—and hopefully valuable treasures beyond my imaginings— underwater and in the lava tubes."

Bradley smiled, his teeth glistening.

"That's good," said Uncle Richard.

"Quentin and I have each other, and I have a year and a half to figure out what I can do to earn a decent living. I feel like I have something to look forward to and work towards, and this is something that Quentin can do with me when he's ready."

Bradley finished his breakfast and as soon as Aunt Benitita could hear him walking around upstairs, she blurted out her greatest fears in a frantic whisper.

"What will happen to our two nephews? Where will they end up? And can we keep them safe and sound in the meantime? I know this isn't the time to share these concerns with Bradley. He already has too much on his plate, but pretty soon he's going to need to know what's going on. The boys need Solana here to tutor them and to teach them how to use their abilities properly. Tristen has got to hurry with his efforts in Scotland. Bradley's coming of age and we're running out of time."

Bradley headed straight over to meet Mr. Sidlau. The conversation with his aunt and uncle fueled his enthusiasm and he couldn't wait to get started. While Bradley was fast-walking to Mr. Sidlau's house, he tried to remember what he'd heard about this guy. He liked to be called Michael and lived alone on the shore by the most remote section of cliffs on the island. He moved in the year after Quentin and Bradley arrived, but Bradley and Quinten had never spoken to him.

Bradley arrived at Mr. Sidlau's property. He looked up at old man Celton's house. It seemed to be a mirror image of Uncle Richard's with one notable exception—a two-story addition that was connected to the main house by a twenty-foot-long second story walkway, with no ground floor entrance.

How weird is that?

The house was also located on a cliff that was at least two hundred feet above the ocean. From the top of the cliff, Bradley could almost see the entire island, but not Uncle Richard's property because of the hilly terrain and the trees that blocked his view.

Bradley climbed the steps to the front door and knocked. He only had to wait a few moments before Mr. Sidlau opened the front door and warmly greeted him.

"Good morning, young man. What can I do for you?"

Bradley introduced himself and quickly recapped his discussion with his uncle. Mr. Sidlau seemed amused by Bradley's enthusiasm and patiently waited for the boy to complete his stated purpose. He politely invited Bradley into his home to finish their discussion over a cup of freshly squeezed lemonade.

"Bradley, it's so nice to finally meet you. I would ask that you call me Michael Robert, or simply Michael will do. Mr. Sidlau sounds too formal and I would hope to nurture an informal relationship between the two of us. For instance, you might not be aware, but I know some of your relatives on your father's side. Did your Uncle Richard tell you?"

Caught off guard, Bradley blurted, "No."

"Well, I can tell you more about all of that later. But first, I'd like to address the reason you stopped by."

"Yes, sir, I'd like that."

The two settled into a sitting room, lemonades in hand, where Michael began his informal job interview.

"I could not have asked for a better visit from anyone today. I'm looking for someone just like you, an enthusiastic, able-bodied young person with a higher than average intelligence. You obviously have all of these traits, from what I just witnessed, and from what your aunt and uncle have told me. But I need to know if you're also adventurous. Are you willing to take direction? And can I trust you with family secrets—secrets that can only be conveyed to others with my consent? If your answer to any of these questions is *no*, my answer to your request is *no*."

"Of course you can trust me. I'm really good at keeping secrets. You can ask anyone who knows me."

"But are you adventurous? Are you willing to learn from another?"

"*Yes,* and *yes.*"

"Bradley, I want you to know I'll expect much of you. It will be hard work, and if I ask you to do something, I'll expect you to do it. Can you do that?"

"Yes, sir, I not only can, *I will.*"

"Well then, my answer to you is *yes*. You have a deal."

"Awesome!"

Bradley and Michael spent the rest of their first meeting getting to know one another in a friendly and open discussion. Michael spoke to Bradley as if he were an adult, something Bradley greatly appreciated.

Michael divulged, "I like living alone here nearest to the ocean and by the most remote section of the cliffs. I inherited this place from my deceased uncle, one of the few properties ever handed down to a family member who wasn't an islander. This property includes many acres of land. A good section of the cliffs is surrounded by abundant, naturally occurring oyster beds that are potentially some of the most productive in the world. These oyster beds are hard to access from the open ocean, due to the large waves crashing against the rock outcroppings just offshore. The beds themselves are protected by this wall of glacial rock that creates the calmer, protected waters where the oysters thrive. You add in the unpredictable seas and weather, and the cost of life and limb to farm the oysters is great. Having not been farmed regularly, the oyster beds have grown beyond measure. I also own the access to the mysterious, hidden lava tube labyrinth, whose size and breadth is still unknown. Many a story has been told concerning folks who ventured into them, never to return."

"Are those stories true?" asked Bradley.

"They're true, as far as I know. The lava tubes are a vast system of caves and tunnels that go everywhere and nowhere, and it's easy to get lost in them if you don't know what you're doing. The tides flood some but not others, and with no apparent regularity, so it's hard to plan an exploration. *But* there is a good side. The water within the labyrinth is warmed by a few degrees from heat that makes its way up and into the caves and tunnels walls. The warmth comes from the remote volcanic activity. It provides enough of a heat source to keep the cove waters surrounding the entrances to the caves slightly warmer than average local temperatures, helping to prevent the adjacent oyster beds from freezing over and dying off during the harsh winter months."

"Do you know what's down there?"

"From what my uncle told me, only he and his father have ever had the decoder key to the labyrinth construct. Unfortunately for me, my uncle wasn't able to pass a lot of what he knew on to me prior to his death. I learned way too little to have a full appreciation of its wonders. The majority of the lava tube labyrinth is unexplored territory that needs to be charted and the attributes documented."

"Are you glad you came here?" Bradley asked.

"The short answer is yes, because after being around so many people back in Lithuania, whence I came, I jumped at the chance to move here. It was the opportunity of a lifetime. I'm so grateful to have had the little time I did with him. I wish I could've gotten to know him better. I felt a bit bitter concerning his early passing, but I'm over that now. I still feel somewhat cheated out of the years I had hoped to spend with him. I would've liked to have been a greater part of his life, because I lost my father at an early age, and my uncle had become, for me, the father I no longer had. As if that wasn't bad enough, when my uncle died, he left me wanting for the knowledge of this place that was known only to him; very little was ever written down. I want you to help me solve the mysteries of my holdings. I think we have much to gain from a partnership."

Bradley hung on every word, as Michael continued to relay his history and talk about the plans he had for the two of them. Bradley couldn't believe Michael had been in Celtston all this time and he hadn't gotten to know him.

Bradley was surprised to find out that Michael was about the same age as his own father. Michael seemed so easy to relate to and he acted much younger. Bradley also felt at ease because Michael's facial features and some of his mannerisms were similar to his father's. The men were about the same height and body type, but Michael had brown hair—not blond.

Why couldn't Uncle Richard be more like Michael?

Bradley's new-found friend reignited the flame in him, and he was starting to feel hopeful that everything would be okay.

Over the first several weeks of their newly formed partnership, Michael gave Bradley a limited tour of the underground lava tubes and showed him the best spots to harvest oysters. Bradley learned how to safely get to the oyster fields and back by foot and by scuba diving in water less than thirty feet deep. Sometimes the tides and other natural phenomena could make accessing the various sites rather tricky. For safety reasons, Michael limited Bradley's initial exposure to the places that were easiest to access.

Michael enjoyed sharing his knowledge of these surroundings. He emphasized, time and again, his most important rule: "No matter what, safety comes first, and then the fun will surely follow."

Michael even showed interest in Bradley's brother, encouraging Quentin to visit and, over time, to participate in some of the easier scuba diving adventures into the external tunnels and caverns. Quentin immediately liked Michael, further validating Bradley's feelings toward the man.

Bradley hadn't felt as safe or content since leaving his jungle home.

Bradley spent the next two weeks waking up at dawn, quickly devouring his breakfast and scurrying off to Michael's. Having less than two months left until school started, Bradley hoped to absorb all he could about oyster farming. Once winter came to the island, Bradley feared his access to the ocean and the lava tubes would cease.

With exactly one month remaining prior to the start of the school year, Michael taught Bradley how to safely scuba dive in deep and treacherous waters, and how to dive inside the outermost, partially enclosed lava tube caves and tunnels. He quickly gained an appreciation for the underwater world, and while he had started off using the basic scuba gear his uncle had given him, he soon found the gear he had been gifted wasn't good enough for the more serious diving. He would have to purchase gear better suited for longer, deeper dives.

While diving was fun and adventurous, it could be equally dangerous. Michael made him study books on dive theory, and then he gave him written and practical tests. The tests validated his understanding and his ability to apply the theory to real scenarios. This continued all summer, until Bradley was able to prove to Michael that he could actually perform the needed skills to undertake more advanced dives. Bradley proved himself more than capable and he easily passed the written and practical tests.

"Bradley, you're a natural scuba diver."

"I love this stuff and it's so fun. I can't believe how much I enjoy being able to go underwater and stay down there. It's so cool . . ."

"I can tell," laughed Michael.

"I don't care about losing my spot on the boats and deep sea fishing any more. I've finally discovered my niche in this world, just like you said I would. Look at me now. I'm a certified scuba diver and a novice lava tube explorer. It's so hard for me to believe how much you've taught me this summer."

"I still have so much to teach you. Overhead cavern and cave diving in these underwater lava tube tunnels is one of the most challenging dive-training specialties. It's really hard to master. It requires more than merely learning skills and retaining knowledge. A diver must be able to prove to the person training them that they can handle themselves appropriately while in confined, stressful and, at times, dangerous situations. Few divers possess these most-coveted certifications or the composure required for such undertakings. Fewer still, even with these certifications, would ever venture into the unchartered and unlit caves and tunnels that lead to who knows where. Bradley, you've proven to me over the summer that you're such a diver. You're calm, collected, and unshakeable. You seem to thrive in the underwater environment. You're everything that I hoped you would be and more. You have proven to be a good dive buddy. I feel I can trust you to save me if I have any issues while diving, and that's what I need in a dive partner."

"I could stay underwater forever. It's so peaceful and surreal."

"Yeah, I know what you mean," agreed Michael. "Before I learned how to scuba dive, I hadn't realized how much my ears and my mind were assaulted from external sources. There's always a modicum of errant white noise constantly bombarding us. Noise that I hadn't been aware of, and that over time I unknowingly manage to ignore. I think that's the case for all of us."

"It is for me," Bradley said. "I can relax underwater. I noticed the assault you're talking about stops when I'm submerged."

CHAPTER NINE

ADVENTURE BEGINS

B radley hurried over to Michael's house, excited to be joining him in exploring an uncharted part of the underwater lava tubes. He could hardly sleep the night before, anticipating the day's exploration.

Michael opened the screen door to allow his beaming trainee to enter, but in lieu of venturing toward the sitting room where they usually started their day, Michael headed up the stairs to the second floor.

"Coming?" grinned Michael.

"You're taking me into your inner sanctum—the addition to the house. But why? Does this mean you aren't going to take me into the unexplored parts of the lava tubes today?

Michael just motioned to Bradley to follow him as he turned and sauntered towards the walkway leading to the addition. Bradley reluctantly followed, dragging his feet.

"You're not taking me where you promised today, are you? Not another lesson. I thought you told me I was ready?"

"Just follow me. I'll explain what we're doing once we're in the room. All you need to know is that you'll be the first person who is not part of my immediate family that has ever been allowed to enter these spaces, *and* has been entrusted with the knowledge I'm going to share with you this morning. Come on."

Without another word spoken, unhappy about the classwork surely to follow, Bradley headed towards the staircase.

He slowly walked up the stairs to the second floor, not sure what to expect and not bothering to look at Michael when he passed him in the hallway. He headed across the walkway, a fifty-foot-long, red oak corridor edged with elaborate cornices atop deep wainscoting. The only decorations were small windows spaced every eight feet or so. But, when he stopped at the nondescript wood paneled door that was the obvious entrance to the sanctum and attempted to open it, he found it locked. Bradley turned to call out to Michael, finding him to be standing right behind him flourishing a very old, ornate, brass key in his outstretched hand. Michael opened the door, turned the light switch and entered the furniture-free room. "Bradley, please shut the door behind you and lock the deadbolt. Now, please come over here. I need to get you entered into the security system."

"You have a security system? *Cool!*"

One of the wooden walls had four round buttons mounted flush, none of which were labeled. Michael pushed the buttons simultaneously and a foldout table popped out complete with a keyboard, display, and what looked to be a small, Rubik's Cube-sized speaker and an eyepiece.

"What is that?" said Bradley, pointing at the eye piece protruding from the inner wall of the hidden panel.

"There are three forms of security protecting this sanctuary. The eye piece you're pointing at is part of the retinal scan and biometrics aspect of the security. We'll do that one last. The other two components are for voice recognition recordation and password authentication.

Your eye shape, color, etc. are unique to you, as well as your voice. In this way we can be certain that you're the one entering the sanctuary. The user identification and password will also be unique to you. You must never write them down or share them with anyone, not even Quentin. Understand?"

"Yes."

But first, I want to talk with you about our family history. You need to know why it is that I'm entrusting you, one who appears to be a complete stranger to me, with this very important Sidlau family secret." He sat on the floor with his back to the wall and slapped the floor next to him, indicating to Bradley that he wanted him to sit, as well.

"*Okay*," said Bradley as he took a seat close to where Michael had indicated.

"Your great grandfather, Justin Alfred Gordon, married my grandfather's sister, Bernice Theresa Sidlau. You're actually a relative of mine. We're distant cousins. Your father was her grandson. Do you understand?"

"I think so, but it's hard to follow. Why'd you wait until now to tell me this?"

"There's so much to tell you, but a lot of it, you're not ready to learn."

"Yes *I am*. I'm *sixteen* years old," Bradley said, visibly agitated.

"You have to trust me when I tell you that you're not, but you will be. You need to calm down and listen to me. You'll be told everything, but you must be told things in the proper sequence, so it all makes sense. Okay, Bradley?"

"I guess so . . . what choice do I have?"

Michael looked at Bradley with a raised eyebrow.

"Alright, I'll be patient. That's all anyone ever asks of me. *Please be patient*. We're sorry we left you in the dark for so long, but you're a dumb little kid who *can't handle the truth*."

"Bradley, until now, you *were* too young to know all that has transpired. No one wanted to burden you, but you've since matured. We believe you're ready to learn some things, things that we had hoped your mother and father would have been here to tell you. But alas, time isn't on our side. It has taken longer to resolve a scenario more complicated than was anticipated. Unfortunately for you, we've no more time left due to external concerns."

"Does this have something to do with my father?"

"I heard from your aunt and uncle that history is one of your least favorite subjects, but I found that learning about one's own family's history, especially your family's history, is much more exciting than that which you learn about in school. There won't be a test afterwards, but I suspect that you'll remember everything I'm going to tell you."

Bradley finally took a softer, more engaging stance, as he too sat back and leaned against the wall.

"Your father's family is from Northern Europe, the Gordons of Scotland. Your father is the legal heir to the *Gordon dynasty*. Your family is an important family in global world politics . . . but that's another discussion for another day. My family, and yours as well, the Sidlaus, also hail from Europe—Lithuania. The people on this island are the descendants of refugees from Lithuania who fled religious persecution, Christian religious beliefs to be exact. They fled many years ago. The three exceptions on this island besides me are you, Quentin and your Aunt Benitita.

"Wow!"

"Hundreds of thousands of Christian Lithuanians were killed, tortured, and persecuted during this genocide. Only a few families were able to flee their persecution and to make it to safety. Their whereabouts have been a tightly held secret for hundreds of years. They have been living a peaceful and productive existence, a life they cherish and a secret they guard most fervently. My uncle's great-great-grandfather led the refugees who fled to this island. He changed his family name from Sidlau to Celton as part of their evasion strategy. Thus, being grateful to their savior, the refugees named the island Celtston in honor of him and all he had done to ensure the survival of their lineage. The island remains left off most charts and maps because it's so small and so insignificant to off-islanders, an ideal state of affairs for the occupants."

"I know you can't tell me the entire story now, but would you please tell me later?" requested Bradley.

"Yes."

"You were right. I am interested and I really want to learn more about my family. Up until now, no one would tell me much of anything, so I quit asking."

Michael continued. "To this day there are families who live in Lithuania who still harbor hate and loathing of the refugees, because they were Christians. They feared the Catholic Church leaders in Rome and other Christian groups who they believed were attempting to usurp their power by expanding Catholicism and Christianity into the heart of Lithuania. The powers that be, at the time, put an abrupt stop to what they considered to be a silent but effective takeover of their country. No war or battle was required to take over the people's hearts and minds. The ruling parties felt their power and control over the population diminishing. The Christian leaders and followers were labeled *usurpers* by the Lithuanian ruling class, and those found to be consorting with them were considered to be enemies of the state, and they were harshly dealt with—men, women, and children. It's believed that approximately two hundred and fifty thousand people were able to escape by scattering to many different countries and places all over the world. The majority were hunted down and killed. No one knows for sure how many of these people actually found a safe haven, because many of them changed their names, as did our ancestors."

"That's a crazy story."

"You're related to your Uncle Richard and to me, so by extension the people on the island are your family. The islanders worked together to build Celtston, and they have survived these many years working as a tight knit community. So, while they're not all your *blood* relatives, they're as close as any family could be. They protect one another and would die for one another."

"That's awesome."

"You and Quentin are refugees and you're hiding to escape harm. Your grandfather and grandmother fled their homeland to save their son, your father, from harm. That's how you ended up living with the Precaveros tribe. Now, history is repeating itself. Your father and mother had to flee their home to save their sons, you and Quentin, from harm."

"Do you think my mother is still alive?"

"Yes, we do. We don't know where she is, but we believe your other grandfather, Chief Solano, knows more than he has been willing to share with us thus far. We think he's been in contact with her. Chief Solano is still not sure who he can trust, so he hasn't confirmed what we believe to be true.

"Your *father* is Tristen, but who you believe to be your grandfather on the Gordon side, Lord Andrew Gordon, is actually your grand-uncle Andrew."

"No way!"

"It's true." It took Michael almost an hour to recap for Bradley his family's history. "A false story was spread that relayed the sad and untimely deaths of your father and your grandparents at sea during a ferocious storm, thus allowing your family to have lived in peace and tranquility until the recent past. None of us are certain what ignited the fires of curiosity that resulted in the extraction team being sent to retrieve your mother, and until all the players are identified and their motives understood, we're keeping you here—safe and sound."

"Who's this *we* you keep referring to?"

"The Celtston elders, your dad, and your grandfather, Chief Solano."

"You guys are all in this together?"

"Yes. You have a lot of people looking out for you, and who care about your wellbeing. A somewhat terrifying aspect of this story is that we're not sure who is hunting your mother, and you, and your brother—and why. The potential exists that it might be the Rosen family—the same one that caused your grandparents to flee Scotland. The Rosen family is powerful and resourceful. We don't know what they're planning to do with any of you once they retrieve you. So, like the rest of the islanders, we need you to remain here until it's safe for you to leave. This is why your communications to and from the island have been limited, and why your dad and your grandfather have taken so long to resolve matters. There's nothing easy about anything they're attempting to accomplish, or anything we've been asking of you."

"I can't believe you're telling me this now. Shouldn't someone have been preparing me to defend myself against these people?"

"Your family, the Misticatos and the Gordons, are relying on your Aunt Benitita, your Uncle Richard, and I to take care of you and Quentin. It's our job to prepare you both for what is to come. I'll be teaching you important life skills that will also allow you to perform the work I do that contributes to the Celtston community. These same skills and knowledge will serve you well when you finally arrive in Scotland. All the young men and women on the island will soon find out that you're set to be one of the island leaders should you perform your duties well, and should it be necessary for you to remain here an extended period of time. I hope this knowledge helps to relieve you of some of the pain and anguish you've been feeling concerning your non-selection for the boats."

"Like I said before, I used to miss the boats, the guys and the deep sea fishing, because I'm a natural fisherman and I love the sea, but not anymore; that's all behind me now. I like doing what we've been doing so far, but I do miss hanging out with my friends and spending time with my cousin, Chance. We hardly talk to each other anymore."

"Bradley, I promise to give you some time off the last week of summer to go camping and to hang out with your friends. Right now, I need to prepare you for your life to come."

"I won't be staying here forever though, will I?"

"Only time will tell what life has in store for you." Michael gestured toward the security equipment, "Let's get your retinal scan inputted, your voice recorded, and your user ID and password setup so we can continue on with our lesson for today in a more comfortable setting."

After little time had passed, Bradley was set up and the hidden door opened, but not from the wall, as Bradley had anticipated. A section of wooden planking clicked down and slid back into a recess in the flooring, revealing a six-foot-wide wooden staircase leading down to a well-lit room. Michael, with Bradley in tow, swiftly descended the stairs. The wooden floor access shut almost on cue from above once they had both stepped off the last tread of the staircase.

After one more retinal scan and voice recognition entry, they went through a thick steel door and down another set of stairs. This spiral staircase was made of stone and built into a circular stone wall, leading down into the darkness.

"Michael, where do these stairs go to? It's so dark down there. I can't see the bottom."

Then as if on cue, Michael flipped a switch that illuminated the entire structure. Bradley felt like he was looking into someone's home from above. There was an entire house below that had no ceiling. He could see every room at once, six walled off sections. It looked like what would have been the perfect home for a ship captain. His office would have been located to the right of the sitting room that was next to the berthing compartment. The quarters were decorated with thick wooden wainscoting and elaborate cornices similar to the second story walkway above. The walls were also adorned with blue, green, and gold striped, wall-papered panels. There was a comfy looking overstuffed bed and heavy looking wooden chairs, with nautical decorations aplenty throughout the house. A large, mahogany desk was placed along the wall in what had to be the office. The smallest room, along the wall in the back, appeared to have an exit door inside of it, and it was filled with large metal lockers.

"This is awesome," blurted Bradley, as he ran down the stairs to get a closer look. It was hard for Michael to keep up with the enthusiastic young man who ran from room to room, commenting on all that he saw.

There was so much cool stuff to look at. Then Bradley saw that two of the largest lockers were labeled *Scuba Equipment* and *Spelunking Equipment*.

"No way!"

"I was wondering how long it would take you to see those. The special equipment we've been talking about is here. Some of your gear is good enough, but for the older and outdated pieces of equipment, there are better choices inside these lockers."

"When can we go through the lockers? Do you have any better dive computers than the one I've got?"

"Whoa . . . hold your horses. Come over here and let's sit down. Let's have a cup of tea and finish our earlier discussion. This could take some time. Do you want a cookie or a muffin?"

"Sure . . . I mean yes, please. Thank you."

Michael completed serving the afternoon tea and biscuits and sat down across from Bradley, while continuing the telling of his family's history in more detail. Michael told him all that had happened to land his family in the Amazon basin with the Precaveros tribe, and how important he and his brother were to the Chivalran and the Veneré."

"Bradley, there's so much more to tell you, but I think what I've told you is more than enough for you to absorb in one session. Let's consider the history lesson over for today. We've been talking for four hours—it's almost two."

"I can't believe it's so late," gasped Bradley. "It's so hard to tell the time of day with no windows to look out where we can see the sun. Will we still be able to get one good dive in this afternoon? I don't see how. High tide is at three-twenty. We'll never make it upstairs and outdoors to the scuba dock in time to allow us to have even one decent dive. I was hoping we'd get at least two dives in today."

"We will, because we'll be entering the water through that doorway. That leads to the main cavern of the internal lava tube tunnel system," said Michael, pointing to the lone door to the left of the lockers. If you follow the correct tunnels, you can get to the outer dive platform from there."

"There's an access to the water and labyrinth through *that* door?" marveled Bradley.

"Let's get suited up. You'll find your wetsuit, gloves, hood, and booties, and your two dive computers in that dive locker, along with everything else you'll need. The tanks, weights, regulators, masks, snorkel, fins, and your buoyancy control device are already down below at the water's edge. I hope you don't mind that I took the liberty of setting your gear up for you to save us some time?"

"That's fine, I'm glad you did."

"You're going to get to try out some of the newer gear we've talked about during our book study."

Bradley raced over to the dive locker and started suiting up. He found that Michael had separated the wetsuits and gear that fit him in one section of the locker and conveniently labeled it *Bradley's Gear*.

"I've never seen you get ready so quickly. Let's go," said Michael.

Upon entering the lava tube system, Bradley was immediately assaulted by conflicting odors.

"This place smells like a mixture of salty sea air with a hint of rotten eggs, and it feels so *dank* in here."

"You're experiencing the best of both worlds. We have the sea smells and we have a smidgen of volcanic activity in far away and remote regions of this labyrinth where there exist a few negligible hot spots. That smell of rotten eggs is actually the faint smell of sulfur. There are enough gaps in the rock strata above that the sulfur is vented to the outside. A short-term exposure to the low levels of sulfur in here won't be harmful to us. But I can't say it enough, what we're doing down here is dangerous stuff. That's why I continue to urge you to not take anything for granted. I want us both to come out of here at the end of the dive unharmed. You let me know if anything concerns you so we can handle it *before* we have a problem. Understand?"

"Aye . . . aye . . . sir," said Bradley as he playfully saluted Michael.

"The lighting in here is great. I can see all the way down to that stone platform," said Bradley pointing downward, "This stairwell is *really* massive. I bet it's as wide as our gymnasium at school. It must be over two hundred feet down to the water's edge."

"It's a smidgen over three hundred and twenty feet down. You need to use caution when walking down these steps because even though they're wide and well built, moss starts growing on damp spots. It's hard to detect and extremely slippery. Just how much buildup we get depends on the outside and inside temperature differentials, and the storm tides that bring damp air higher up within the tunnel system. The moss forms when there's too much moisture for those two blowers up there to remove it all." He pointed to the upper extremities of the enclosure. "Use the banister at all times and tread carefully. If you get hurt, your Aunt Benitita will hunt me down and kill me. I could probably work something out with your Uncle Richard."

Bradley laughed. "I'd be more afraid of Aunt Benitita than Uncle Richard any day."

"Follow me, young man."

In no time at all, Bradley and Michael were on the lower stone platform and looking at all the equipment on the landing.

"Why are there two of all these pieces of gear? Am I supposed to pick one of each?"

"Bradley, remember the sections we read on technical diving?"

"Yes."

"Well today we'll be doing a technical dive of sorts. This dive requires more equipment. Can you tell me why? You passed your tests on this subject matter."

"Redundancy, as back-ups, but I didn't think we'd be doing *that* kind of diving any time soon."

"You're going to be learning the practical elements of some of it. Remember when I told you the diving we'd be doing today would be harder and that you had much to learn? I need for you to pay close attention to everything we do here today. You must gain a thorough understanding of the theory to become proficient in the practical aspects of what you're learning. Your life could literally depend on it."

"Yes, sir."

"Cavern and cave diving are what we'll be doing today. You'll be learning skills that only commercial scuba divers and technical divers use. It's much more complex than the recreational diving we've been doing the last few weeks."

"I thought you already showed me how to dive this type of scenario?"

"I showed you accessible cavern diving with large overhead ceilings and multiple egress points that allowed you to enter and exit the cavern at will. That is not what we'll be doing today. You'll be diving in low overhead cave structures with only one known entrance. If you have a problem, you yourself need to be able to solve it. This is why we're bringing extra equipment: two masks, two computers, twin air tanks, a side mounted bail-out tank and two emergency *stage* tanks. The *stage* tanks will be positioned at waypoints within the tunnel system we'll be diving as a prudent safety measure."

"Do you think I'm ready for this?"

"We're not going far within the labyrinth today, and the deepest water within the cave system is maybe fifty feet below sea level—if that. The majority of water depths will range anywhere from four feet to around thirty feet, give or take a foot or two. This means that we won't need mixed gases, thus removing one of the greatest complications of a more advanced cave diving scenario. However, we do have to have all the gear we need with us should we experience any problems with any of our essential pieces of equipment. I've already shown you how to dive with all of your extra equipment and how best to use these extra pieces of equipment, should the need arise. We'll be focusing on how to get neutrally buoyant with all of the additional stuff you'll be carrying. Once I feel that you've achieved the appropriate level of proficiency with your equipment and have relearned your peak performance buoyancy, we'll dive one of the tunnels, that one over there to be specific." Michael pointed to the mouth of the smallest tunnel of five, spaced out like the fingers of a hand.

"I'm sorry, but we won't have any time to play around today during this dive, but next time we will. First things first, let's get this gear on and enter the water. It's a lot harder to get into and out of the water carrying extra tanks and burdened with the bulkiness of the rest of the additions to your ensemble. We'll take it one step at a time. If you feel uncomfortable in any situation, you let me know and we'll slow it down until you feel like you're ready to proceed. Understand?"

"I do," confirmed Bradley.

"Let's go," directed Michael.

Bradley walked carefully behind Michael as he followed him down the submerged part of the half-circle shaped stone staircase that slowly plunged them into a nice, calm body of water. The area was the size of a small community pool and was about twenty-five-feet deep. Bradley felt like he was overburdened with extra gear. He was tall but not husky, and the additional equipment felt like it was way too bulky. It got in the way of him comfortably relaxing his arms by his sides.

"I don't see how I'm supposed to be able to keep track of this extra baggage, and the height of each of these steps makes me feel like I'm going to face-plant any minute," Bradley complained, as he cautiously descended each step, one at a time.

"Take it easy. You'll be fine," reassured Michael.

Once waterborne, it took Bradley at least two hours to figure out how to achieve buoyancy control with double tanks, which was more challenging than the single air-tank dives that had become second nature to him. His initial awkwardness diminished when he calmed down and focused. Everything seemed to align and he started to enjoy himself again.

Once Bradley was under water, he regained the serenity that he only seemed to have when he was scuba diving. He began looking around to become familiar with his surroundings. As far as he could tell, he was in an underwater oasis. The water was crystal clear.

Michael caught his attention and motioned for Bradley to come over to him so that they could spend a few more moments practicing a few skills. Not being able to speak under water was initially challenging, but in no time at all he learned the hand signals required to effectively communicate the essentials.

Michael signaled to Bradley to follow him into the tunnel opening—the pinky of the five fingers of tunnels. They slowly entered the tunnel. Bradley was careful to frog kick. He kicked sideways in a smooth horizontal back and forth motion thus keeping his fins off of the silt covered tunnel floor. If he hadn't, the silt would've risen and clouded the water so badly that it would have made it near impossible to see through the floating waterborne *silt-storm*.

Even though the water was crystal clear, if not for the fact that Bradley and Michael had bright dive lights that illuminated their paths, they would have been in total darkness.

Bradley was proud for maintaining the ample distance between he and Michael at all times, allowing each other space to maneuver.

The dive went well and without incident, but they got started later than they had originally planned and returned to the surface. Bradley felt exhausted after experiencing the day's challenges.

The two divers were able to quickly disassemble and clean up their equipment, store it away and head back to the sanctum for a post-dive debrief.

"Bradley, you did well. I saw no evidence of claustrophobia. You didn't silt-out the dive site and you maintained the proper safe distance. You'll make a good cavern and cave diver. However, we only accomplished the most basic skills today; it'll take many dives to make you a qualified technical diver. You still have much to learn."

"You don't have to worry about me getting overconfident, I am surprised I didn't *freak out*. At first I was a little bit scared, but I did what you told me and calmed myself down. Then everything seemed to click after that. I want you to know that I really appreciate you taking the time to teach me how to do this. Thank you."

"You're welcome. You make my job easy."

CHAPTER TEN

SPURT OF ENERGY

B radley and Michael were finishing their end of day review, dissecting the last dives and cave explorations, when Michael gave Bradley the good news.

"You've done so well that you've earned the right to spend the remainder of your summer vacation with your friends. I have to leave the island for a few days to take care of some business. This time off will be good for the both of us."

Bradley protested. "But I'm still not sure of several of the spelunking techniques, and I need more scenario practice on cave diving disasters . . ."

"You and I both need some rest *and* relaxation. Whether you want to or not, we're taking some time off. We can dive all year long, since the lava heats the stone and keeps the waters within the labyrinth temperate, even in a Celtston winter. I've set aside the majority of my weekends for you. Enjoy yourself and your pals. Sleep in a few days."

Once Bradley got over his panic of not having totally grasped everything he needed to know about his new career prior to the

start of the new school year, he calmed down and decided to make
the most of his reprieve from training. The first thing he did was to
contact his three best friends, all of whom were so happy to learn he
could go with them on their next camping trip that, coincidentally,
was already planned for two days later.

"Whoopee! You're finally coming with us," yelled Skeeter, as
soon as Bradley had come by to let him know he was free. "You look
so . . . *happy*, yeah the word is happy."

"I think, for the first time in a long while, I *feel* happy."

The next thing they knew, all four friends, Bradley, Skeeter,
Kyle, and Ed Moe—and Quentin, who was invited to tag along
too—were off to the woods to their secret lair in the thicket. While
the island was large enough, over seven miles wide in some spots,
there were few locations on the island that hadn't been trod upon
by the island inhabitants of one generation or the other. The boys
had found evidence of others having been in their lair, like the
remnants of an old matchbox, but it was ancient. They estimated
it was probably fifty years old. All that mattered to them was that
nothing new had been found since they claimed it.

As usual, once the boys had arrived at their destination, they
split up to take care of the chores needed to ensure they were
prepared for their stay in the wild. Two boys headed off to find
firewood, another one to fetch the kindling needed to start the fire,
and the last two were sent to fetch some fresh water from what was
considered to be the Celtston equivalent of Shangri-La—a flowing
waterfall feeding a clear pond of pure spring water, surrounded by
multiple green shades of foliage of all sorts. The spring water would
be used for their powdered hot chocolate and their only source of
drinking water for the entire weekend.

Bradley and Quinten were sent to get the water and were looking
forward to having some fun rummaging through the foliage and
fallen trees in the hilly and rocky part of the island. Unbeknownst to
the adventurers, there were others in the area that had been looking
for them. Teddy Nopar and his two sidekicks were hoping to have

some fun at their expense and had prepared the perfect booby trap in hopes of scaring whichever of the boys were sent to fetch the water. They pre-staged a suspended pine log by carefully tying two double knotted, concentric loops at each end, using a heavy chord of twisted hemp. The log was situated at just the right height to be swung towards an unsuspecting hiker in hopes of startling them.

"Look, there they are," said Nopar. "It's Bradley and Quentin, and they're by themselves. *Man* did we get lucky," whispered Nopar as the threesome hurried to conceal themselves in the shrubbery. They watched Bradley and Quentin jumping adeptly from tree to tree, shouting to one another and laughing at their near missteps.

"Those two don't have a *clue* that we're here," Nopar whispered, grinning. I can't believe we've already found them. I thought it would take us hours. Good thing we decided to hide around the falls. I told you guys they'd need to get water."

Bradley and Quentin finally arrived at the little Shangri-La. There were big leafy water lilies, and the spring's water was so clear that they could see the rocks on the bottom, making it difficult to determine the actual depth of the water.

"Quentin, these trees are so tall, they must be hundreds . . . no thousands of years old."

"All I know is that I feel good when we're out here. I don't feel so anxious. I like the quiet—no people and I finally get to spend some time with you. You've been with Michael so much lately. I hardly ever get to be with you anymore."

"I know, but I have to do what I've been doing. This summer was all the time I had to prep for my new career, one that, when you're old enough, you'll be able to do with me. We can start our own business together. We'll call it Gordon and Gordon, or the Gordon Brothers," declared Bradley, patting Quentin on the back.

"I'd like that," said Quentin.

"Oh man, here's the last jump. Let me go first so I can show you where best to land."

Bradley positioned himself to make the final jump, by far the most difficult leap of the journey. He had to hop from one fallen oak tree to the next. The two trees were located at least thirty feet above the water, on opposing ledges of two adjacent overhangs. There existed little room for error.

Quentin was focused intently on watching his big brother make the jump, one he himself had never made before, when his brother seemed to get discombobulated right before he touched down on the other side. While Bradley did safely land on the fallen tree, he seemed to lose his concentration right before he landed. Luckily, he fell forward away the water. Seeing that his brother was unhurt, Quentin burst out laughing.

"You're usually like a cat," he chortled. "I've never seen you fall before."

As soon as Bradley recovered, he stood up and frantically yelled, "*Quentin, get down now! Duck!*"

Quentin barely hit the ground when the big log flew towards him, cockeyed instead of headlong. It would have hit him hard had he not ducked.

"Are you okay?" pressed Bradley.

"Yeah, I'm okay."

"Quentin, get up and jump over here, *to me.*"

He jumped safely into his brother's arms.

"Nopar swung that log at you, but he didn't push it right. I could *feel* his fear. He was afraid that he was going to knock you out of the air and onto the rocks below instead of into the water," Bradley said.

"You could have *killed* him, Nopar. What's *wrong* with you?"

Not a sound was heard, save the soft roar of the waterfall. Nopar and his pals froze, not moving a finger, while Bradley continued with his admonishment. "I can't see you right now, but when I find you, I'm going to make you pay for what you just did. You *coward*, come out and face me!"

All the taunting in the world wouldn't have made Nopar reveal himself. He didn't want Bradley to have the proof that he was actually there. Nopar had come to the realization that he could've actually harmed Quentin, and he didn't want any witnesses. As it stood, it would be his word against Bradley's, and his buddies could provide him a good alibi. He remained silent and didn't move a muscle.

Bradley and Quentin, believing Nopar to have run away, finally calmed themselves and went about finishing up their business, including tasting some of the pure cool clear spring water. It was sweet and well worth the journey to retrieve it. Once the water was collected, they decided to take the longer, more easily traveled walking path with their burden of heavy buckets.

As soon as Bradley and Quentin headed back towards their camp, Nopar jumped up and started to dust himself off, flabbergasted.

"How did Bradley know what happened? How did he know what I was thinking? You heard him; Bradley warned Quentin. He told him *exactly* what I was thinking, but I didn't *say* anything. You saw what happened?"

"We don't know what you were thinking Nopar. How could *he* know what you were thinking? Bradley must have just seen you when you let go of the log," said one of the boys.

"No. No he didn't. I couldn't see Bradley. He had already jumped when I pushed the log. I know it sounds crazy, but it seems as if the log hung there in mid-air as if something were . . . holding it in place . . . it should have hit Quentin long before Bradley had a chance to say something."

"We were ducked down so we wouldn't be seen, and we couldn't see what you're talking about. You sound a little bit crazy right now. There's always a slowdown of an object when it reaches its height of travel before it falls back to earth," said Bill "We learned that in physics."

"I didn't push the log *up* so it could fall down and hit him. I pushed it *toward* him. It *froze* in midair. It stopped moving then it continued on its path. It should have hit him. Mind you, I'm glad it didn't, or I would've been in a lot of trouble, since that stupid log went all cockeyed, but something really strange just happened. You're telling me that neither one of you saw what happened?"

Nopar looked at his two buddies, waiting for one of them to admit that they'd seen what he had, but no confession was forthcoming.

"This isn't over. I'm going to find out what just happened. I'll show you who's losing it," scoffed Nopar, stomping off into the woods, leaving his buddies standing there, both shaking their heads in disbelief.

Bradley and his friends finished out their end-of-summer vacation camping adventure with no other nefarious interruptions or incidents. They had fun and enjoyed the precious time they spent together—so much so that they regretted not having found the time to get together more often.

Unbeknownst to Bradley, when he saved Quentin, he had sent out a powerful signal that transmitted a unique frequency, which was detected by others with sophisticated monitoring systems.

Bradley was woefully unaware of his special abilities, and certainly had no clue they could be detected.

CHAPTER ELEVEN

JAY

The weather in Scotland had been unseasonably warm and free of rain during July and August, quite unusual, but nonetheless welcomed by many, because the past year had been wet and cold. After two months of temperatures over seventy-seven degrees Fahrenheit, and several days reaching into the upper eighties, most were hoping for some relief because they lived in homes, attended schools, and worked in environments without air conditioning.

Gordon Castle and the associated township were teaming with highlander residents going about their business. The popcorn clouds with the backdrop of the deep blue sky, the smell of the fresh cut grasses, and the view of the beautiful purple heather on the surrounding mountain hillsides would have made the perfect scene location for a movie production.

The soccer field-sized castle square was surrounded by a cobble-stone walkway and pillars covering the entire area. The full complement of the Gordon Chivalran was meeting for their daily morning muster, their *stand-up meeting*. Attendees stood while they discussed the turbulent happenings and the general goings-on in their realm of responsibility.

This realm included the northwestern left quarter of Europe and all outlying islands in the North Sea, from the western border of Germany over to the outermost islands of North America. Other northern land masses up to but not including Greenland and Iceland, plus a few outliers, were also part of their domain, the majority of these uninhabited.

This forum was to be a quick daily tag-up where pertinent real-world issues were discussed, and when needed, appropriate actions would be taken to address those items of potential interest—or so the new recruits were told.

The day started out a bit serene and a tad boring, especially for some of the new recruits. Many were disappointed that they hadn't been involved in any intrigue.

Lord Brian Michael Gordon, the son of the late Veldor Gordon, and leader of the Gordon Chivalran, had the arduous responsibility of providing the Chivalran with assignments, and when feasible, to assign tasks to new recruits that would test their mettle and ability to address all manner of threats.

So far, nothing much happened since Justin John "Jay" Gordon arrived. A tall dirty blond, blue-eyed, very fit, and handsome young man, he happened to be one of the newest recruits. Jay arrived only a few weeks earlier but was already starting to lose his zeal.

Finally, something of interest occurred. The meeting was unexpectedly interrupted by the arrival of a courier that pulled Brian's attention away from the gathering. A double-wrapped, standard letter-sized envelope was hand delivered to Brian. He had to pull out his knife to free the contents. After a quick review of the document, Brian called out to the attendees.

"Thank you all for your patience while I discuss a brief matter with the leadership council. Please do take this time to pour yourself another cup of coffee. Members of the High Council, please join me over here for a briefing. An incident has occurred in our jurisdiction that requires our attention. Thank you."

As soon as the Council assembled, Brian shared the info he had just received.

"We have much to do over the next few weeks. Getting ready for the larger Chivalran training days is a top priority for us, but we can't ignore our basic responsibilities. We have a validated frequency hit and we need to send someone to check it out. Is there a recruit who can handle this by themselves and with no local oversight?"

Unanimously, Jay Gordon was nominated for the task at hand by those assembled.

"Good choice. He's too new to be of any real benefit to us during the training scenarios this go around, and he has shown the most promise out of this batch of new recruits. Let's get this muster over so we can start transport of the recruits to the games."

Brian resumed his place on the platform.

"Everyone, please gather around. We're ready to resume the meeting, and I have something I'd like to share."

A few minutes later he was able to conclude the mundane discussions of the day, ending the meeting with one final assignment.

"Infrequently we receive requests to look into anomalies that occur. Today is one such day. This is a perfect assignment for a new and promising recruit, but this person will be pulled out of the training days with the other regiments and will be temporarily assigned an additional duty. We have chosen a person who has promise and one that can be trusted to handle matters without a mentor present. Jay Gordon, please come forward and receive your orders from Lord Donald MacAllister Gordon. Mac, please raise your hand."

Mac waived to Brian.

"Jay, please see Mac after our meeting and he will fill you in on the details of your first assignment."

"Yes, sir," replied Jay.

"Chivalran, you're dismissed," announced Brian.

Jay immediately sought out Lord Gordon.

"Hello Jay," said Mac.

"Good day, Lord Gordon."

"Jay, I'm your uncle and this isn't a military organization, so please just call me *Mac;* everyone else does."

"Sir, I don't want to seem ungrateful, but I was really hoping to take part in the training scenarios and this assignment is going to pull me from the games. Is there any way someone else could take on this duty?"

"Simply speaking, the answer is *no*. But not for the reasons you might be thinking. You're so new that you wouldn't have been taking part in the more interesting portions of the training scenarios anyway. You haven't the experience needed to do so. You would've been in a back room taking notes and helping to run messages back and forth between the actual participants. This assignment is going to save you from that drudgery."

"So, I *have* to take the temporary duty assignment and I should be honored I was chosen," said Jay, with a hint of disappointment.

"Correct. You were unanimously selected by the Council to take this job because you have promise, and we know we can trust you to handle things on your own. You *should* be honored. Take this assignment in the vein that it was given and be proud that you're going on your first assignment, and solo at that."

"Yes, sir."

"You'll be going to Celtston Island to look into an anomalous signal our communications team picked up. This is important, because there you may find a special abilities candidate that we are as yet unaware of. If you do, you'll be successful in the execution of your first assignment. If you don't find a potential candidate, you will still have been successful. In this part of the world, we have had several erroneous hits due to the magnetic phenomenon in the area. These errors tend to manifest especially when the Aurora Borealis is prominent, which it is at this time. This shouldn't take you but a few days. If you're able to sort things out expeditiously, you might still end up making the last few days of the training scenarios. I think you'll find them to be of the most value to you anyway," concluded Mac.

"Thank you, sir."

"You've been instructed on how best to engage in this type of scenario and we're hoping you're able to practically apply that which you have learned. I'm anticipating that you're ready to leave, since you should've packed to move out to the training grounds this afternoon. Your boat departs in two hours. All the information you need is in this package." Mac handed Jay a thick folder. "Read it, memorize it, and do not take it out of the castle. The information in this folder is to be provided back to the comms detail monitoring this incident, prior to your departing for duty. Any questions?"

"Yes, sir, just one. Who will be my liaison back here should I need to consult with anyone?"

"You are quite the lucky fellow. I'll be your liaison since the others will be immersed in the games. I know I don't need to tell you, but I'll remind you just the same: this could result in you becoming aware of very sensitive information. You need to be careful how you choose to communicate any findings that you might have concerning any potential candidate. I'm expecting a status update from you by seventeen hundred every day you're on mission. Anything, I mean *anything*, that appears to be sensitive in nature should not be handled over the airways. It's best you return and deliver that type of update in person, since you won't have a courier working with you. Understood?"

"Yes, sir. I'll gather my things and head down to the docks."

"Safe travels, Jay."

Jay turned around on the spot and headed toward his quarters, mulling things over. *I guess I'm not surprised that as of late there have been several false alarms in this area. So why should they waste a seasoned Chivalran to check on the source of a routine signal detection. I won't be surprised if this is just a false alarm, after what Mac told me. Yeah, I've been unanimously selected. Let's send a novice to investigate this energy spurt with the anticipation it will be a total waste of his time . . . no problem.*

On the flip side, Jay was happy because he was at least going to be doing *something* versus watching others having all the fun. Fortunately for him, he had family on the island, and he was looking forward to spending some quality time with Michael Robert Sidlau, his first cousin on his mother's side of the family. Jay rarely had opportunities to hang out with him except for the infrequent family events when luck would have it that they both attended.

This trip won't be so bad after all, thought Jay. As soon as he reached his room, he contacted Michael and made arrangements to stay with him for a few days while he checked out the happenings on the island. Michael seemed pleased Jay was coming, and so very gracious a host to receive him on such short notice.

CHAPTER TWELVE

STRANGERS

B ack on the island, things weren't so cheery. As soon as Michael hung up the phone in Captain Nopar's office, he told him of the impending visit from his cousin—a Gordon Chivalran who was en route to perform a routine investigation into an anomalous signal that was detected in the area.

Captain Nopar immediately summoned the small cadre of elders for a private meeting in his office. His office was an unassuming, small, wood-framed building located at the edge of the town's marina, consisting of two austere rooms sitting atop twelve-foot pilings. Windows spaced one foot apart from each other covered all four exterior walls, affording the room's occupants a clear view in all directions. The windows were covered with thick draperies, and the single-bulb lamp was dimmed.

Michael informed the elders of what little he knew about the upcoming visit.

"Jay Gordon is my cousin and basically a good guy. I don't expect too much trouble from him. For one, he's new to the Chivalran and this is apparently his first field assignment. I think it's quite advantageous that he'll be staying with me. We'll be able to stay informed concerning the status of his investigation, and we'll be the first to learn of any findings that may arise."

One of the elders asked, "What will we do with Bradley and Quentin while Jay is in town performing his duties? Should we hide them until he leaves? What do you think?"

"I don't think that he is aware of their existence. He made no mention of either of them. I'd say we do nothing for now," Michael replied.

"I thought about that. I think it prudent to hide them in plain sight. They live with us and there exists no reason why anyone would think they were related to anyone other than a Northcutt. Everything should be fine," added the boys' Uncle Richard.

"Okay. It sounds like we have a good strategy. It's going to be your job to keep us informed," said Captain Nopar, pointing at Michael and Richard. "We'll meet here at the same time every day, until he departs, to discuss anything disconcerting that we hear or see.

"We need to be vigilant and ready to handle whatever might come to pass—the sooner the better. I cannot express the importance of quickly addressing and retiring any and all concerns that arise so that we can keep things contained. I need to know that everyone in this room understands the gravity of this situation."

The attendees responded in unison, "We do."

"I've already received port notice of the incoming vessel that'll be bringing our guest; he arrives early tomorrow afternoon."

It seemed like no time had passed before Michael found himself standing at the docks to greet his guest.

"Cousin Michael, I'm so glad to see you," Jay said as the men shook hands. The visitor wasted no time with small talk.

"Who do you recommend I start interviewing? Who are the few key folks who might know something, or could help me successfully complete my investigation in the shortest time possible? Should I start with Captain Nopar? I heard he knows everything and everybody."

Michael laughed at his cousin's enthusiasm. "Jay, I'd like to suggest we first get you settled in at my place, and *then* we can have a nice lunch and talk about exactly what you're looking for. I'll help you figure out the best list of folks for you to interview. Does that sound good?"

"Yes, it does. Please excuse my exuberance. I want to hurry and complete this task so I can get back to a special European cross-Chivalran training event that I've been looking forward to taking part in. Being assigned this ancillary duty has greatly restricted my ability to participate. If I quickly finish my work here, I might be able to get back in time to at least be involved in the end games, the most valuable part of the training scenarios . . . or so I've been told. As much as I wanted to come and visit with you, I must admit, I'd much rather partake in the Chivalran games. I hope you understand."

Michael picked up Jay's large duffle bag and motioned to Jay to follow him to his golf cart, the primary form of transport for the older or overburdened islanders. They dropped off Jay's duffle bag at Michael's and headed back into town to enjoy a nice lunch, as they settled in at the local island café for a strategy session. In no time at all, Jay had the list of key folks to interview. Michael helped him with the needed introductions.

When folks on the island found out that Jay was related to Michael, they were friendly and looked forward to meeting him. For the most part, Jay found himself getting all the islanders up to speed on the latest happenings in the world outside of Celtston more than he learned anything of any real value from them. He hadn't learned of any incident that appeared related to the anomalous signal he was investigating, but a few of the islanders told him about some interesting happenings linked to the two boys known locally as the *Northcutt nephews*.

"If you want to know more, I'd recommend that you talk to your cousin, Michael; he's the one adult that seems to know the boys best," said one of the interviewees. "He's taken a real liking to the older of the two—Bradley. You may also want to interview Captain Nopar's boy, Theodore, who we call Teddy. He claims to have some interesting experiences with Bradley and his younger brother."

Jay did more snooping around and learned of the two brothers' vague history. The boys came from the Amazon basin area of Brazil, and they had been sent to live with their aunt and uncle when their mother mysteriously disappeared many years ago, Jay was told. No one seemed to know what had become of their father.

Jay surmised that the source of the anomaly, should it be human, might be the older of these two boys. He had heard the story about Bradley's mysterious ability from the harbor master's son and the other boys present that day in the woods. He also learned that Bradley was working for Michael, his host.

Jay started to formulate a crazy idea in his mind after thinking about what his father, Michael Patrick Gordon, had told him.

His father had gone on a mission to South America for the Veneré about eight years earlier. That op was the very reason Jay had decided to join the Chivalran. It was full of intrigue and adventure— exactly what Jay was looking for when making a career choice.

The idea that what my father did years ago might actually be related to the happenings on this rock in the middle of the North Atlantic is unbelievable. I have to get to the bottom of this.

He interviewed Michael one afternoon when they were enjoying a cup of tea and biscuits, sitting comfortably on the two oversized, white wooden rockers on Michael's back porch. The two men seemed to be in their own worlds, enjoying the day, rocking away while overlooking the ocean. Then the questioning began.

"Michael, would you mind if I asked you a few questions about what I heard during a couple of my interviews? I'm especially interested in learning more about the Northcutt family and their two houseguests, their nephews. I understand Bradley is the older of the two brothers, the younger being Quentin, and Bradley is your protégé?"

"Sure. I was wondering when it would be my turn for an interview."

"How long have you known the Northcutts?"

"I've gotten to know them pretty well over the seven years that I've lived here. Before that, I had seen them on and off when I'd come for my two-week, annual visits with my uncle, prior to his death. Our friendship has grown and strengthened since I moved here. I've gotten better acquainted with the entire family; good people."

"What do you know about their two nephews?"

"I was asked by Richard Northcutt to help train Bradley, the older of the two boys, and *yes* he is my protégé. I'm teaching him how to be a commercial scuba diver and spelunker. Unfortunately, Bradley wasn't chosen to work on the boats, the main source of income for most of the islanders. It was perfect timing, because I needed a partner to help me tend to my vast oyster fields, and I've been blessed with a hardworking young man."

"Don't you find it interesting that these two boys look a lot like Lord Brian Michael Gordon, except for their green eyes? If I didn't know better, I'd say they were Veldor's descendants. What do you think? Do you know their parents? Where are they? Who's the blood relative, Benitita or Richard Northcutt?"

Michael was taken aback by Jay's accusatory tone, but he decided to take the high road and merely answer the questions received to the best of his knowledge.

"Benitita is their blood relative."

"I see. You wouldn't by chance know their *last* name?"

"By your tone of voice and your line of questioning, I think you already know the answer to your question, but to confirm your suspicions, their last name is *Gordon*."

"I've been entertaining a ludicrous scenario that I quite frankly didn't expect to actually have any merit, but I'm starting to get the feeling that I might be on to something here."

"Jay, let me save us both some time. Okay?"

"Please do," scoffed Jay.

"I'm sure you've already figured out that the boys are Tristen Gordon's sons, making them Lord Robert Clifton Gordon's grandsons. Tristen is in Scotland, as I suspect that you're aware. He is attempting to reintroduce himself to the Gordon clan and to figure out if he's welcome. And while he's working things out with the Gordon dynasty and Chivalran leadership, he has entrusted his sons' care to the Celtston Island elders. They're here for safekeeping. I suspect that by now, you've also figured out that Tristen is married to Solana Jeju Misticato-Gordon, who is the sister to Benitita Misticato-Northcutt, the boys' blood relative, as I told you."

"Once I started talking with folks, I couldn't ignore what I was hearing, what I've learned. This has been a lot to take in all at once. I don't think anyone will believe me when I tell them what I've discovered here," gasped Jay.

"I was hoping we wouldn't have to have this discussion," Michael said.

"I see. When were you planning to let the rest of us in on the secret, Michael?"

"While I've never met Tristen or Solana, having gotten to know their two boys, they must be good people. I believe it's Tristen's and Solana's right to decide what should or should not be shared concerning their sons. We promised to keep these boys safe and hidden, and that's what we've been doing."

"You know this is *big* news. Everyone should've been told. Why didn't you let the Gordons know that you have our kin here?"

"Jay, I'm related to the Gordons, to you, you're my family—*the reason* why I'm respecting Tristen Gordon's request to keep his secret. It's up to him to decide when to make this public. This news is not mine to tell. I would have suspected that Tristen would have told the Gordons by now. The question you should be asking yourself is why haven't they shared this with you? There's something really disconcerting going on, and Chief Solano and Tristen Gordon are attempting to get to the bottom of it. I think it best you return to Scotland and confront your father and uncles. I believe that Brian and a select few of the Gordon elders are now aware of the boys' existence, but I don't think that anyone has been told where they're hiding. Don't expect me to share any other information with you on this matter. I'll help you with the specific investigation that you're here to address, but that's all you can expect of me."

"I can't believe that I've been kept in the dark. The others know and decided not to let me in on the secret—but why? I can't worry about that now. I need to spend my energies getting to the bottom of the matter I was sent to address."

"I think that's best," said Michael.

"If you don't mind, I'd like to continue with my line of questioning, now that I understand my boundaries. I'll keep my inquiries specific to this investigation, as you have requested. I agree, I should talk with my father and my uncles concerning any further inquiries into the ancestral Gordon family matters."

"Thank you."

Jay continued. "I know that you're part of my family, even though right now I'm not so sure that you believe that to be the case, or why would you be keeping anything from me? Why wouldn't you trust that I would have the boys' best interests at heart? I would *never* do *anything* to hurt them or cause them any harm."

"The only reason I agreed to let you stay in my home is because you're my family. I'm in a tight spot right now. Two different factions of the same family are keeping secrets from each other. I promised to keep these secrets as well, and for good reasons. It's my belief that you, too, will understand when the truth becomes known. You'll be asking yourself why I even shared the information that I've already shared with you thus far. I've told you way more than I should have. The boys' safety is of the utmost importance. The decades-long fight with Rosen and his family is secondary to me. Please don't insult me by questioning my loyalty to family again."

Jay softened his tone. "It's not for me to judge you, but I still can't believe you didn't let any of us know. What you've done or not done is not a matter for me to pass judgement as to whether or not it was the right thing to do. I'll leave it to those higher up in the ranks than I to decide. All of this is much bigger than me, apparently, because I haven't been told *anything* about *any* of this."

"Fair enough . . . so what other questions do you have for me?"

"How well do you know Bradley Gordon?"

Michael was surprised to hear Jay attach the name Gordon to Bradley. He had always referred to him as Richard Northcutt's nephew.

"I've seen Bradley and his brother around the island from time to time over these past years, but like I've already told you, I only met him recently. His Uncle Richard asked me to help him out by teaching him skills he could use to earn a livelihood when he graduates from school, since he wasn't chosen to crew any of the boats—the primary source of income on this island. Bradley's a good student and he's quite the scuba diver and spelunker. He works well with me. If I had a son, I'd like him to be a clone of Bradley. He's a smart kid, follows my instructions, is integrity based, cares for his friends and family, and he's loyal to them—all characteristics I admire."

"I'm only here to investigate the source of the anomaly we detected, so let me cut to the chase. Have you ever seen the kid do anything strange?"

"Nothing I thought to be strange. What do you mean, by *strange*?"

"Trust me. You'd know what I mean by strange if you had seen anything. Don't worry about it. I was just curious," said Jay. "But thanks for your candor. I think those are all the questions I have for you right now."

"I'm sorry I couldn't be of more help to you. For the boys' sake, you have to be very careful with whom you share the knowledge you have gained. I hope you take this into consideration when you make your report. I implore you to provide an in-person, verbal report to your leadership, versus a written or oral report to a wider audience—especially one that is disseminated over the airways, when prying eyes and ears may intercept the communique," pleaded Michael.

"I'll be careful. What I've already learned today is dangerous enough. If I find out that there exists anything else to report concerning these boys . . . well . . . let's just hope I don't."

Michael did not delay in reporting his discussion with Jay to the island elders early the next day. No one was happy to learn of the findings thus far. Like Michael, they were aware of the boys' potential. They themselves were not aware of any abilities that Bradley may have manifested, save the obvious telepathic connection between he and his brother—thought to be similar to the connection a set of twins have from birth.

"We might have placed Celtston in Rosen's cross-hairs by hiding these boys on the island, should it be revealed that they have any special abilities of note. It's a real possibility that we'll be found as culpable in this affair as Chief Solano and Tristin Gordon," worried Captain Nopar.

"The information flow and questions from Jay should dry up after his little talk with me yesterday," Michael said. "He knows I'll protect the boys at all costs, and that I'm not willing to tell him anything about the boys that I think might cause them angst or harm."

"I sure hope so," said Uncle Richard.

"Don't get me wrong. Jay *is* dedicated to family and now that he knows the boys are family, I believe we can trust that he'll do them no harm. In the meantime, I'll work to regain a modicum of trust with him so I can re-establish our communications. I think it's safe to say that you can no longer count on me to know what he's doing and what he's planning to report out to the Gordon Chivalran—that boat has sailed."

Captain Nopar added, "We must proceed as if the belief that no one knew what had become of the boys has now been shattered. This information is being widely communicated to the broader community. Why do I make this assumption? Because, unbeknownst to Jay or to any of us, another stranger has arrived on the island who I now believe to be a Chivalran as well. He arrived under false pretense. He feigns interest in our island geology, but his actions betray him."

The Celtston B&B innkeeper and island elder, Ms. Donna Kay Layton, a tall, mature woman with emerald green eyes and long, flowing blonde hair, reported, "This stranger hasn't contacted any of us. I would've thought he would have at least checked in with one of us out of respect by now, but alas he hasn't. After spying on him these past few days, since he's staying at my B&B, it's my belief he's investigating the source of the anomaly too. What's interesting is that while he and Jay arrived in town within days of one another, I've never seen them together. Jay appears to be unwitting."

"I've seen this fellow before off-island. I'm pretty sure his name is Seth McLeod, and if I remember correctly, he's a member of the McLeod Chivalran or some such organization," offered Captain Nopar.

Donna Kay continued. "So, his name is *Seth* . . . interesting. His reservation is under a company name and is being paid for by a company credit card, so I didn't know that. I've seen *Seth* observing Jay during his interviews. I know he's aware of the fact that Jay is conducting an investigation of sorts, but for some reason he hasn't reached out to him. I wonder why? Seth has been asking folks similar questions to those that Jay's been asking. I overheard him talking to a few people. He did ask if they had ever observed the boys doing anything out of the ordinary. I haven't heard him mentioning anything about their parentage. So, I don't think that he's put the two together—at least not yet."

"Who sent this guy? And why doesn't Jay know he's in town?" fretted Uncle Richard.

"Most of the Chivalran all know the others of their ilk, at least those that have been around for a while, but Jay is a brand-spanking-new recruit. I would suspect that's why he doesn't know this other guy. The scarier thought to me is that Seth might not even be a Chivalran." warned Michael.

"Richard, I think in order to protect the boys it's time for you to have a conversation with Bradley. He needs to know what's happening so that he can do what needs to be done to protect himself and Quentin. I know you're doing what you can, but the boys aren't always with you or Michael. Things are starting to get too complicated for us to manage, and we're going to need his help. We *have* to bring him in on this," Captain Nopar said.

"I'll talk with him tonight, but I wish there was something else we could do," Richard said.

"Let's go and find out what we can and report back here, same time tomorrow. Meeting adjourned," said Captain Nopar.

The attendees gathered their belongings and, as had become the custom, they left the building one at a time, every few minutes, to lessen the chance that anyone would see them leaving together.

CHAPTER THIRTEEN

THE ARRANGEMENT

Bradley awoke in an exceptionally good mood after partaking in a wonderful dream, the details of which were already beginning to fade. He had quickly jumped out of bed, dressed, and headed towards the smell of sage sausage links and sweet buttermilk pancakes wafting throughout the house. As he turned the corner at the bottom of the stairs to head down the hallway to the kitchen, he was surprised to see his Uncle Richard sitting alone in the kitchen

"Good morning. Are you taking the day off? Did I oversleep?"

"No, you're fine. Come on in and have a seat. There's a stack of pancakes, sausage links, and three fried eggs warming for you on the stove."

Bradley stopped in his tracks, "What's going on? You have that look. Is everyone okay?"

"Yes, boy. Come sit."

"*Okay*," said Bradley slowly sidling over to the kitchen nook and taking a seat across from his uncle. "Whatever I did, I'm sorry. I didn't mean to do it. I promise . . . and I won't do it again."

"You're not in trouble, but I do have something serious to discuss with you. It has to do with your family and the two strangers in town."

"I didn't know there were two strangers. I only know about one. I think his name is Jay. He seems to be a good guy, from what I've heard. He's staying with Michael. I think he's his cousin or something like that."

Richard gave his nephew the background on the visitors without being overly specific about Jay's objective.

"I don't get it. What are we supposed to have done? Does this have anything to do with my mother's disappearance?"

"The main reason we're so worried about these two guys is that we don't have a full appreciation as to why each of them is here. We think Jay is less of a concern because he's related to you. He's a Gordon, and he has been open and honest with us, but he knows little about your circumstances. He was astonished to learn who your father is. You have a complicated family history. We believe it's safe to assume that Jay has your best interests at heart."

"Jay knows who my father is? Why didn't he say something to me? Is my dad okay?"

"Bradley, of course your dad's okay, but I need for you to stay focused. The other stranger hasn't talked to you or to Quentin, right?"

"No, he hasn't."

"But he has talked to many people about the two of you. He's the one we're concerned about."

"So . . . has anyone *asked* him what he's doing here?" probed Bradley.

"You see . . . that's part of the issue. He hasn't contacted any of us—you, your brother, your aunt, or me. He *seems* to be talking to folks as he gets an opportunity, but we think his interactions to be more deliberate than that. The information he's sought thus far primarily concerns you. We don't know who sent him or what he's attempting to find out. His questions aren't focused around you potentially being the source of any energy fluxes, as are Jay's. This stranger's inquiries are all over the place. He's been asking about your friends, your hobbies, and other such things."

"I have so many questions, but I can't get past the most basic one. You keep saying *we*, who's *we*?"

"The Celtston Island elders."

"Oh . . . and Michael is one of the island elders?" asked Bradley.

"Yes. He took his uncle's place when he moved here and assumed the ownership of his property and his island oversight responsibilities."

"I didn't know he was an island elder. He's been talking with you about me?"

"Only as it relates to taking care of you and ensuring your safety. He doesn't share personal information or any of your confidences with us."

"Still, why didn't he tell me this? Why did you both wait so long to let me know? Why do you keep treating me like a *child*? I'm sixteen years old. If you can't trust me, how do you expect me to trust you?" chided Bradley.

"Calm down. Getting all riled up isn't going to help us with the situation at hand. We need to be able to discuss what's going on. We wanted to let you enjoy your childhood for as long as possible, but that's no longer an option. I'm so sorry about that. So, here we are, and we need to lay out a plan of action on how best to approach this situation. Are you with me?"

"Once again, I have no choice; so I'm with you."

"It's this behavior that makes me not want to share things with you. If you'll act like an adult, I'll promise to treat you like one from now on. No more outbursts, no more drama—promise me," admonished Uncle Richard.

"I promise to act like an adult if you promise to treat me like one. No more secrets; this has to stop. If I knew all this was happening, I would've been more careful."

"*More* careful? What do you mean?" asked Uncle Richard.

"You know. I'd avoid talking to the strangers, and if I ended up having to talk to one of them, I'd make sure I didn't say anything I shouldn't."

"You and Quentin have special abilities. I'm not sure what they are nor to what extent they have developed, but I can see that you're extraordinary. You two have a connection with each other. You seem to know what the other is thinking without saying a word. This is obvious to even the casual observer; there's no hiding this fact from anyone. I don't know what talents you may have beyond that, and I think it best not to pry into these matters. But I need to know, have you experienced any issues handling your abilities? Has anyone seen you manifest any of them? Has anything happened that you want to share with me? Is there anything that we should know? We can't protect you if you don't let us know what's going on with you."

"Nothing that I think you should be concerned with," said Bradley.

"Something brought these two men to the island and it had to have happened recently. None of us know exactly what that was, but they don't seem to want to leave until they find whatever, or whomever it is they're looking for. Their inquiries have led them to believe the issues are centered on the two of you. If you don't feel comfortable talking with me, please talk with your Aunt Benitita or Michael. They'll be helpful, I promise. The situation is starting to get serious now. You need to understand that whatever is happening won't end with these two guys; it's just the beginning."

"Uncle Richard, I'm not lying. I haven't done anything. I really have no idea why they're here."

"Son, I believe you. But what I am concerned about is that you might not be aware that you're manifesting these abilities. I'm asking that you think about the past few weeks. Did anything happen that scared you? Or that caused you any discomfort? If something comes to mind, please let us know about it—*okay?*"

"I will."

"Alright then, I've said what I needed to say on the matter, so unless you have something to discuss, I think we're done here. I have to get to work," concluded Uncle Richard, as he stood up and headed out of the kitchen.

Bradley quickly gulped his breakfast down and ran out of the house and over to Michael's place, trying not to be late for their eight o'clock start time.

"Hey, Bradley!" yelled Michael from his front porch. "Pushing it a bit, aren't we?"

"I'm on time . . . aren't I?" sassed Bradley as he started his climb onto the front porch stairs, skipping two steps at a time, then finally settling into the chair he had claimed as his own. He liked the oversized, white wooden rocking chair that was separated from Michaels' twin by a nice, glass-topped, white wooden table.

Once settled, they talked about Bradley's discussion with Uncle Richard. It didn't take Michael long to help Bradley appreciate the situation to an even greater extent. Bradley gained a better understanding as to why they had deemed it necessary to keep him in the dark for so long. By the time they finished talking, he felt grateful for the island elders' efforts on his behalf. Michael was able to allay Bradley's fears, while effectively relaying the gravity of the situation so that Bradley would be ever vigilant.

Once the more dire discussions were completed, they were able to get to the topics that they both enjoyed—scuba diving and spelunking.

"Bradley, I've found that teaching someone how to play any sport or tradecraft has really helped me to gain a greater proficiency in that sport or tradecraft. For this reason, I want you to pick one—and only one—of your friends that you believe will be a good dive buddy for you. Someone that you'll be able to teach the nuances and subtleties of scuba diving and spelunking. They'll be allowed to dive in the outer reaches of the lava tube system, and in the parts of the externally accessible caverns and tunnels—the ones that you and I have started to explore. You'll need to get this person trained quickly, because I need the two of you to finish drawing and detailing the maps of the cave systems that I've already started. While you're doing this work, depending on what you find, you might actually earn yourself some money. You have about five weeks or so when diving outside is viable. Are you interested? Any questions?"

"I understand, and yes I'm interested. I do have a fair few questions for you."

"I'd be disappointed if you didn't," laughed Michael.

"I pick Kyle."

"*Really?* That didn't take you long to decide. I thought you'd pick Skeeter or Ed Moe."

"They're not serious enough for this sort of thing, and we only have a few days to learn a lot of material. Kyle is really smart and should be able to learn the lessons pretty easily. Besides, Skeeter is the bravest, but he plays around too much, and even though Ed Moe is my very best friend of the three, he's blind as a bat because of his one funny eye. I think that's what makes him so afraid all the time. I'm convinced that he sees two of everything, but he won't admit it."

"I'm glad you made that determination on your own," said Michael.

"Don't sound so surprised."

"I'm not surprised. You've come a long way since we first met."

Bradley nodded and continued. "Will you be able to give Kyle the gear he'll need?"

"This is another reason why I'm glad you chose Kyle. You two are about the same height and weight. Ed Moe and Skeeter are half-a-head shorter than the two of you. Your choice makes things much easier, as far as outfitting your dive buddy. You'll be lending him your spare gear. Choose wisely what you plan to share. We have plenty of new masks and fins in the outside gear locker. The two masks and fins that work best for him are his to keep. He can store the gear you assemble for him in one of the unlabeled lockers on the dock."

"Sounds good, and now for my last dive buddy question. Will you be teaching him any of his coursework, or am I to do all of his training and certifications? *And* do you have the books and the tests for him to take?"

"I want you to teach him and test him, and you'll be the one to decide if he's ready to be your buddy. This will cover the classroom work, the confined water skillsets, and the open water scuba diving practical skill assessments. I'll give you the needed course materials and training slates, along with all the gear, equipment, and other training aides. If you need or want my help, just ask. Once he passes the basics and you're ready to start the cavern and cave diver training, that's when I'll get involved."

"Perfect. What days will you and I be meeting, so I can schedule Kyle's training?"

"You and I'll meet Saturdays and Sundays, leaving you all five of the weekdays to work with Kyle for the last two weeks of the summer. When school starts, you can dive with him when you're not diving or spelunking with me. It'll be different each week. We'll play it by ear."

"Great. I'll ask Kyle today if he's interested."

"Not so fast. There's one more item to discuss. We touched on it when we first met."

"Aww . . . we were doing so well Michael. Why'd you have to go and get all adult on me?" teased Bradley.

"This is a serious matter and it involves you. I cherished every moment I had with my uncle. He was such a good man, so genuine, kind, and his intellectual prowess unmatched by anyone I've ever met. He taught me many of the hidden secrets of this land that became my inheritance, but we never completed the exploration of either the shoreline water ways or the vast cave systems prior to his death. I have so much more to learn. I've been slowly exploring and uncovering these wonders every day, but I've only scratched the surface of what I like to call the *Celtston Labyrinth*. I've been limited by time and Mother Nature's whims these past few years. High seas and unpredictable water conditions have made it near impossible to make much progress. Fortunately, this end of summer has been the mildest since I arrived here. Right now, I'm overburdened with too many responsibilities to take full advantage of the limited time I have until the onslaught of winter, but you're not."

"I can't wait to go inside all of those tunnels," exclaimed Bradley.

"That's a good thing, because I'm hoping that you and Kyle can do something I've yet to accomplish—complete the mapping and documenting of the five finger caves and tunnels that make up the *hand* that is the entrance to the labyrinth. I don't need you to spend much time looking into the pinky, index or ring fingers, where we did a few of your training drills. These three are pretty well documented. I've been in parts of the other two caves and tunnels, the thumb and the middle finger, and that's how I know that some of the features and key attributes, information, and warnings are missing from the documentation. I've been trying to rectify this situation working alone, and it almost cost me my life one day, but luck was on my side and I made it out safely. I don't want *luck* to be a major part of our explorations. I choose to create an executable plan where my dive buddy and I are safe, and we've taken all necessary precautions to mitigate our risks to the maximum extent possible."

"You have maps for all five caves. You just need us to fill in the missing data? I'm surprised they haven't been completed after all of these years."

"There is a lot of information, and I would say the person or persons who amassed it all most likely considered it adequate enough for their purposes. But there are too many notable attributes and warnings missing for ours. There's nothing that references the mysteries of this place: seasonal anomalies; the tides that affect what can safely be accessed and when; depths of water-rise in the caves; potential dangers to avoid, etc. . . . there is so much more to learn and to discover."

Michael continued, "My uncle told me that he didn't possess the complete knowledge of his holdings, even though he spent his entire lifetime attempting to accumulate this knowledge. He died at seventy-six years old and while he knew more than his father perchance, he only scratched a fraction of the surface left to be discovered. I'm hoping you and Kyle will be able to help me to start this work in earnest while I'm otherwise employed, to include entertaining the two strangers in town. Are you up to the challenge?"

"I sure am! Thanks for trusting me to do this," said Bradley.

"I'll pay you for each completed map and associated documentation, pictures and notations of all features and attributes—once I've approved the final product, that is. You can decide if you want to share your earnings with Kyle. I think you providing free scuba lessons and equipment should more than compensate him, but it's up to you."

"Fair enough."

"I've been thinking a lot about what I want to do here. Starting where my uncle left off is just the beginning. I'm hoping with your help, I'll complete the exploration of the entire labyrinth structure within ten years."

"I'm *so* glad that you're letting me help you," said Bradley.

"You're not just *helping* me. The work that I'm asking you to do represents the beginning of our partnership. In lieu of you setting up a business elsewhere on the island, I want to share half of the profits of all the treasures we unearth with you. *Plus*, I'll handsomely reward you for mapping out the uncharted portions of the labyrinth, especially the hardest to access, like the innermost dry sections of the lava tubes. I haven't even ventured into those areas yet. As you've started to learn, they extend from below this house to *Lord* knows where. While I inherited many acres of land and naturally occurring oyster beds—potentially some of the most productive oyster beds in the world—my uncle led me to believe that my real inheritance lies below these lands and has yet to be revealed."

"That's too much. It would be wrong of me to expect to receive all of that from you," countered Bradley.

"You and Quentin are family. I want what I have to be kept in the family; it's as simple as that."

"I guess this is okay for now but, depending on how everything works out in the end, I might not even be here. I might still get to go home."

"We'll see what the future holds for you. But in the meantime, I do need to share with you the stories of the untold treasures and lost artifacts that go back centuries. These treasures are thought to be buried in the labyrinth somewhere. My uncle found only a spattering of relics, but these finds validated for him, and now me, that the stories had some truth to them. I'm asking you to take part in this wondrous adventure with me. What do you say? Are you with me?"

"Of course, but I'd like to take this one step at a time. Right now, you pay me for my efforts and *if* or *when* I earn it, we can discuss more compensation. Deal?"

"Deal," confirmed Michael.

"Wow! Look at the time, I need to get going. I can't wait to tell Kyle!"

Bradley reached down to gather his belongings from the floor, pausing to look up at Michael, "Thank you. Every time I'm feeling a bit out of sorts, you seem to do something that helps me to pull myself up and off of my pity pot."

CHAPTER FOURTEEN

LONG JOHN

K yle found Bradley on the outside cave diving platform, setting his scuba gear up, awaiting his dive buddy's arrival. "Yo there, Bradley, how goes it?"

"It goes well, my friend," replied Bradley.

"I couldn't wait to get here. I had to finish up a few chores for my dad before he'd let me come over. Sorry for making you wait."

"Perfect timing, I just got here myself. We couldn't ask for a better day to start our mapping projects. I've been thinking about how we should go about this. I want us to start mapping the longest and hardest to access caves today, because I think as the fall weather starts to arrive, these caves will most likely be the least accessible."

"Sounds good to me," said Kyle.

"Michael told me that he never made it to the end of the longest cave, the middle finger, but he was pretty sure he was close to the end when he ran into a few challenges and had to turn back. Come to think of it, he never went into the specifics of these challenges, but he did tell me that he used his experiences as the basis for the development of all of the emergency training scenarios that he made us go through, so we should be well prepared."

"I'm glad to hear that," said Kyle.

"He spent a lot of his time taking water samples and checking the integrity of the cave walls the entire time he was doing the dive. That's one less thing for us to do. *Plus*, he made sure that the traverse line was in place and that the permanent tie off was sound, so we have a good tag line to follow into the cave system."

"That's even better; more time for us to explore," smiled Kyle.

"Michael told me that he started to run low on air, so he would've had to call the dive anyway. We want to make sure we don't make the same mistakes. We're going to use our rebreathers today to ensure that when or if we start experiencing *nature,* as Michael called it, we're better prepared to handle it. I don't want to take any chances. He was solo diving, and that dive made him decide to ask me to be his buddy. He said, and I quote, *diving in caves should be a shared experience.*"

"Whatever you decide is fine with me. I'm just glad to be here," said Kyle. "I still can't believe that we never thought to try this stuff before now. I'm not telling *anyone* else how much fun this is, or everyone will want to scuba dive with us. Whenever anyone asks me about what we're doing, I always act as if it's really hard and scary, especially when I'm talking to Skeeter and Ed Moe. Now neither of them even wants to try it."

"Kyle you've done your job well with those two, but did you have to scare them that badly?"

"Yep."

Bradley *cracked up* at the quick and affirmative response.

"After all the stories Chance told me about other people's diving exploits, diving wasn't even a consideration for me," said Bradley.

"I know what you mean. I've heard those stories too."

"Kyle, let's get suited up. Remember to grab the underwater slate and pencil, and I'm bringing the underwater camera. Let's go over our Michael-approved dive plan. I made sure to include extra air tanks with regulators that we'll place in the second cavern of the tunnel system. They'll be our emergency stage tanks."

"Better safe than sorry," Kyle said.

"It's so funny to me that we seem so far underground when we're actually seven feet above sea level on this platform. I'm glad we don't have the need to use mixed gases. Their use seems way too complicated for me, and I think all the extra planning required would take the fun out of the dive," said Bradley.

"You're right, but I'd still like to dive really deep one day when I feel a bit more confident, and I'm more experienced, and when I have one hundred dives under my belt. I especially want to make sure I have a solid handle on my buoyancy and all."

"You have great buoyancy control. You could do it now if we needed to. I'm glad you agreed to be my dive buddy. You're the only one I trust, with the exception of Michael, on the entire island. Now let's quit talking and get to work."

"You sound like Michael. You better be careful. He's rubbing off on you."

Bradley and Kyle finished suiting up and moved their gear into the water. The water felt a tad bit cooler than last week, an omen of the colder weather to come.

They quickly went about the business of their buddy checks to ensure each other's gear was properly assembled and functioning and ready for the descent into the water, especially since they would be going into waters within the cave system that neither of them had been in before. It was really hard to tell which of the two boys was more excited about the adventure.

"You did study your copy of the partial map of this cave, so you'll be more comfortable going on this dive?" asked Bradley.

"You bet I did. That reminds me, when I was going over the copies of all the maps you gave to me, I realized the cave nomenclature being used. Cave A, Cave B, and so on just isn't going to cut it. This isn't the only tunnel system in this area, and from what Michael's told us, we could soon run out of letters of the alphabet. I had an idea how to fix this. I think we should start referring to each of the caves by names, and I came up with some names for these five if you're interested?" proposed Kyle.

"What'd you have in mind?"

"I wanted to use simple but easy to remember names like *Long John* for the cave we're diving today since it's the longest of the five. What do you think?" asked Kyle.

"I like it. *Long John* it is."

"Great. That'll be the first change to the map of this cave and tunnel system. Cave A is now *Long John*," said Kyle scribbling a note on his pad."

"Now that we've settled that, let's make sure we're on the same page concerning what we're about to do. I'll be leading the dive. You follow just like we did during our training scenarios. If you have any issues or concerns, *I mean any*, you get my attention like you've been taught, okay?"

Kyle nodded.

Both boys put their masks on, turned on their dive lights, stuffed their mouthpieces in, and gave the other the okay sign. They made a fist with their thumbs pointing downward as they descended into the cool, clear water of the cavern. The wetsuits, with their gloves, booties, and hoods, kept them warm enough, but the cool water had to enter their wetsuits in order to become a warm insulating layer.

The boys conducted one last look at each other's gear, being the good dive buddies that they had become. Then they headed toward the cave tunnel entrance, Bradley in the lead, with Kyle following. When Bradley reached the mouth of the tunnel, he pointed down to a metal eyebolt that had been tapped into the rock. Here the quarter-inch thick traverse line that would be their guide to the tunnel system they were entering was permanently tied off.

Bradley loved the solitude. When diving, all the noise ceased in his head and he could think and relax. He could see every rock, nook, and cranny in the cavern with their bright dive lights, and the fish and other sea life in the cavern were deep maroons, bright yellows, vibrant purples, blues, greens, and brilliant whites. The water was so clear. It was as if they weren't submerged after all. This was the first dive Bradley had led that wasn't a training scenario; he could finally enjoy the dive unencumbered.

Bradley and Kyle slowly went into *Long John's* tunnel entrance and were relieved to find it to be almost five feet in diameter—plenty of room. It seemed like only minutes passed before they reached the first cavern and were able to surface and get a good look around. Bradley was grateful that Michael had already confirmed that this part of the cave system had quality, breathable ambient air due to the porosity of the lava rock formations that made up the Celtston labyrinth.

The boys found that there were no words to describe the cavern surround. The ceiling was at least twenty-nine feet high and the cavern was oblong in shape—about fifteen feet wide on the short side, and twenty-three feet wide on the long side. The stalactites were not uniform and a few of them were pretty extensive.

"Bradley, I'm surprised how fresh and clean the air smells in here. Let's turn our lights off to see if we can see any sunlight leaking into this place." It took only moments after the dive lights were turned off for the boys' eyes to adjust.

"Look at all of the crystals in the stalactites. They look like bright white Christmas lights," blurted Bradley.

"They're twinkling like the stars on a clear night with no clouds . . . this is *so* cool. I've never seen anything like it. This must be the phosphorescence Michael was telling us about. It's so beautiful. Look at the ones over to the right, up there on that really big stalactite. They're multicolored," Kyle said.

"I could stay here all day," Bradley said. "But we only have four hours planned to revalidate what's on the maps and to add missing attributes. We need to take the photos, make notes of water height, temperatures and all. Let's get going. We have three more of these internal caverns before we get to the end, and I want to hurry and get to the next cavern so we can drop these stage bottles off."

"Yeah, you're right. Let's get going. There's so much to see; now I understand why it took Michael so long to get through here," said Kyle.

"To be fair, I would like for us to take turns doing the different duties. I'll take pictures and note unique optics, while you take the physical measurements this time, and we'll swap for each of the caverns?" offered Bradley.

"I like that idea," said Kyle.

The boys were overwhelmed, and despite the many distractions, they quickly went to work.

"Who'd have thought that this splendor was underneath the mound of dirt and rocks above?" said Bradley.

"I can't believe we're already at the entrance to the tunnel leading to the last cavern on the map, and we have so much air capacity left in our rebreathers. We've been breathing surface air more than diving. I'm really surprised at that," noted Kyle.

"I know, crazy huh?" agreed Bradley.

"With all the beauty we've seen today, what's the chance this cavern would have such an entrance? Going down the shoot of that little waterfall and being tossed in the air at the end of the slide we just went down was *awesome*. Someone cut that smooth rock trough we went through or that could've been a dicey fall from that height. I'm glad there wasn't a pile of rocks waiting for us instead; that's about a seven-foot fall without the shoot, I'd guess." deduced Kyle."

"I'm having trouble coming up with the words to describe what it looks like in here for the report. It's so hard to capture what we're actually seeing. I'm making sure to take a lot of pictures. There's so little ambient light. I'm not sure even the pictures will catch the vibrancy of the colors," said Bradley.

"I'll make sure to draw a picture and to get as many dimensions as I can," said Kyle. "You know we're going to have to climb up those rocks next to the falls to get back through to the tunnel. That'll be interesting with all of this gear on."

"Another reason Michael wanted me to have a dive buddy," said Bradley. "Let's hurry, so we can get to the end of the tunnel system and finish the map. I want to have some time left to look around some more."

"I'm on it," said Kyle.

Both boys went to work, and in less than twenty minutes they were ready to enter the last part of the tunnel system noted on the map.

"Okay Kyle, you ready?"

Kyle followed Bradley as he submerged and entered what they thought to be the final tunnel of the cave system. Bradley stopped without warning and Kyle, busy validating measurements and making notes of the rock strata and silt mixture and depth variances, almost ran into his fins.

Bradley signaled for Kyle to back out of the cave.

Kyle signaled back to discern if Bradley was okay before he responded in the affirmative to his direction.

Once Bradley responded with the okay sign and he reconfirmed his signal to back out, Kyle slowly turned himself around, careful not to damage any of his equipment as he headed back to the cavern from where they had come.

As soon as Kyle hit the surface, he already had his mouthpiece out and quickly swam over to Bradley so he could check on him to make sure he was okay, "What's wrong?"

"I'm fine. This tunnel is different. Couldn't you feel it?"

"No, but you were ahead of me. I couldn't see what you could see."

"The descent was slight at first, but once I got to what I thought was the final cavern entrance, I realized it was actually a bend in the tunnel heading downward, and right before the bend the traverse line ends. It looks like the tunnel drops about eleven feet, then heads to the left. I want to look at the map so we can get our bearings.

We're entering new territory here and I want us to go slowly, and make sure we don't do anything we'll regret later."

"I'm with you," said Kyle. "Do you think we should keep going without a traverse line to follow?"

"Sure, why not? We built time in our dive plan to allow us to get to this tunnel systems end point. We're going to start laying the remainder of the traverse line. I have the line and eyebolts right here," said Bradley, as he pulled the eyebolts out of his gear pouch and freed the looped rope from the clips attaching it to the back-plate of his harness.

The boys reviewed the map and figured out their location in relation to *Long John's* entrance. Then after reconfirming that they both had sufficient air capacity, they headed back under the water to explore the unexplored. The two of them couldn't have been more excited, because they were now entering uncharted territory. It was great. Diving under the earth, they weren't exposed to too much sun and a sudden downpour common to this area couldn't affect them—or so they thought.

Bradley and Kyle slowly inched their way to the lower part of the tunnel, careful to keep the line taut as they made the left turn. While the water was clear and the tunnel seemed to maintain its size in width and height, Bradley couldn't see the tunnel's end. He remained calm and slowly moved forward allowing ample time for Kyle to continue with his efforts, but the lack of an end in sight started to make Bradley anxious.

Where's this tunnel leading?

He perceived a change in the water's color about twenty feet in front of them. He could barely make out a hint of low-level light coming through, like in the other caverns.

Once he entered what he thought to be the last cavern in this tunnel system, and Kyle finished his data collection, the two boys surfaced. They were happy to have reached the end and were ready to complete their work for the day by documenting the cavern's overhead details. Then they could finally have some fun.

Kyle started to look around. "Bradley, I think the water is starting to rise in here. Am I right?"

"It is. I'm not sure what's going on. Let's say we finish this job another day. I think we better start heading back."

"I'm ready. Let's go," said Kyle.

Both boys put their mouthpieces in, gave the ready-to-descend signs, and started heading to the cavern exit, but soon realized there was a strong current pushing the water into the cave. They were finning, but not getting anywhere. The water turned murky, making it hard to see within the walls of the tunnel. Bradley signaled to Kyle that they needed to surface, but before they made the attempt, both boys were swept back into the cavern by the ever-increasing flow of water.

"Both boys grabbed hold of the others' harness straps so that they wouldn't get separated and quickly made their way to the surface. Bradley shouted out to Kyle, "Get on the ledge over there," as he pointed to his right. "It looks like there might be another, smaller tunnel's entrance up there. I'll be right behind you. Hurry!"

In no time at all, both boys had climbed to safety with the help of the other. They took a moment to collect themselves. Their hearts were pumping *way* too fast. They needed to stop and assess the situation just like they were taught in their emergency training scenarios.

"What're we going to do? The water's still rising in here. It's coming in faster now," fretted Kyle.

"I'm not sure, but I'm glad Michael changed our dive plan to include rebreathers, so we have a lot more dive time. We should be fine. Based on the tide tables I looked at this morning, I think this must be the floodtide coming in. This cavern ought to provide us sanctuary until the tidal water recedes. If I'm remembering correctly, we have about two hours from now until the tide starts to turn. We're going to have to wait it out here," said Bradley.

Kyle smirked, "Well so much for your *plan* Bradley."

"You're right, but I think we'll be fine here. The water is still rising, but it seems to be slowing down. In the meantime, we might as well see where that tunnel up there leads."

"Well, let me check my schedule to see if I can accommodate your request," teased Kyle.

"We'll only go as far as we can with our gear on to be safe. Since this is an uncharted part of the cavern, we'll need to keep breathing through our rebreathers until I test the quality of the air in that tunnel and where it leads. We'll carry our fins with us. Look there, the water level is starting to rise above the sill we're standing on. I think we need to see if we can find some higher ground to wait this out. You go first. I'll be right behind you," Bradley said.

Kyle was more than happy to be doing something, as he and Bradley put their mouthpieces in and climbed to the tunnel entrance. He stopped prior to entering and removed his mouthpiece.

"You do think that we'll be okay? Are you sure it's wise of us to go even deeper in here?"

"Kyle, we should be fine. Michael has our dive plan, so he knows what tunnel system we're in. I think our going up in elevation couldn't hurt. It would be smart of us to find out exactly where that tunnel leads. Wouldn't it be nice to know if we had another way out of here?"

"Alright," conceded Kyle.

"Change of plan Kyle my boy; you follow me. I'll take the lead," said Bradley, when it became clear to him that Kyle was reluctant to go first and looked a tab bit uneasy.

Bradley pulled out his meter to test the quality of air at the mouth of the tunnel before entering and was relieved to find the air breathable and consistent with the prior tunnels. He signaled to Kyle that the air was okay to breathe.

"I'll keep this meter handy and take samples of the air as we move forward. Be ready to stuff your mouthpiece back in if you see me doing so."

Bradley and Kyle moved slowly through the tunnel as Bradley continued to lay the traverse line.

"I'm sure happy we found this dry tunnel and it's going up in elevation; that's way better than going downward," beamed Bradley.

By the time they reached mid-tunnel, they were wading through a half foot of water.

"The cavern we just left must be completely submerged by now. Thank goodness we pursued higher ground," noted Bradley.

"Unfortunately, the slight elevation gain in this tunnel isn't enough; the water is still rising," said Kyle.

When they reached the end of the tunnel, the boys were pleased to find an open cavern with no water present. It was the same size as Celtston's small one-room post office building. The sight surprised them so much that they momentarily forgot their seemingly dire situation.

"This place looks like it used to be an underground storage room or someone's office." said Kyle.

"It's obviously been submerged more than once. Everything's covered in silt and all the stuff in here has been tossed about. The only thing sitting upright is that huge desk over there. Look at the chairs and what looks to have been books at one time strewn all over the place." exclaimed Bradley.

"That desk looks like it weighs a ton. How'd they get it in here?" pondered Kyle. "I suspect they brought the wood in here and built the desk in place?"

"I bet you're right. You know, Michael wasn't too happy with himself when he didn't get to finish his dive, but now I'm starting to think he was lucky to have ended his dive when he did," said Bradley.

Kyle gasped. "Look, the water is starting to come in here and it's rising pretty fast. There's nowhere else for us to go!"

"Kyle let's practice stopping, thinking and assessing our situation. What do we know?"

"There's nowhere else for us to go," replied Kyle.

"And . . ." coaxed Bradley.

"So, I guess we're going to have to wait it out here," said Kyle.

"What else do we know about this situation?" asked Bradley.

"We've got plenty of air," said Kyle.

"And you have a good dive buddy; that'd be me," said Bradley as he smiled and pointed at his own chest. We'll only use the rebreathers when the water reaches our chins. We've hardly used any air capacity so we're *good-to-go* for at least two hours, and if we can make it at least halfway back we have our stage bottles tied off and waiting for us. You good with that?"

Kyle was frantically looking around the room and working to calm himself down, as he witnessed the water continuing to flow inward. He was finding it hard to relax, but he did manage to respond in almost a whisper, "Well, in the absence of any other options—yeah—I suppose I'll have to be."

"Kyle, look at me," Bradley said. "Let's get up on the desk. This will give us more time to breathe the ambient air. We'll wait for the water to rise enough to float us on top of the desk so that we won't have to try and climb up there with our gear. Let's put our fins back on right now. We'll be able to easily fin up there in a few minutes."

"Alright," submitted Kyle.

It took the boys five minutes with the help of the other, but they finally found themselves standing on top of the desk. They had reached the highest spot in the room.

"It looks like we have about twelve feet from the desktop to the overhead, but I don't think we'll need it, because the water is actually starting to level out."

"Bradley, once the water stops rising, we're going to need to conserve our air. Pretty soon we're going to have to start breathing off of our rebreathers because what little air is in this cavern won't last for very long."

"Don't be silly. This is a big space and once the water stops rising, there should be plenty of air in here. We shouldn't have to worry about air to breathe. We'll be able to leave before that becomes a problem for us, mark my words."

The boys stood chest deep in the rising current, and just when it seemed to have leveled off a violent surge of water rushed into the room and seemed to lift all of the submerged contents off of the cavern floor, save for the desk they were standing on. Something smashed into Bradley's leg, knocking him off balance and causing a sudden sharp pain. He slipped off the desk before he could put his mouthpiece in his mouth, and he went down, disappearing under the cocoa colored water.

Bradley bobbed to the surface gasping for air. He quickly inflated his buoyancy compensator, allowing himself a few seconds to catch his breath and to regain his composure.

"I thought I was a goner," panted Bradley.

"That makes two of us . . . you okay?"

"I'll live, but I don't think I want to do *that* again."

"Get back over here and quit playing in the murky water."

Bradley swam over to the desk with little effort.

"Kyle the current's gone; I don't feel it anymore." He reached the desk. "Help me up . . . Please."

"Give me your hand so I can pull you out."

Kyle lifted Bradley to safety, and the two boys took a moment to breathe and relax. "I don't think I can take another moment of fun-filled excitement," said Kyle.

"I'd suggest that you put some more air in your BC, so you won't have to experience the thrill I just had. It's really overrated," warned Bradley.

"Good idea. All I want to do is to get out of here. My fun meter *is pegged* for the day," declared Kyle.

"Well now that we're going to live, I need to tell you something," said Bradley.

"*What now!?*" exclaimed Kyle.

"When that box or whatever it was that hit me and knocked me off the desk, it tore my wetsuit. I think it may have cut my leg, but I can't tell how bad it is. It's probably fine for now, but hopefully there isn't anything in here with us that likes the smell of my blood. Plus, my temperature gage is showing that the water temperature has gone down to sixty-six degrees with the influx of new water, and the cold water is leaking into the hole in my wetsuit. I'm starting to feel a bit chilly."

"You're kidding me—*right?*" beseeched Kyle, looking at Bradley, hoping he'd start laughing and telling him he was just joking.

"We've got to hurry and do something! All the rescue diver scenarios showed that if you get hypothermia you could *die*, and Captain Nopar told us that a shark can smell *a single drop* of blood from miles away—and you sound like you might have a serious cut down there!"

"Calm down. I didn't tell you to make you freak out. I told you because I need your help to try and cover up the tear in my wetsuit. If we do this right, it will minimize the bleeding and prevent the cold water from free-flowing into my wetsuit. I have a doo rag in my gear pouch."

"That looks like the head wraps those motorcycle dudes wear in the movies," said Kyle.

"Not the same thing," responded Bradley as he filled his BC with air to its capacity. Now he was able to float atop the water on his back, with his legs outstretched in front of him, his fins helping to buoy his legs up. This pose allowed Kyle to reach Bradley's leg more easily so he could tie up the breach in his wetsuit, and to make an assessment of the damage done to his leg.

"Something pretty sharp hit you right here in the calf," said Kyle feeling around the wounded area to discern if the damage was limited to the cut he could see. "The cut is not long, but it's deep. I bet you'll need a couple of stiches. It sure looks like it hurts, and the dirty water in here isn't going to help it heal."

Kyle patched up the suit as best as he could by tying the rag tightly around the tear.

Bradley rejoined him on top of the desk when he almost slipped off again. Whatever had hit him was apparently now resting on the desk in the area Bradley was hoping to occupy. Luckily Kyle was close enough to grab his harness before Bradley face planted back into the water.

Bradley stuffed his mouthpiece in and quickly descended, clumsily resurfacing moments later holding an old rust-free metal cigar box-sized container.

"This box is made of a heavy metal alloy of some kind or a composite. I've got to see what's inside, but we're going to have to wait until we're back at the dock before opening it, on the off chance this box is watertight, and the contents are still intact. I learned all about this in the cool forensic diver books Michael had me read. I don't want to ruin what's inside by opening it now."

"That's a good idea," said Kyle.

"I've got a dry-bag in my gear pouch as well. I brought it just in case we found any treasure. It has taken a lot of effort, but we've finally discovered our first treasure chest," beamed Bradley.

"Now what do we do?" asked Kyle.

"Now we wait out the tide."

The boys remained precariously perched on the desk for three hours.

"I feel like it has been days," Kyle said. "I need to get out of here. I don't think I've ever stood this long in one place my *entire* life."

After the water started to recede, the boys took photos and measurements, because they didn't want to have to come back here any time soon.

They were finally ready to depart with their treasure when Bradley received a frantic impression from Quentin. It was as if Quentin was a hologram standing in front of him in the cavern. Startled, Bradley jumped back.

"What's going on over there?" Kyle asked his diving buddy.

"Nothing, everything's fine. Could you just give me a minute? I just need a minute," begged Bradley.

Kyle nodded.

"I'm just going to take another look around if you don't mind," feigned Bradley.

"You've got to be *kidding*. I want to get out of here. I'm going *crazy*. I feel so claustrophobic in here right now."

"Just a minute—*please* Kyle."

Kyle could see that Bradley wasn't okay, but he relented. "Sure . . . take whatever time you need."

Bradley moved across the room and pretended to study a pile of debris on the floor while he mentally engaged Quentin.

"Where are you?"

"I'm at Michael's house with everyone else. You're way overdue. They're getting ready to go down to the docks to get a search party assembled to go looking for you. They all think you're dead or something, but you're okay—right?"

"We're fine. Only a few cuts and bruises, but we're doing great."

"What happened to you?"

"We got stuck six caverns back in the longest tunnel by a flood tide. The water surged in and inundated the tunnel system. We found high ground and we've been waiting for the tide to ebb so we can get out of here. We'll be heading back in a few more minutes. I figure it'll take us about two hours to get back to the dock."

"Thank God! I was so scared. I felt your fear. I thought I felt you get hurt. I know that sounds crazy, but then I couldn't feel you anymore. I thought I lost you."

"I got a small cut on my leg. I just need a few stiches. Don't tell anyone you reached me. No one can know we can talk with each other like this. Understand?"

"Yes, but not even Uncle Richard, Aunt Benitita or Michael? They're all so worried about you."

"It's important that you tell no one. We don't know how they'll take it."

"I won't say a word," promised Quentin.

"Who's with you now?" asked Bradley.

"Half the township is here, including Captain Nopar and even the two strangers are here. Did you know there were two strangers in town? I only knew about Jay, but not this other guy. Jay seems okay, but I don't like this other guy very much."

"Yeah, I found out about him the other day. You and I haven't had a chance to talk. We have a lot to talk about once I get out of here. I'll see you in about two hours."

"Bradley . . . Bradley . . . Come on! Are you okay?" shouted Kyle as he shook Bradley by the shoulders.

"Huh, yeah . . . I'm fine—just fine," said Bradley emerging from a daze.

"You were totally zoned out just now. I couldn't get you to look at me. You really scared me. Are you sure you're okay? Did you hit your head when you went under? Let me see."

Kyle started to examine Bradley's skull.

"I'm good," said Bradley as he gently pushed Kyle's hands away. "I didn't hit my head. I just started thinking about how long we've been gone, and I bet there's an entire island of people who are worried sick about us; I know Quentin will be. You know how upset he can get. I just hope he's okay."

"Wow! I didn't even think about that. My parents will be going bonkers. Can we *go* now?"

"Yes. You can lead us out of here since I'm wounded."

The receding tide helped pull them through the submerged cave and tunnel system, making their exit almost effortless; they hardly had to fin at all. They reached the dock area in less than the anticipated two hours. Upon arrival, they hit the surface and heard cheers of joy from the islanders who had made their way down to the dock surround. A search and rescue team was gearing up to start searching for the two missing boys. The boys could hear everyone calling out to them.

"Thank goodness you're alive and well."

Kyle responded, "Bradley hurt his leg. I need some help getting him up to the dock."

Michael jumped into the water.

"Bradley, Kyle, you boys okay?"

"We're fine. I'm probably going to need at least three stitches, but other than that, we're both okay," responded Bradley.

"We've all been so worried about you. Well, at least I was until your Uncle Richard showed me Quentin in deep thought after he had been acting kind of crazy just moments prior. He suddenly calmed down and smiled, when only a few minutes earlier, we thought we were going to have to sedate him. I knew then that you were okay, and here you are."

"Michael, we have so much to tell you *and* something to show you," whispered Bradley.

"We'll get to that later boys; don't let anyone know that you've found anything."

Uncle Richard and the others helped to pull Bradley up the ladder and onto the dock while Kyle and Michael pushed him up from below.

"Michael, what an *awesome* adventure," beamed Kyle.

CHAPTER FIFTEEN

QUENTIN

Bradley lay awake with his eyes closed, feeling unrested after tossing and turning all night, his mind replaying frantic scenes of near drownings. Instead of attempting to go back to sleep and dream of something pleasant, Bradley dressed and headed downstairs for breakfast. He was starved because he'd gone to bed without supper, since he was so exhausted after yesterday's great adventure. That's what yesterday's events were to him now, and he was looking forward to his next one already. Then he remembered, *Today's the first day of school. Bummer.*

Sure enough, everyone in the house was already awake and in the kitchen. Bradley could feel the positive energy from his cousins, and even Quentin. He could hear everyone talking excitedly about what they felt the day would hold for them. Quentin wasn't talking, but he was at least listening—and for him that was engaging in the conversation.

As soon as Bradley arrived in the kitchen doorway, he was greeted by everyone

"Good morning, sunshine," his aunt said. They all laughed.

Bradley couldn't have stopped himself from smiling if he'd wanted to. He was happy to be alive, and grateful for his loved ones.

"Good morning to you all," as he pretended to bow to royalty.

"I thought I was going to have to wake you up," said Aunt Benitita. "You feel okay?"

"Yeah, I'm good. I've got a little bruising around my cut, but that's about it," said Bradley, as he turned to look at Chance. "I can't believe this is our *last* year of school. We're going to have to make it one for the history books."

"No, you don't. I mean you don't have to. You could have fun without any more excitement. I think we've already had our fill of excitement for the entire year, after yesterday's exploits," declared Uncle Richard.

It wasn't long before everyone finished their breakfasts, dressed, and the young ones raced off to school. They barely made it in time, arriving as the bell tolled, indicating the start of the first day of school lessons. Bradley patted Quentin on his back at the main door, and they all headed off to their respective classrooms. The township was so small that all the children, from preschool to seniors, took their lessons in the same complex. Bradley's senior class consisted of twelve students, and his class was larger than average. There were approximately eighty children in the entire school.

In no time, Bradley found himself bored to death in his English Literature class. Only an hour had passed since he arrived at school and he was already looking forward to his lunch break. He couldn't wait to see his pals.

As soon as the lunch bell sounded, he, Kyle, Skeeter, and Ed Moe headed towards the lunchroom in hopes of being first in line. Being seniors meant their classroom was closest to the school's dining hall. The boys jostled each other to be first in line. Bradley won, of course, followed closely by Skeeter.

Bradley was salivating because of the smells that had been wafting throughout the building since early morning, when the cooks started making the home-cooked midday meal. "Look at that fresh baked sourdough bread, buttered and lightly toasted—*mmm, mmm, mmm*—my favorite. Oh, and look at the main course, the juiciest roast beef with gravy and fresh vegetables of all kinds—*awesome*."

"You and your vegetables; my mother *makes* me eat them. I don't get why you like them so much." said Ed Moe.

"These are so different from what I ate back home. Brussel sprouts are my favorite," said Bradley, shoveling a large portion of everything he could onto his plate. Once his plate was overflowing, he headed back to their table so he could start chowing down. It was great being seniors, now they could sit in the best seats in the room, located nearest to the windows and farthest away from the gaggle of noisy little kids.

Kyle's and Bradley's great adventure was the first topic of the day, followed by Skeeter's fishing trip with his father, and ending with Ed Moe's days of imprisonment where he was forced to do an outrageous number of extra chores. His fault, of course, since he let his father's cows out by leaving the gate open—again.

Bradley found himself daydreaming. The idea of fencing in an animal was still so foreign to him, even after so many years away from the Amazon. He found it tragic, but it was normal for the islanders. It didn't seem to bother anyone but him, so he never discussed it, but he did make a promise to himself that he wouldn't ever cage an animal, even a poor creature that was going to be their meal someday. *Shouldn't they be allowed their freedom until then?*

Bradley was rudely brought back to the conversation by a piece of bread hitting him on his cheek, thrown by Ed Moe.

"Are you listening to me?"

"Yeah . . . I hear you," responded Bradley picking up the piece of bread and returned fire. He hit Ed Moe right between the eyes, "Now, what were you saying?"

Soon the conversation turned to Nopar, who was now pointing over at the boys and talking animatedly from two tables down, but Bradley ended the conversation before it really gained any momentum.

"I hate talking about that guy. You're going make me upchuck if you don't stop."

CAPOW! Rang throughout the lunchroom as everyone quickly turned towards the source of the noise. A bench had been knocked over and two boys were entangled on the floor, punching each other as they rolled over and over.

"It's Quentin! He's fighting Mathew Demko!" yelled Skeeter.

"*Oh no,*" said Bradley rushing over to pull the two boys apart. Fortunately, Chance had beaten him to it, arriving just in time, because Quentin had gotten the upper hand and was hitting Mathew hard in his face.

"Quentin, what's going on?" said Bradley panting hard from his sprint across the room.

"He started it! He's always calling me names. He won't leave me alone—he deserved it!"

Bradley grabbed a hold of Quentin's arm and pulled him away from the fray. "Thanks, Chance," and then he looked down at Mathew with concern. "Are you okay?"

"I'm fine," said Mathew slowly standing with Chance's help.

"He's such a weirdo. I was just *playing* with him. I didn't call him any names, just ask anybody here. He just freaked out! I don't know what he's talking about."

"Coach is coming," an onlooker called out.

The crowd dispersed back to their tables, quickly taking their seats. As far as the kids were concerned, nothing was broken so there wasn't a need for adult intervention.

What Bradley found most interesting was the fact that the dining staff didn't engage and offered no assistance. They were adults too, and they provided no response to coach's inquiries.

"Is everything okay in here? What happened?"

Most of the kids just shrugged.

At the end of the school day, Bradley and Quentin waved goodbye to Kyle, Skeeter, and Ed Moe as they headed home. They were quick to leave the school grounds as soon as they were dismissed, to preclude any follow-up from the lunch-time brawl.

Chance ran to catch up with them to find out what really happened.

"Hey, you two . . . hold up . . . wait for me."

"Quentin you got lucky this time; no one reported the fight, so my parents don't know it happened. But, from what I've heard Mathew is pissed, and he still wants his pound of flesh from you," reported Chance.

"Yeah, I know. He kept giving me the evil eye all afternoon. I acted like I didn't know he was doing it," said Quentin. "The problem is no one else heard him call me the names, so I'm alone on this one . . . again."

"Quentin, you always have a tough first day. Everything's going to be okay. Let things die down, and in the meantime, ignore them and don't respond. This will all blow over," said Bradley. "Mathew will be reluctant to do anything with the two of us around."

Quentin had unfortunately been correct. His scuffle was just the beginning of many more to come between him and his other classmates; his feuding was not limited to Mathew Demko.

The next few of Bradley's and Quentin's school days were uneventful, giving Bradley false hope that Quentin had finally settled in like every other year. He needed some time to adjust to being around so many others; it always overwhelmed him.

Bradley felt the same way about crowds, but he was able to pretend that people didn't exist when their presence became too much. He would need to coach his younger brother on how to do the same.

Despite the episodes at school, Quentin was handling the world pretty well—or so Bradley thought as he was excitedly running to Michael's house after classes were done for the day. Michael had finally returned from his week-long off-island business trip, and Bradley and Kyle were going to get to open their treasure box.

Bradley spied Michael and Kyle sitting on Michael's porch with a pitcher of lemonade and a few glasses brimming with ice.

"Good afternoon," shouted Bradley, as he reached the top of the hill.

"Get on over here and have a seat. We were just going over what happened to you two in the tunnels," Michael said.

"Crazy, huh?" said Bradley, as he jumped up the stairs and landed two-footed on the porch.

"I was just telling Michael about the box hitting you and you falling under the water," said Kyle.

"Well carry on, I didn't mean to interrupt the most exciting part of your story," said Bradley.

"You're *too* much," said Kyle shaking his head.

Kyle recounted how the water rushed in and Bradley disappeared beneath it. "It seemed like he was down there forever . . . I thought I was going to die in there all alone. I was so glad to see him surface."

"I knew you loved me," teased Bradley.

The boys conveyed their misadventure in full, describing their discovery in detail.

"You boys did exactly the right thing. You stayed calm and waited out the tide. Very impressive," he congratulated.

"We even have pictures," Bradley said.

"If you'd have ever told me there was another room in that set of tunnels, I wouldn't have believed you. This is the first I've heard that it exists. I can't wait to see this desk you speak of. Based on what you've told me, I suspect they probably built it inside the cavern. There's so much to explore in the Celtston Labyrinth. Now, let's go see what you found," said Michael. "It's time to open up the treasure box."

CHAPTER SIXTEEN

TREASURE REVEALED

ichael's workshop was unsurprisingly orderly. Bradley carefully pulled the box out of his backpack and gingerly handed it to Michael.

"I can't wait to see what's in here. The suspense of not knowing what's in this . . . what'd you call it? . . . an *antediluvian* box . . . it's been killing me all week," exclaimed Bradley.

"Yeah, tell me about it. I've had dreams about the treasure every night since we found it," said Kyle.

"It won't hurt you two to wait a few more minutes while I make sure there's no booby traps on the box that may somehow cause harm to its contents, or any of us," warned Michael. "Please have a seat on a stool so you can *silently* watch me do my thing."

Michael placed the treasure box on the workbench as Bradley and Kyle leaned in as close as they could.

"Here we go," said Michael, as he commenced the inspection of the box.

Michael conducted the external examination of the box, followed by an X-ray. Fifteen minutes later, Michael breathed a sigh of relief and announced, "I think it's safe for us to open the box."

The two boys jumped in unison from their stools to stand as close as possible on either side of Michael as he slowly unclasped each of the eight metallic clips, two on each end of the lid. Then he ever-so-gently used the thinnest metal file Bradley had ever seen to crack the seal all around the lid of the container. The vacuum that had been holding the contents securely and dryly, released.

Michael opened the lid, and the look of disappointment showed on all three of their faces when he pulled out the contents—an unofficial looking paper document.

"That's it? I thought for sure there'd be diamonds, rubies, or some great treasure," moaned Bradley.

"No kidding," complained Kyle.

"Hold your horses you two, before you get so downtrodden. Let's read the letter. This could be a clue, or help lead us to the real treasure," said Michael as he methodically pulled apart all four pages of the letter. It was hand-written, with no date.

"This writing appears to have been done with a quill and ink. I'm guessing it might be quite a bit older than it appears to be at first glance, but *look*, it's written in English—American English— so it can't be *that* old," reasoned Michael. "I don't think the word *globalization* was used in this context prior to the nineteenth century. And look at this reference to the *old country*—Scotland. I'm pretty sure this document was written within the last fifty years." He then turned the paper over and back again.

"Still, I would've thought it had been written by my uncle, but I don't think that's the case because this handwriting doesn't look like his. His lower-case *f*s are a simple curve with a slash from left to right. These fs are too loop-de-looped to be his," Michael said.

"Michael, would you *please* read the letter out loud to us already," pleaded Bradley.

"Yes. Sorry about that. We have plenty of time for forensics once we learn what is written herein."

"*Thank you,*" blurted both boys.

"Bradley, Kyle, I'm going to ask you to indulge me a minute while I read the letter by myself first."

"*No way . . .* you're kidding!" cried Bradley.

"You can't do that to us. You're *killing me,*" complained Kyle.

"Boys, I need to make sure there's nothing personal in here, or private family related information. I'll sit over there and read," he said, as he motioned to the comfy recliner. "While I'm doing that, you two can get a closer look at the box," said Michael.

"Alright, but *please* hurry," begged Bradley.

Both boys took a quick look and sat impatiently while Michael read the letter, and then reread the letter with a brow that became more furrowed with the turn of each page. When he got to the last page, he flipped it over. And flipped it back. And flipped it back over again. "This letter can't end like this; the story is incomplete."

"What's going on Michael? Your face is all scrunched up and we saw you read the letter twice. What does it say?" Bradley asked.

"You're not going to believe it. The letter is meant for a Gordon's eyes. You're a Gordon, so it must have been left here hoping you or another Gordon would find it someday. Unbelievable," exclaimed Michael.

"You've got to be joking," said Bradley.

"I wish I were. I read it twice and I'm not really sure what it's attempting to relay," said Michael.

"Can we see it," asked Kyle.

"Certainly . . . here you go," said Michael handing the letter to Bradley. "Be careful with it so you don't tear it."

Bradley and Kyle quickly settled in on their stools, shoulder to shoulder, and began reading. Similar to Michael, on the last sheet of paper, they turned it over, and over again, hoping to find the end of the story.

"This is all about *my* family, my grandparents, my parents and it makes mention of their two sons—the heirs to the Gordon dynasty. Are they talking about me and Quentin? And what's this cryptic clue or whatever it is?" said Bradley as he pointed to the last page of the letter.

To the isle of Scots, you must go,
To glean who is true to you, or foe,
Hardships you will most certainly bear,
The price you pay for seeking those who care,
Whilst useful knowledge you will gain and a glimpse of the future you will see,
In what seems like no time at all you will be forced to flee,
Or risk aiding the great dynasty from which you hail
Most assuredly to fail!

"I'd say it's a Scottish ode of sorts, but it's written in English not Gaelic. I don't understand how it's supposed to lead you to any end game?" deliberated Michael. "It sounds more like a doomsday prophecy."

"How could anyone know all the information that's contained in this letter? Even my father didn't know some of this until after my mother was abducted, or left us, or is who knows where. What's going on here, Michael? Is this your idea of some sort of a joke?" accused Bradley, jumping off of his stool and shaking the letter at Michael.

"No, Bradley, I would never do something like this to you. I honestly don't know what's going on here, but I promise to help you find out."

"How could anyone have known we'd even find the box? We only found ourselves in that part of the tunnel by accident," Kyle said.

"What does this mean? Could they be *more vague?*" complained Bradley.

"Bradley, we're going to have to get some help to figure out what's going on," said Michael.

"I don't see how anyone could have known any of this stuff, and we ended up in that cavern by happenstance. There's only one way in or out of there," said Kyle.

"I'm at a loss for words," admitted Michael.

"I need to get home. I'm going to take this letter with me tonight," challenged Bradley. "I want to reread it after I've gotten some sleep and I've given myself time to clear my mind."

"Certainly. After all, the letter is for you, but I think it wise we print a copy of the letter that you can take home with you, so we can keep the original safe here in the sanctuary," suggested Michael.

"That's probably the smartest thing to do," Bradley agreed.

Michael quickly made a copy of the letter, handed it to him, and locked up the original. The three compadres headed out of the workshop. They soon found themselves standing outside on Michael's front porch. They somberly said their good nights and headed off to their respective abodes, Michael turning around and walking back inside.

As soon as he entered his foyer, Jay called out from the other end of the hallway.

"What was that all about? A few hours ago, you three appeared to be happy and excited, and now you look to have lost a close friend. Has someone died or something?"

"That would've been easier for us to absorb than what just happened," said Michael.

"I'm listening," responded Jay.

"I'm not sure what to do here, but I do know when I'm out of my league, and I could really use your help in understanding something of a delicate nature. I don't want to offend you, but I need to know if you did something, or if you didn't do it, who do you think is the mostly likely culprit? This is a Gordon dynasty matter after all."

Jay perked up, "A Gordon dynasty matter?"

"I need to be assured that you'll keep this *close hold*—not to be shared beyond the two of us without my consent."

"How could you think you've the right to make me promise to keep knowledge pertaining to the Gordon's a secret. I'm a Gordon. That knowledge is mine."

"Actually, it pertains to Bradley and *his* immediate family, making it his. He has allowed me to share this information with you, and he only asks that you respect his request to not share it further without his express permission."

"He's just a boy," argued Jay.

"He's also the heir apparent to the Gordon dynasty, and in this matter, I am acting as his intermediary."

"Go ahead," said Jay.

"Pledge your silence now or I'll seek help elsewhere. You seem always to want to challenge me. I don't have the luxury of time. I need your help now or not at all. What's it going to be?"

"You're right. I apologize. I don't know why I was so quick to anger . . . a discussion with you for another day I suspect . . . but for now, I promise to do my best to help you figure out whatever it is you're attempting to noodle through. *And* I won't share your confidence unless Bradley authorizes me to do so."

"Come on Jay, I could use a cup of tea, can I get you one? This is going to take us a while to discuss."

"A good cup of spiced tea sounds perfect right now."

Michael provided a synopsis of the contents of the letter found by the boys, purposefully not mentioning the ode. He wasn't sure why, but somehow these details seemed meant exclusively for Bradley.

"This is outlandish! Who could have known all of this? I'm more worried than I already was about the boys . . . especially Bradley. I've heard some incredible stories concerning him and Quentin. Getting the two of them to Scotland forthwith is not only the most prudent thing to do, but it would place them under our direct oversight and protection. From what I've learned, Quentin requires special attention and we'll make sure he gets it."

"Jay, who do you think could have written the letter and left it in the cave for them to find? And how on earth did they get in there to deliver it? Whoever this was, had to have been following Bradley and his friend into the cave system. No one was around to protect them, and this intruder could have done them real harm. Bradley and Kyle almost didn't make it home alive the other day."

"Even more reason for us to send Bradley and Quentin to the Gordon castle. No one will get near them inside the fortress walls."

"They're not going anywhere until their father asks for them to be sent. We're supposed to be keeping them safe here at *his* request, but unless we have the entire picture of what's actually happening, we don't even know who or what they need to be protected from. In lieu of locking them up in Celtston's one-room jail and placing armed guards around them, I'd like to make up a non-intrusive protection plan that can allow them to live their lives as freely as possible, while we take the proper measures to ensure their safety. Can you help us to do that?"

"Michael, I think I need for you to come clean with me first. *And* I need your assurance that this conversation stays between the two of us—not to be shared with anyone else. Not Captain Nopar or any of the Celtston Elders, including Richard and Benitita, and especially not Bradley. He has enough on his plate. Agreed?"

"That's a tall order. Their safety is our shared responsibility. The others need to know what they're up against."

"I'll agree to us filling them in on a *need-to-know* basis, but for now this all stays with the two of us."

"Agreed," promised Michael.

Jay recapped all that had happened since he left Scotland, including how he felt shut out by the Celtston inhabitants, Michael being one of them. This exclusion made him more curious and caused him to delve more deeply into the boys' lives than he would have.

After hearing what Jay had to say, Michael felt compelled to tell him a little secret of his own.

"There's another stranger in Celtston who showed up within days of your arrival, but he's never engaged us. We don't know why he's here, or where he came from. He's told folk that he finds Celtston quaint and welcoming. He has decided to extend his holiday for a few more weeks—no departure date mentioned."

"What's his name?"

"Seth McLeod. Have you ever heard of him?"

"No, I haven't, but I have a scheduled phone call with my Gordon liaison this evening and I'll ask about him. Do you have any other questions for me?"

"Not yet, but I'm sure I'll have more over the next few weeks," said Michael.

"My number one goal has become to ensure the safety of Bradley and Quentin, and you need to know that I've figured out that Bradley is most likely the source of the anomalous signal. You've heard of the Chivalran and the Veneré, correct?"

"I know of them, but I'm not really sure what each of them actually does or the extent of their influence. *And* I really don't understand why you would come to the conclusion that Bradley had anything to do with this anomaly issue?"

"We've got a lot to discuss, but I have to obtain permission to share any more with you. Please allow me to talk with you tomorrow after I've discussed what has happened with my contact this evening?"

"Okay. I'll stand by, but in lieu of waiting until tomorrow, let's plan to get back together tonight after your phone call," proposed Michael.

"Okay. See you later," Jay said.

Michael sat there alone for some time attempting to absorb all that had transpired, considering the various possibilities and potential meanings behind them. He ended his pondering with one concrete conclusion. *All I know is that I'll do whatever it takes to keep Bradley and Quentin safe and out of harm's way—no matter what I need to do, or to whom I have to do it.*

CHAPTER SEVENTEEN

SETH

As promised, Jay Gordon reported back to the Gordon Chivalran liaison, Lord Donald MacAllister Gordon, that he had found the source of the energy variance but didn't divulge names or the extent of his findings.

"Mac, I need to be allowed to return to Scotland to talk with the Regiment's High Council in person concerning my findings."

"Based upon all that you've shared with me today, your request is most certainly granted," replied Lord MacAllister.

"To make my status report more meaningful, I'd also like to ask permission to engage Michael Robert Sidlau to a greater extent. I need his help, and in order to gain his support, he needs to know more about the bigger picture and exactly how the Celtston incident fits into the larger scheme of things. He is, after all, a member of the Gordon family. Intimate knowledge of the Gordon Chivalran and the Veneré should be no stranger to him."

"Jay, I know Michael and I've always trusted him. Your endorsement of his character is good enough for me. However, you have my permission to engage him to a greater extent with one *serious* caveat. Michael must be told that once he takes part in our undertakings there is no turning back. In the past, he hasn't been willing to assume this burden. It's imperative that you get his affirmation that he understands what this all could mean to him personally. I know that what I'm saying sounds like a stark warning, and that's exactly what it is. It's vital he commits prior to you sharing anything more with him."

"Understood. Thanks, Mac."

"Your transport home will arrive on the outskirts of the township, north of the port, prior to first light. You know the drill."

As soon as Jay hung up, he sought out Michael.

Jay found Michael reading in his study. He was sitting in a lush, blue silk-covered, overstuffed, high-backed chair with his legs propped up on an equally comfy ottoman, listening to soft classical music and sipping what looked to be Courvoisier. The familiar smell of the burning hickory in the fireplace reminded Jay of home, and for a fleeting moment he was envious of Michael's seemingly peaceful lifestyle.

"Please come join me." Michael motioned for Jay to take a seat in his chair's counterpart. "Luckily, it just so happens there's enough of this fine aperitif for us to share a few," said Michael pouring a snifter of Courvoisier and offering it to Jay.

"*Mmm . . . mmm,* there's nothing better than the smell of a fine liqueur," said Jay.

"Well, I'm going to assume by your demeanor that the conversation went well this evening," Michael said.

"Yes, it did. I had a very productive discussion with my liaison, Lord Donald MacAllister Gordon, who goes by Mac. You've met him before, correct?"

"Yes, he's a good man," Michael said.

"He was very interested in what I've found out to date, even though, due to the sensitive nature of my findings, I wasn't able to share all of the specifics. Mac is receptive to me bringing you up to speed on the scenario at large, especially as it relates to pertinent information associated with this case, but only because it was *you* with whom I wanted to share the information. After all he's family."

"I'm glad to hear that," said Michael.

"He wanted to make sure I let you know how serious the sharing of the information with you is, and to emphasize the ramification that it could have on you and potential future impacts to your way of life. You'll be read into something that once done cannot be undone. Are you sure you want to know? This knowledge comes with baggage, intrigue, and awareness of global affairs that makes it hard for you—well, me, in my case—to sleep at night."

"I'm certain," replied Michael.

"What I'm asking of you cannot be taken lightly. Once you are read into this domain, you'll become an asset that could be called upon to assist us, or to take part in some of the intrigue at any time. There are several very bad actors involved in many of the cases. Do you understand, and are you willing to take on these added risks to your somewhat mundane and uneventful life?"

"I can handle whatever you have to tell me. I think I might know some of it already, if not to its full extent. I must confess something to you. Until now I haven't been willing to take on this added responsibility. I know members of a few of the Chivalran regiments besides the Gordons, and I have a very close friend who is involved in other ways. I've never revealed any of their secrets, and I won't share anything I learn with anyone, not even Bradley, as you have requested," promised Michael.

"Well then, let's get started."

It took Jay several hours to get Michael knowledgeable concerning all of the Gordon family affairs, to gain an understanding of how the other Chivalran regiments fit into the picture, especially the Misticatos' roles and responsibilities and the small part that the Veneré was known to have played for certain. Jay was pleased that Michael was clever enough to ask the right questions and to focus on what mattered in the conversation, and Jay happily noted that any instance that had anything to do with Bradley or Quentin clearly was of interest to Michael.

"Michael, if nothing else, I truly believe from this discussion that you wholeheartedly care about the two boys, and for that I'm eternally grateful to you and pleased we have you on our side. That said, I'm leaving first thing in the morning."

Michael sat forward in his chair. "You're leaving *now*, at this critical juncture?"

"The only reason I feel it's okay for me to depart with Seth in town is because you and the Celtston elders are here to provide Bradley and Quentin the security required to keep them safe. Seth is alone here, and I'm confident that you'll be able to handle him. Key for me is that you'll watch over and care for my nephews while I'm gone as I would have done."

"You know that I will," Michael said.

"I'm not sure when or if it'll be me who returns, but someone will be coming to retrieve the two boys within the month or so, or sooner if we deem either of them to be in any danger. In the meantime, Mac has a team working an exfil plan for whom I referred to as *the two boys,* just in case a need arises. I didn't tell Mac their heritage. That was too sensitive a detail to share over the wireless, but Tristen is with Mac now, so I suspect he's privy to whom we've been referring," Jay surmised.

"I've personally come to care for Bradley as if he were my own son, and Quentin by extension. But do you think it wise to leave before we know Seth's true intentions?"

"Yes, I do think it wise and let me tell you why. It all has to do with the answer to the one question you asked of me earlier today—who is Seth McLeod? Mac knows him, and the only time he sounded concerned during our conversation this evening was when I mentioned his name. Seth is the personal security chief of Rosen, the head of the Veneré. Rosen considers him a member of his family. Seth is extremely loyal to him, and Rosen only sends him to handle *delicate* matters."

"Knowing this, you still think that the boys are safe for now?" asked Michael.

"After talking with Mac, it's my belief that Seth and Rosen are not aware of Bradley's and Quentin's heritage, or more would've happened by now. The more likely scenario is that since this is an island whose inhabitants are related to the Gordon Family, Rosen is having an independent assessment conducted of who might be the cause of the anomaly—to ensure no conflict of interest arises when the time comes to unveil the source."

"So why is he asking so many questions specifically about them?"

"The boys are of interest to Seth because of all the talk in town about the camping trip incident with Teddy Nopar. Plus, add the fact that they live in Benitita Northcutt's home—*Solana's* sister. Mac thinks that more than likely Rosen is making sure Solana isn't the source or, what we believe would be of equal interest to him is if Benitita is the source of the anomaly."

"So, he's looking for evidence to ensnare the Misticatos," Michael said.

"That's what Mac believes. We think this will all blow over when he has evidence that supports someone other than Benitita having special abilities. Benitita has been living in Celtston for over twenty years since she married Richard Northcutt, and nothing has occurred until now. That alone should have ruled her out. Moreover, Solana is not here in Celtston, so there's nothing for him to find. These suppositions allow us to draw yet another important conclusion. Mac thinks it's fair to assume that Rosen doesn't have Solana, as he had once feared possible," Jay said.

"I'm glad to hear that. Later, I'd like to hear more about Solana, but for now please continue."

"Anything that might embarrass a member of the Gordon family, even indirectly through association, is of interest to Rosen. Mac told me that Rosen would benefit if he could further tarnish the reputation of Chief Solano and his family. Any dispersion cast on the Misticato Chivalran could aid Rosen in removing one more obstacle lying in his path: he needs to gain the support of the

Chivalran regiments against Chief Solano, and by extension the Misticato Chivalran."

"Jay you were right, this is a lot for anyone to take in all at once. I'm glad we're sparing Bradley these details," said Michael.

"I doubt we'll be able to shelter him for much longer. When and how we choose to engage him will be one of the discussions I'll be having with the Gordon Chivalran Regiment High Council. We haven't been willing to discuss the entire affair in the open, but much has been going on behind the scenes, apparently. I suspect that the Gordon Chivalran leadership is not yet ready to bring this discussion to the Council at large, and most certainly not to the Veneré, until we're positioned to ensure that a positive result for the Gordons will be forthcoming."

"Please make sure your leaders have a full appreciation for the precarious nature of our situation," beseeched Michael.

"I will. They know that Rosen and his family have a lot to lose by Tristen's, and now the boys', return to Scotland. If Rosen's father's accusations against Tristen Gordon are found to have been false, the boys and Tristen will be in great danger. You can trust me when I tell you that Rosen is a shark and if he smells blood in the water—especially if it's his own—no one will be safe. If you should be concerned about anyone, it's him. Rosen is the wildcard in all of this: a very powerful man with endless human and monetary resources and much to lose."

With that last ominous proclamation, both men leaned back in their chairs, looking aimlessly into the fire, sipping their liquors and lost in their own thoughts concerning what the future might hold.

Not too far away, in Scotland, a similar discussion was occurring. Initiated by a phone call from the local Celtston B&B, Rosen and his trusted confidante, Seth McLeod, spoke on a secure satellite phone system. Seth couldn't wait to contact Rosen with his good news.

"I found Solana's boys. They're living here with her sister's family, the Northcutts. The two boys are a spitting image of their grandfather, Lord Robert Clifton Gordon. With one exception, they both have Solana Misticato's sea green eyes, with a hint of blue. The Precaveros people all have dark brown, almost black eyes, with two exceptions: Solana and her sister Benitita, who take after their mother. I find it remarkable how much the boys look like a young version of all the paintings that I've seen of Lord Gordon. No *wonder* we couldn't find them. They don't look like Solana. We've been looking for a person that hails from the Amazon with a bronze complexion. What a mistake on our part."

Rosen could hardly contain his excitement.

"I knew I could count on you to find them. I never would've thought to look for them in Celtston, but now, after having learned this, it makes perfect sense. I'm glad I listened to you. Your hunch that they might be hiding up there with Chief Solano's other daughter has paid off."

"That's not all I have to tell you. There is *so* much more. I hope you're sitting down for this next piece of news. While the two brothers haven't revealed anything special to me as of yet, I've heard tidbits all over the island concerning the two of them doing weird or unexplainable things. The talk of late centers on what the folks are referring to as the strange events that happened during a recent camping trip. Apparently, one of the local boys played a trick on Bradley and Quentin. The trick had the potential to cause series harm to one of the brothers, from what I've heard, but the two of them made it out safely due to some inexplicable intervention. Apparently, a kid known as Teddy was looking forward to inflicting pain on one of the brothers but was traumatized by what happened. No one is talking specifics and when they see me lurking around, they change the discussion to some benign topic, because of their obvious mistrust of strangers. I haven't learned enough to prove anything, but I know the older boy, Bradley, may look like his father, but I believe it's more likely that he inherited some key attributes from his mother—the special abilities of most interest to us. I'm going to have to recreate a scenario like the camping trip so I can get him to reveal his abilities. I have a little something planned to ensnare him tomorrow. I'll report out the results of my efforts at our afternoon status call."

"Seth, call me as soon as you have *any* evidence. Don't wait to call me at our scheduled time, understand?"

"Yes sir, will do. Good night."

"Great work! Thank you," grinned Rosen, barely able to contain himself.

Seth hung up and started working on his plan for the coming day. He couldn't afford any mistakes. He wanted his plan to be flawless. Rosen was counting on him.

CHAPTER EIGHTEEN

ENTRAPMENT

Seth hadn't completed his plan until nigh after three o'clock in the morning, and he kept rerunning the different scenarios in his mind. He finished the last sip of his java and stood to retrieve the gear needed for his scheme to *out* the boys. It hadn't taken him long over the past few weeks to construct a solid schedule of their typical daily routines.

I'm dealing with unsuspecting children with the mundane agendas that one would expect a child to have. Getting them to reveal their abilities shouldn't be too difficult, he thought.

He soon arrived at the scene of the crime to be, a large, well-maintained two-storied, bright cherry-red painted building with white trim around the windows and doors of wooden construct. The perfect spot for the *great reveal* to take place.

After taking a quick look around outside, he squeezed himself inside the heavy, unlocked sliding barn door. Once inside, Seth quickly slid the door closed. He took a moment to allow his eyes to adjust to the minimal lighting available to him from the sun that shined into the barn via the few grey, opaque paint-covered windows. The barn was well winterized and sealed to withstand the severe weather that typically visited the island during the frigidly cold winter months, so no light showed between the wooden slats.

There's not a single light fixture in here. I guess they do their work during the day and aren't in need of them, reasoned Seth, as he looked at his watch and discerned that he had ample time until his targets arrived. He found himself a bale of hay and took a seat, allowing himself the opportunity for his thoughts to wander for a few minutes.

I'm glad to be coming to the end of this mission. I have so much real work to do elsewhere. I can't wait to get off this rock that's literally out in the middle of nowhere.

He couldn't handle sitting still, so he decided to take one more look around. He stood up from his brief respite, rechecked his work, and finished prepping his final ensnarement.

Well, it looks like everything is good to go. No surprises. A typical barn with hay in the loft, wooden slat boxes stacked and bordered by bales of hay, ready for transport. The barren stalls will provide plenty of room for the scared animal scenario to play out.

Seth completed the installation of an expendable miniature audio system and speaker, set up to mimic a wounded puppy. He finished setting up his innocuous monitoring paraphernalia, pinhead-sized cameras, so he could catch the actions and reactions of the boy from all angles, within and outside the barn. He didn't want to miss anything.

His hardest challenge was figuring out how to get a seventeen-year-old boy to *out* himself without attracting any undue notice from the other locals. It would've been easier to scare the heck out of a teenager in a big city; an assault would rarely attract any attention from onlookers and those that did notice usually wouldn't feel compelled to interfere for fear of putting themselves in harm's way. It seems that in heavily populated areas throughout the world, self-preservation reigns supreme. But he knew the citizens of Celtson would not hesitate to help the boys should the need arise. If he was exposed, there wouldn't be any putting that genie back in the bottle.

His only other concern was that he might miss capturing Bradley expressing all of his special abilities. *What if the scenario isn't intense enough?* he pondered. He had to pull it off without harming the participants—well, at least not inflicting any *permanent* damage to either of them.

Quentin's over-protective big brother will have to do something to save his little hapless kin from danger. And if luck is on my side, I'll even catch Quentin revealing a special ability of his own. Two birds with one stone . . . I'm going to have to deploy protective extrasensory measures on the off chance they inherited their mother's talents, so I don't tip them off before I've ensnared them. I've got plenty of time before I need to worry about that.

Seth went through his plan of attack and recapped all the necessary prep work one last time: *flash charge for the fire starter in place; video equipment up and operational; listening and audio equipment up and operational. All that's left for me to do is to move to my external site to watch the show that's about to start from afar.*

Seth perched in a nearby hundred-year-old evergreen, safely tucked away like a predatory falcon. His perfect bird's eyes view of the barn and its surroundings revealed there wasn't a soul in sight. He sat on a branch wide enough for his legs to lay comfortably outstretched in front of him. He leaned back against the tree trunk as he took a long, enjoyable breath of fresh pine-laden air, while reveling in the warmth of the sun soaking into the skin on his face. He slowed his pulse and entered into a meditative state to prepare himself to defend against any impending mental infiltration attempts.

The school bell rang. Quentin quickly gathered his personal belongings and sprinted out of the classroom, down the school hallway and was first to push open the two double doors leading to his freedom. He looked quickly left then right, glancing from the top of the stone stairway leading down to the cobblestone street before hopping down the steps two at a time. He was soon on his way to where he could finally get some alone time—peace and quiet—beauty to behold aplenty.

He was already getting lost in the solitude of his own head as the distance grew between him and the myriad of other school kids. The nervousness, anxiety, and negativity that consumed him when he was near the other children slowly dissipated as the distance between them grew.

The township wasn't laid out neat and tidy like one might expect. The Celtston buildings were constructed as and where they were needed. Quentin ran along the zigging and zagging graveled streets on his way out of town.

He was happy to see the big red barn, indicating he was close to the edge of town. He found himself smiling from within. *I made it the whole week and I didn't have to hurt anyone.* He slowed his breathing and could feel his muscles relaxing as he inhaled the fresh air.

He stopped a minute to look at his favorite building, the big red barn, not to admire it, but because he thought he heard something inside. *I'm sure I heard a whimper, like there's a scared animal in the barn . . . there it is again . . . a puppy . . . I think it's a puppy.*

Quentin looked around outside of the barn and saw nothing. Then he heard the whimper again. *How could a puppy get inside? The door is closed. Why isn't it locked?* Then a louder more fearful yelp came from inside the barn, as if the animal was injured.

No one was in sight and there wasn't anyone to ask for permission to enter the barn. As he approached the barn door, he heard the puppy cry out like something was hurting it. Forgetting all that he had been told about respecting other people's property, he pushed the sliding door open a few inches, just enough to allow himself to squeeze his head inside for a look around. Unfortunately, it was too dark, so he opened the door a bit more and stepped inside to allow for his eyes to adjust to the low lighting.

He started running around the first level of the barn looking in the stalls to the right and left of him, when he heard another whimper coming from the back of the barn, behind a stack of wooden slat crates near some hay bundles.

"Here puppy . . . come here little fellow. It's okay . . . I'm here to help you. "

After looking around and finding nothing, he reasoned that the dog must be outside behind the barn. He dashed toward the barn door when without warning, it slammed shut. Followed by a loud *click*.

Somebody had locked him inside.

Quentin began yelling, "I'm in here. *Please* let me out!" When he didn't get a response, he yelled louder, "Please let me out of here! There's an animal that's being slaughtered! I have to save him! Let me out of here!"

He started banging on the door with his fists, but no one responded. Quentin pleaded one last time out of desperation, "Please let me out of here . . . please unlock the door!"

Quentin continued. "Why are you doing this to me? Are you still out there?"

He stood with his forehead leaning against the door and his arms outstretched above his head as if he was praying for someone to save him.

What's that smell? As he turned around to look within the barn for the source, he soon eyed smoke. *Oh my God, the barn is on fire.* He could see flames emanating from the back of the barn and the fire was spreading fast.

"Help! Somebody help me! There's a fire in here—let me out!"

Quentin went into full panic mode. First, he tried to open the windows, without success because they had all been painted shut. Then, he attempted to break a window by pounding on it as hard as he could with his already swollen fist, only to realize the windows were too thick. It would take a hammer or some such tool to break them or to pry them open. *I can't believe there isn't a rake, a shovel, a hoe or an ax in this stupid barn . . .*

Then Quentin remembered, *there's a loft, maybe there's another way out up there.* He swiftly climbed the ladder to the loft, looking for another exit. He realized something he never noticed before: there were no windows on the second floor. They had all been planked over. He quickly climbed back down the ladder and started pushing on the door until he was exhausted. He slid to a sitting position on the ground and all his remaining energy seemed to drain out of him as the heat intensified.

If someone doesn't come to help me soon, I'm going die in here.

Out of desperation he tried to mentally call out to Bradley, as he'd done when Bradley was lost in the tunnels. Unbeknownst to him, his panicked state hampered his ability to connect with his brother. All Quentin knew was that Bradley was in training, and that he wouldn't be coming by this way *any* time soon.

Quentin was starting to have trouble breathing as smoke filled the barn. He started coughing uncontrollably. Breathing caused a burning feeling in his throat, and his eyes began to sting so much so that he was having trouble keeping them open.

Quentin was so used to Bradley taking care of all of his problems that he rarely found himself having to solve his own dilemmas, but he knew that he had to do something on his own this time, or there wouldn't be a next time. With this sobering thought came an idea. *All I need to do is to get some fresh air in here so I can breathe. If the air is coming in it could also let the smoke go out, and then maybe someone will see the smoke and come to save me . . . but how? My belt buckle should do the trick.*

He unbuckled his belt and detached his tapered, rectangular shaped metal buckle from the leather strap. *I can use it to pry the sliding door away from the wooden framing. I just need a crack for the air to come in.*

Quentin dug the thin knife blade-sized buckle into several places and finally located the only spot where he was able to jam the thinnest part of his buckle between the door and the trim, creating a small enough gap to allow a miniscule amount of smoke to vent.

Quentin was starting to feel lightheaded and overcome by the fumes that forced him to his knees. He sat there with his mouth as close as he could get to the tiny crack, where he gasped for what little air he could suck in.

Bradley was sitting in the back of a classroom with his three best friends, awaiting their instructor. He sat quietly at first, dreading the beginning of the first day of the *Life After School Program* that was established to teach the young high school graduates how to manage their finances and run their adult household. For Bradley, it was the first coursework that he found had the potential to be of value in the real world.

"Skeeter, I really don't have any idea where Quentin and I are going to live once I graduate," said Bradley.

"Your Uncle will help you out Bradley. Quit worrying about it," said Kyle.

"No really, I haven't a clue where we're going to live. We don't have a house and we don't have enough money to build or buy a house. My Uncle doesn't have a house for us to move into on his property. He's always talking about where Chance will live. He's building Chance's house next to the main house. Uncle Richard has never mentioned anything like that to me. As far as I'm concerned, he acts like Quentin and I aren't even a consideration of his."

"We'll help you build your house. You can build it right next to the one I'm going to build. We'll be neighbors," said Skeeter. "Besides, I think my father wishes you were his son instead of me anyway. He's always talking about why can't you . . . *blah, blah, blah* . . . like Bradley."

"I have a job prospect that up to now has resulted in no income. How am I going to make money diving? It's a lot of fun, but—"

All of the sudden, Bradley jumped up from his desk, his brow furrowed, his eyes wide open, a look of total fear on his face.

"Somethings wrong with Quentin; he's in trouble!" Bradley darted out of the classroom without another word.

"What just happened?" spouted Kyle.

"Should we follow him?" Ed Moe asked.

"Class is going to start in a few minutes. We can't all miss this class. Bradley will come and get us if he needs help. We should stay here," said Kyle.

Skeeter jumped from his chair. "You two take good notes for us and let the instructor know we had to leave because of a family emergency. I'll catch up with Bradley to see if he needs help."

Bradley knew all the places Quentin frequented when he wanted to get away from the fray of people. As soon as he cleared the school building, he began running as fast as his size twelve feet could carry him in the direction of one of Quentin's favorite hiding places, the place that he hoped he'd be. He sensed his little brother's fear.

All of a sudden, Bradley found it hard to breathe. He began coughing and had to stop running to catch his breath. He was feeling lightheaded and was sweating.

Why am I having trouble catching my breath? What's going on with me?

He closed his eyes, placed his hands on his knees, taking several deep breaths to compose himself and focus. As he slowly stood, he couldn't believe what he was seeing: smoke was ahead. It looked to be coming from the big red barn.

Just then, Skeeter caught up to him.

"Skeeter, run and get the townspeople, the big red barn is on fire! I have to go and find Quentin. You have to hurry!"

Skeeter spotted the smoke and immediately dashed off to alert the town fire brigade.

Bradley ran equally as fast in the other direction. He could feel his heart racing and he soon realized why—Quentin was inside. *He's having trouble getting air because of the smoke.*

As he neared the barn door, Bradley could hear Quentin coughing and then he heard Quentin call out to him in total desperation.

"Bradley, I'm locked in—open the door! The fire's almost to me and this door is the only way out of the barn!"

"Quentin, I'll get you out of there! Just give me a minute to figure out what to do! Skeeter is already on his way to get the fire brigade!"

Then Bradley heard Quentin undergo another coughing fit, and he jumped into action. First, he tried to pull open the large metal lock on the barn door, to no avail. Then he pounded on the windows with his fist in hopes of breaking one of them, but was unsuccessful.

"I can't breathe—please hurry!" gasped Quentin, almost inaudibly. "I don't want to die!"

Bradley's rescue diver training kicked in. *When you get yourself in a serious situation, the best thing to do is to not panic. I've got to stop and think about what to do here so I can figure out the right steps to take next. I need to calm myself. I can't think, and that's not helping me to save my brother.*

Fighting back his tears, he worked to maintain his composure as he attempted to guide Quentin into a safe place within the danger zone.

"Quentin, take your shirt off and put it over your mouth. Close your eyes and keep them shut. Lay as close as you can get to the sliding door's opening down in the dirt. Hang tight little brother. I'm going to get you out of there . . . I promise!"

Seth watched from afar, frustrated that Bradley hadn't displayed any special abilities. He'd shown no extraordinary talent at all. *I'm going to have to intensify this catastrophe or I'll be leaving here empty-handed*, and with a push of a button he elevated the threat level of the scenario.

Suddenly, Bradley heard an explosion from inside the barn.

"Quentin, are you okay? What was that? Answer me!"

"Quentin!" yelled Bradley while making another futile attempt to yank the lock off the barn door.

Suddenly, Uncle Richard came sprinting around from the backside of the barn carrying large bolt cutters.

"Uncle Richard, thank God you're here! Quentin is trapped in the barn!" shouted Bradley.

"I know, son," Uncle Richard said as he ran up to the sliding door and cut off the large metal oversized padlock. Uncle Richard and Bradley pulled the sliding door open with one big tug. They found Quentin's limp little body just inside the door, face down in the dirt with his face wrapped in his shirt. He didn't appear to be breathing.

Uncle Richard reached down and picked Quentin up and carried him out into the fresh air. As soon as he was in the open, he gave Quentin a big bear hug to prompt his breathing.

Quentin gasped and coughed, sucking in the smoke-free air. The boy made a very weak attempt to rub his eyes with his shirt to try to clear some of the debris from his soot encased eyelids. He began to sob uncontrollably.

Where'd he come from? thought Seth, as he quickly climbed out of the tree and exited the area. *What is their Uncle Richard doing here, and how did he know to bring those bolt cutters? Rosen is not going to be happy about this. There wasn't any smoke to warn of any dangers. I need to call him to discuss what just happened. I need to come up with another tactic . . . this was an epic failure.*

Within seconds of Quentin's rescue, the town fire brigade and the medical squad showed up with Skeeter in tow. In no time at all, a bucket brigade went to work, and the fire was put out without any external structural damage to the barn——a miracle.

Quentin required immediate medical attention; discussion concerning what happened would wait until later.

The fray caused by all the people addressing the fire and tending to Quentin lasted only about an hour, but when it was over the ordeal left Bradley and Uncle Richard feeling completely and utterly exhausted as they walked shoulder to shoulder toward the medical center.

"I'm so glad you came when you did. Quentin would have *died* if it weren't for you," lamented Bradley.

CHAPTER NINETEEN

CELTSTON ELDERS

Uncle Richard, Captain Nopar, Michael, and Bradley visited Quentin in his recovery room. They chatted about what took place leading up to the incident in the big red barn.

Quentin couldn't wait to tell Bradley what had happened, as he looked up into his brother's red and swollen eyes.

"It was a trap. I thought I heard a yelping puppy inside. It sounded frightened, and when I went inside the barn to look for the puppy, he squealed really loud—like something was trying to eat him alive. That's when someone locked me in the barn. I didn't *see* anyone . . . I know it wasn't anyone from school because I ran out of the building ahead of everyone else, or I'd have thought it was Mathew Demko who did this to me. He hates me."

Quentin sobbed, tucking his head into Bradley's chest. The two brothers held onto each other as tightly as a drowning person would grab on to flotsam.

"If you hadn't come for me, I'd be dead."

"Quentin, you're safe now and I won't let *anyone* hurt you," assured Bradley fighting back tears.

"Quentin, I promise, we're going to find the person who did this to you, and they'll pay for what they've done," swore Uncle Richard.

"Bradley, I couldn't feel him, and I don't have any idea who it was," whispered Quentin so that no one else in the room could hear.

"I know . . . I know," reassured Bradley.

"Boys, we're going to need to talk with you both later, after the Celtston elders meet, but Quentin you have earned some much-needed rest, so we'll be on our way and you can get to it," said Captain Nopar. "Bradley, could you please step into the hall with us for a moment? We have something to discuss with you."

Bradley gently brushed Quentin's face, "I'll be right back," and he followed the elders into the hallway.

"Bradley, did you see anything we should know about?" asked Captain Nopar.

"Nothing," replied Bradley.

"Teddy told me that you jumped out of your chair and ran out of the afterschool program. What made you run out of the classroom? He said *you looked like* your *hair was on fire*," questioned Captain Nopar.

"I don't know. I just got a feeling that something was wrong with Quentin and I know to trust my feelings when it comes to him. I went to look for him in case he needed me, and boy am I glad I did."

Captain Nopar continued. "Bradley is there anything else about this situation that you think we should know?"

"I can't think of anything else, but there is something that's bothering me. Normally, Quentin would've been walking home with Chance and me after school. The only reason he wasn't with us is because we're both enrolled in the graduating seniors' afterschool program; today was the first day. How could someone have known that he'd be alone today?"

"We've asked ourselves the same question," said Uncle Richard. "He was lured into that barn. The fire brigade found no evidence that there was ever a wounded animal of any kind in or around the barn, and we haven't the forensics to determine what actually started the fire. They couldn't tell."

Michael added, "We need to devise a plan that will allow us to keep the two of you safe. We need to meet with both of you as soon as possible. How does this evening work for you? That will give us time to discuss the ramifications of all that has happened amongst ourselves first."

"That'd be fine," said Bradley.

"Please plan for the two of you to be at my office at seven." Captain Nopar said. "It's time we had a candid discussion."

"Quentin should be released by then. We'll be there. He needs me now, though," said Bradley turning and heading back inside the room. The three men departed the medical center and headed to their clandestine meeting of the Celtston elders.

Several of the island elders were already in the harbor master's office milling about, too nervous to take a seat, bouncing off one another as they attempted to walk about the tiny office. When Michael, Uncle Richard, and Captain Nopar arrived, everyone quickly took a seat at the only table in the room. They all started offering their opinions generously, but Michael was able to speak above the cacophony.

"Jay Gordon is innocent. He is *not* the perpetrator. Your thoughts concerning him are misplaced. For one, Jay's related to the boys and genuinely cares about their safety and wellbeing. Secondly, he's no longer on the island. He snuck out of port on a boat that arrived and departed prior to sunrise this morning, which was *before* the incident occurred."

"Michael's correct. It was my turn to follow Seth around today and I saw him enter the barn, where he must have set up the trap for Quentin," confirmed Uncle Richard. "I didn't know that was what he was doing, or I would've stopped him. When I saw the fire and that he locked Quentin in the barn, I ran to the blacksmith's to get bolt cutters."

"Why hasn't he already been arrested, then?" said one of the other elders.

Captain Nopar responded. "Not so fast. We need to talk about the bigger picture of what is going on here, first. Michael has something he needs to share with us. Over to you Michael."

"I've been authorized by the Gordon dynasty leadership in Scotland to share sensitive family history concerning Bradley, Quentin, and their parents. It is a tale which must be kept secret and cannot under *any* circumstances be shared outside of this room— understood?"

Everyone nodded.

It took Michael no time at all to get everyone up to speed.

The Celtston elders, to a person, sat with their mouths agape after hearing what Michael had to say, sensing the ramifications of providing the Gordon boys shelter. One thing became glaringly apparent to them: they were in *way* over their heads.

"So, what you're telling us is you suspect that Rosen himself, *the* high chair of the Veneré, sent his personal security chief to Celtston, and it's *he* who has done this to Quentin," spluttered Donna Kay.

"Yes," confirmed Michael.

Uncle Richard added, "If it weren't my turn to follow Seth around town today, I fear the outcome would've been dismal. Panic overtook Bradley and he couldn't figure out how to get into the barn. The fire brigade would've arrived too late to save Quentin from the smoke inhalation. The most disconcerting aspect of all of this is that Seth was willing to do anything to obtain the knowledge he seeks, even if it meant harming the boys. This man is desperate— making him extremely dangerous."

"What are we supposed do? What's *our* next step? I think we need to find out as much as we can about this man," Michael said.

"What do we know thus far?"

"I believe it's safe to conclude that his backer is in fact Rosen," Uncle Richard said. "The Veneré itself is investigating what was supposed to be a routine anomaly detection, and I believe we can assume that they don't trust us or they would've sought our assistance."

"We're the ones who need outside assistance," said Donna Kay looking around the table to see her concerns mirrored on the faces of her counterparts.

"Michael, what do you think we should do? We can't let Seth's actions go unpunished!" pleaded Uncle Richard.

"While I agree with you, I'm concerned that if we take any adverse actions against him, we run the risk of putting everyone on Celtston in Rosen's cross-hairs," countered Michael.

Captain Nopar added, "If we're careful how we handle this we can still claim ignorance of the boys' circumstances. Once we openly engage against Rosen's point man, and by extension against the Veneré, we'll be overexposed. I don't believe any of us wants to be in that position. Am I right?"

"He almost *killed* Quentin today. He's a nefarious man who needs to be dealt with, and I mean now!" exclaimed Uncle Richard, standing up and slapping both hands open-fisted on the table.

Captain Nopar countered, "Richard, please stop your inflammatory rhetoric. We have to be smart about this. I agree with you. I think we all do, but our responses cannot be emotionally charged. Let's figure out a plan of attack that won't place all of our families in harm's way."

"We don't know and I'm not sure we'll *ever* know all of the facts," Michael said. "But since they seem to be operating under the radar, I think it's safe for us to assume that they don't want exposure—at least for now. We can use this against them. We'll beef up security around the boys. We'll claim ignorance of Seth's part in the entire affair *for now*, and we'll wait out Jay's return. Remember that we're not alone. We have the Gordons on our side, and they have significant resources of their own."

"You're suggesting that we don't do *anything* until we hear back from Jay Gordon?" challenged Uncle Richard.

"That's right. I sent Jay a letter via courier right after the incident occurred to make him aware of what happened. One more topic for him to discuss with his kin concerning the boys' futures while he's in Scotland," confirmed Michael.

Uncle Richard leaned back in his chair, looking as if he'd eaten a bowl full of sour lemons.

Captain Nopar said, "At this moment in time, we're only guilty of allowing Richard and Benitita's nephews to come live in our community," Captain Nopar said. "As far as anyone knows, we're not privy to all of the rest of the shenanigans. I'd like to keep it that way, agreed?"

Once he obtained affirmation from all the attendees in the room, Captain Nopar continued.

"After much thought and consideration, I believe we need to address this incursion on three fronts. First of all, I think it's time for Benitita to visit her homeland. We require Chief Solano's wise counsel and I want to hear it directly from him. I want to know what he would recommend we do. We need to get Benitita on a boat out of here tonight—an unannounced departure."

"Richard, can you please take care of informing Benitita?" asked Michael.

"Will do, but I want you to know that we both figured it was just a matter of time before she'd be asked to go, so I'm certain she'll do it," Uncle Richard said.

"That's good news," said Captain Nopar, tipping his head to Uncle Richard.

"Now for the second subterfuge. I think we should wait to take any actions until we hear back from Jay. We've already sent him the news of today's incident, and he's aware of the boys' history and all that has transpired between the Gordons and the Rosens, as we've already discussed. I think it prudent to let the Gordons take any actions that could be perceived as antagonistic—especially as it relates to a Veneré asset. We should be hearing back from Jay within a day, if not sooner," Captain Nopar said. "If there are no objections, and I don't see anyone with their hands up, we'll consider this an integral part of our ploy." Captain Nopar looked around the table to see if there were any dissenters.

"Good. Now for the third pillar of our stratagem, I'd like to suggest that we engage Bradley *and* Quentin. The three of us," as he pointed to Uncle Richard, Michael, and himself, have already taken the liberty of asking the boys here to talk with us this evening. We need to collectively figure out the best approach to keeping them safe until the first and second pillars of our stratagem become realities. As much as I hate to do it, we need them to be made aware of the dire nature of this situation so that they don't do anything that could unintentionally place them in harm's way."

"I think we're all in agreement," said Michael, looking around the room and receiving a nod from all present—except for Uncle Richard, who was staring at the wall.

"What do you think about all of this, Richard?"

"You know they're just kids. Benitita and I have done our best to shelter them for all of these years, but the time of their living a carefree life of children is over. I don't think we have any other choice."

"Since we're all in agreement, I think it prudent we discuss what we intend to talk to the boys about, what we'll be doing, what we need for them to do, and what we project will be the most likely outcome of all of this," Captain Nopar said.

With that, he and the rest of the Celtston elders dove into their strategy session.

Bradley and Quentin sat on two tall, padded wooden barstools with comfortable wooden backs. The stools were in the middle of the harbor master's office, a place the boys had never before entered. They faced a half-circle of six chairs, occupied by the Celtston elders. Once everyone had taken a seat, Captain Nopar opened the discussion.

"Bradley and Quentin, are you comfortable?"

"Yes, sir. We are," responded Bradley.

"Good. Boys, we feel we have been negligent in our duties to protect you, and more importantly, we have been too slow to recognize that the time has come when we must talk to you about a very serious matter that concerns the two of you." Captain Nopar stood up and began walking around the room, looking down at his shoes.

"I find myself in a rare situation—very rare indeed. I'm at a loss for words. I was trying to figure out how best to tell you that your entire world is about to change. The two of you are caught up in intrigues in which one would expect only the old and wizened would partake."

"Do you know what happened today?" asked Bradley.

"We think we do, and I'll get to that in just a moment. I suspect that some of what I need to tell you will be hard to understand, so I'll go slowly. We want to answer all of your questions. Please don't hesitate to stop me if there's something you don't understand."

"But first, we need to ask you a few questions to ensure that we have all of the facts. Is that okay?" asked Michael.

"Yes," said Bradley.

"Do you know why the two strangers came to town?" asked Michael.

"No," replied Bradley.

"Have either of them asked either of you any questions?" asked Michael.

"No, but what does this have to do with what happened after school today?" questioned Bradley.

"One thing we have all figured out is that we believe the two strangers are here because of you," Captain Nopar said.

"Because of me?" gasped Bradley.

"Yes, you. The reason they came to Celtston is to investigate a rare signal they detected from here. The signal was first sourced on the very day that you had an altercation with my son Teddy, while you were on a weekend camping trip with Quentin," Captain Nopar said.

"Teddy tried to kill Quentin that day!" Bradley huffed. "Quentin and I didn't do *anything* wrong."

"Bradley, please don't misunderstand me. You're *not* on trial here. We need to understand exactly what happened during the camping trip. What *you* did," said Captain Nopar.

"I didn't *do* anything," Bradley repeated.

"I know something happened, because my son told us *his* version of it. Now we want to hear yours. You're not, nor will you be, in trouble," Captain Nopar said. "So just relax."

Bradley grimaced and said nothing.

"My son claimed that something extraordinary happened that day when he came to see us while we were in session. He told us his version of the story, and we collectively came to the conclusion that Teddy wanted to take the attention off of himself for what he'd done, and to place it on you—his attempt at a pre-emptive strike. As a result, I've already punished him ten times over for what he did that day. There's no question that he could have hurt Quentin."

"Let me try," offered Michael, seeing Bradley's reluctance to say anything. "Bradley, could you please give us a *play-by-play* of what happened before, during, and after Teddy Nopar swung the log at Quentin. Tell us what you were thinking about, how you were feeling, and what the two of you were doing throughout the incident. Don't leave anything out. We want to know what happened from right before the incident until you and Quentin returned safely back to your campsite. No detail is too small. We know the two of you were sent to fetch the drinking water for the weekend. Start your story when and where you were when the first inkling of trouble came to you, if you would, please."

Donna Kay leaned forward in her chair and spoke softly.

"Bradley, everything is okay. You can trust everyone in this room. We're all here because we care about you, and we want to figure out how best to protect you, like we promised your father and grandfather we would do."

Bradley sighed.

"We were jumping over a tricky part of the waterfall from one fallen tree trunk to another until we reached a high crevasse above the spring. Quentin and I stopped to look at all of the cool plants. It was sunny and nice out that day. We were having fun. You know where I'm talking about . . . right?"

He continued, "To make sure it was safe, I jumped first and just as Quentin was going to jump, I felt excitement coming from Nopar. He was getting ready to throw something big at Quentin. So, I yelled at Quentin to duck and right at that same moment, I saw this big log swinging toward him from out of the corner of my eye. It came from nowhere. Luckily, the log seemed to slow down, like it got tangled on something, and Quinten was able to duck, or it would have knocked him down. Then I yelled at him to hurry and jump across to me, and he did."

"What happened then?" asked Captain Nopar.

"I grabbed Quentin and yelled at Nopar. I didn't see him, but I knew he was there. He never came out of hiding," said Bradley. "He could have really hurt Quentin . . . killed him, even. He was such a *coward*. He wouldn't even show himself."

"Did either of you actually ever *see* Teddy with your own eyes?" asked Michael.

"No, but it *was* him. I *know* it," exclaimed Bradley.

"Bradley, relax. I don't doubt that you *knew* it. Teddy told us he was there and what he'd done. We're merely attempting to ascertain how *you* knew it without having actually *seen* him," said Captain Nopar.

"I guess . . . except for with Quentin, this was the first time that I ever could tell what another person was doing that I couldn't see. But somehow, I knew he was there and what he was doing and what he was thinking. In my head, I saw him pushing something big and dark at Quentin. For some reason I knew it was really happening."

"But you never actually *saw* Teddy with your eyes?" ask Uncle Richard.

"No . . . I guess I didn't . . . I hadn't really thought about that," said Bradley.

The silence in the room was unsettling, until Quentin spoke up.

"Bradley and I always talk with each other in our heads. We've been doing it since we were little kids. But our parents told us not to tell anyone. We've always been afraid that they'd act like you're acting right now. Everyone already calls me names and gives me a hard time. Now it's going to get even *worse* when they find out I'm even more of a *freak* than they already think that I am."

Captain Nopar tried to ease the boy's concern. "First of all, the conversation we're having right now, in this room, is between us. *No one* will be told anything we discuss unless *you* allow it. Secondly, it's important that you understand what it is that you are able to do when you're communicating with each other that way."

"It's *no* big deal. Why do you *care* so much?" challenged Bradley.

"What you're able to do is rare," Michael said. "Twins have been known to have a special connection between each other and on rare occasion others have proven some proficiency, but the level of ability depends on the individuals involved. You and Quentin have a strong brotherly connection similar to twins, and you both have a heightened ability. It's called *telepathy*. You two are telepathic. But Bradley, you have expanded your ability to hear the thoughts of others, Teddy for example, which makes your ability even more special."

"You could *feel* Teddy, but he didn't report having the same connection with you. You had a one-way communication," noted Donna Kay.

"Yeah, I can confirm that," Captain Nopar added. "Remember when he reported what happened to us? He didn't know how Bradley knew he was there, or how he knew he was swinging the log, or how the log stopped in midair. He kept telling us that something weird happened, but to tell you the truth, I stopped listening to him when he told me that he had almost killed Quentin."

"Bradley, what happened to the swinging log? Why do you think it stopped in midair?" asked Donna Kay.

"I don't know. It was as if it ran into something that I couldn't see, and it got stuck for a few seconds. I really don't know what happened," Bradley said.

"I think there is a possibility that, in your heightened emotional state, you were somehow able to influence the log's motion. I believe that you were able to stop it from hitting Quentin," said Uncle Richard.

"I've never done anything like that before," exclaimed Bradley. "And if I could do something like that, why couldn't I help Quentin get out of the barn?"

"I don't have an answer for you just now, but I'm quite certain you did stop the log in midair, somehow. In so doing, in your heightened emotional state, you emanated a powerful surge of energy at a unique frequency, and that frequency was likely the source of the anomaly that was picked up by the Chivalran. It's the reason the two strangers have come to Celtston," Michael said.

"Are we in trouble?" Quentin asked.

"You're not in trouble. You're helping us to understand the two of you better. We're blessed to have you with us," reassured Donna Kay. "You're helping us figure out the best way to protect you."

"The signal you emitted is unique to human sources and was picked up by those who monitor the earth looking for that specific type of signal anomaly," Captain Nopar said. "This is why the two strangers were sent here. Their job is to find the source. We now know you are the source, and believe that this stranger, Seth, has figured this out as well. What has us worried is that he was sent by the same man that tried to kidnap your mother so many years ago. We want to protect you from him . . . from them. We sent word to your father and to your grandfather to let them know what has been happening. In the meantime, we need your help in developing a strategy that will help us to keep you safe while we wait to hear back from them."

Both boys sat there, looking distraught, their eyes wide open, their lips pursed, and their faces ashen. "What's going to happen to me—to us?" fretted Bradley.

"I think there's a good chance that you'll be leaving the island to go meet up with your father," Michael said. "There are few places in the world that are safer than behind the Gordon castle fortress walls in the Scottish highlands. I believe this to be the most likely scenario."

"Apparently, up until now, your talents—whatever they all are—have been masked by the high magnetic characteristics of this part of the world and the continual bouts of bad weather. Both of you have been shielded from exposure to the outside world, thus keeping you safe from harm. We don't know why it's come to be, but it appears your abilities are getting stronger and as a result, you sent out a signal that surpassed the masking abilities of the island. We can't hide you here any longer," said Uncle Richard.

Michael added, "I suspect that Seth was attempting to get you to reveal your talents, but due to your Uncle Richard's intervention, he might not have obtained the evidence he sought. I think he's probably going to try and get what he needs from you before he leaves the island, and I expect that he'll be departing within the next few days. He must know that we're at least suspicious of the part he played in recent events, and that his time here is limited before we take action against him."

"We could get lucky and with his failure, he could call the trip a bust and leave without further attempts," said Donna Kay. "But we doubt that's what will happen."

"Bradley and Quentin, we hate to do this to you, but you two can't be alone until we get this resolved. That means that you follow the buddy system. Someone should be with you at all times, understood?" Captain Nopar said.

"How long do you think that'll be?" asked Bradley.

"We should know something within the next few days. It won't be that long," said Michael.

"Do you understand what I said about being accompanied at all times?" reiterated Captain Nopar.

"Yes, sir," said Bradley.

"Quentin?" asked Captain Nopar.

"Yes," whispered Quentin.

"Boys, I think we're done here for today. You may leave. Thank you for coming. Everything *is* going to be okay. Be careful and enjoy your remaining days in Celtston.

On the other side of town, Seth finally deemed it safe enough to return to his room in the Celtston B&B, and reluctantly called Rosen to discuss what had happened. He wasn't looking forward to reporting on his epic failure to obtain the evidence he thought would be so easily gathered.

"Good evening, Seth. I'm assuming something went awry, or you wouldn't be calling me at this hour."

"It didn't go as planned. It was a bust," said Seth.

"Talk to me. What happened?" pressed Rosen.

Seth provided Rosen with a play-by-play of all of the events, with a focus on what didn't go as planned.

"I see, and now I'm realizing that I probably should've sent a Chivalran experienced in such matters to accompany you."

"I did what I could. The plan was flawless," protested Seth, feeling insulted by Rosen's apparent lack of confidence.

"I wouldn't have sent you alone if I didn't have complete faith in your abilities, but I was remiss in thinking that a man who has not had to deal with such matters would be prepared to witness some of the subtleties that you were exposed to. You think yourself a failure, but in actuality you've captured evidence not apparent to you. Let me help you understand your success."

"I didn't capture *anything*. Didn't you hear what I said?"

"How do you think Bradley came upon the barn? How is it that he *knew* to come to save Quentin? Wasn't he supposed to be in class? But yet, there he was."

"He and his brother have some sort of telepathic tie to one another, like twins, and I took advantage of that connection."

"And how did Quentin know Bradley was outside the barn? He hadn't called out to him to let him know he was there yet, correct?" continued Rosen.

"That's right," said Seth.

"You were able to exploit their unique ability to communicate with each other. You were able to show that this connection exists between the boys; moreover, you've captured both boys exhibiting this telepathic ability."

"I didn't even realize it," said Seth. "Well, at least something was accomplished today."

"So now you understand why it would've been beneficial to have a Chivalran with you who's used to tracking Arcanums. They're trained specifically for such an instance. My realization that I was remiss in providing you all of the tools you needed to be successful is not a slight on you, but a regret on my part for not having fully thought this through," admitted Rosen. "I was so intent on capturing the evidence that I let my exuberance cloud my thought process."

"Listening to what you've told me, I can't make any assumptions concerning this kid's abilities. My error was assuming I knew what they were. I was trying to get him to open the door with his mind, but apparently that isn't one of his abilities. I won't make that mistake again," Seth said.

"That's smart. Many new initiates appear to manifest their abilities when in stressful or frightful situations, and because these talents are so new to them, they themselves are unaware of what is actually happening and the roles these talents may play," said Rosen.

"I need to make my next attempt more personal to Bradley. I'll leave his little brother out of my next endeavor."

"You have less than a day and a half to make it happen. They mustn't have any evidence that ties you directly to any of what has transpired, or they would've been all over you by now. But you're the only stranger left on the island since the Gordon Chivalran has departed, from what you've told me. I suspect he did so to report his findings, which are too sensitive to be discussed over the airways. I wonder if he realizes yet that he's located Lord Robert Clifton Gordon's grandsons. I'd like to be privy to *that* discussion."

"Yeah, me too," agreed Seth.

"For now, I need for you to set the trap to ensnare Bradley Gordon once and for all within the allotted time. No later than end of day tomorrow would be preferable. In the meantime, I've already sent a vessel that will be anchored offshore within thirty-six hours. They'll be awaiting your call for pickup. That's all the time you have to complete this mission."

"Understand. I won't let you down. I still have almost three hours of daylight left and I plan to use them to our advantage. Thanks for the lesson learned. I'll report out as soon as I've something worthy to transmit," said Seth.

"You've done well, Seth. Thank you."

CHAPTER TWENTY

TRISTEN

On the other side of the north Atlantic Ocean, Jay arrived in Scotland and was engaging in discussions with the Gordon Chivalran, unbeknownst to Tristen, who they hadn't seen fit to invite—at least for now.

Tristen found himself once again sitting alone in his enormous castle accommodations. The Gordons had welcomed their wayward son, but they had not yet received him with open arms or included him in sensitive family matters until, they made certain of his intent and loyalty to family and kin.

Tristen was more than satisfied with his lodgings. He found himself living in a massive stone fortress, truly fit for the royalty of old. He was assigned a three-room apartment within the castle. The rooms had twenty-foot ceilings and tapestries made with the regal Gordon colors of thick navy blue and green stripes, overlaid with perpendicular yarn-thin single stripes of white and yellow. There were thick, padded royal blue and red oriental carpets throughout, and an intricately carved king-sized solid red oak poster bed that only the most skilled woodcarvers could've made. The bed was covered with draperies enshrouding a plush mattress ensemble.

The bedding was changed daily and smelled of the fresh

outdoor-hung sheets of his youth. The ambiance was completed by a grand Lewisian Gneiss stone fireplace that could easily facilitate the burning of a cord of birch. Even with this finery, he still felt alone and isolated. The castle's other occupants still considered him an outsider, and he was treated with suspicion.

He often found himself taking long, hot baths in the morning, because he had nothing better to do until the Chivalrans were done with their morning regimental duties. Until he was fully accepted by the Gordon clan, he most certainly wasn't welcome in any of the Gordon Chivalran gatherings, which meant that he was not welcomed in their meetings—especially emergency meetings, like the one that had been called late this afternoon.

Tristen came to realize that his favorite place in the entire castle was the spacious bathroom because of the sunken bath. Eight feet square and three feet deep, it was made of pink quartz, with its own armchair of like stone built into the wall of the tub. The bathroom was always stocked with luxurious soaps and soaking salts of all manner of scents and colors.

Tristen submerged himself in the warm, musk-scented whirlpool bath, which was lulling him into a meditative state of complete tranquility. As had become his norm, he took in a deep breath of air and found himself outstretched, floating atop the thick film of roiling bubbles.

He was experiencing a feeling today that he hadn't felt for some time, a sense of anticipation after so much waiting and so many unfortunate delays. He now allowed himself to entertain *hope,* because he had received confirmation from Lord Brian Michael Gordon that the Gordons were finally going to recognize him as one of their own. He reflected on all that had transpired thus far.

I can't believe I've been here for so long. The time has gone by so fast. I hope it turns out that my time spent here gaining my families' trust and systematically unveiling the duplicity of the Veneré has been worth it, at least for the sake of Solana and my boys.

Why can't I quit wishing that my parents' well-executed escape plan had failed? I guess I'm still resentful of how I found out about all of this at the most inopportune moment possible. I have to let go of my anger. I now know that all they wanted was to keep me safe.

I don't understand how Uncle Veldor let his Chivalran duties convince him to betray his own brother. How could any of the Gordon Chivalran support what he did, and how could they think it was right and honorable? How can I trust such people? I understand that none of the other Gordons were ever told of our circumstances or surely we would have been pursued, but to what end?

I accept the fact that Chief Solano was also unwilling to expose the Precaveros people, and by extension the Misticato Chivalran, to his role in helping my parents to escape from the Veneré. I truly believe that if our whereabouts had become known at that time, harm would have befallen us.

Tristen forced out another full breath and fully submerged himself under the water. *I've been so petty and self-centered blaming my father and Chief Solano for keeping this all a secret from me. I have to let it go. I need to start doing something of import, something meaningful, or I'm going to go insane. Once again, here I am, waiting for an unplanned meeting to conclude. They've been in that meeting for hours now, what could be so important?*

He emerged from the water just in time to hear a knock at the door. "Please come in," yelled Tristen.

A young teenage boy opened the door, slowly poking his dark brown haired, blue-eyed visage into the room.

"Sir, you're wanted in the council chambers. I'm to bring you there forthwith," informed the page.

"Thank you. If you don't mind waiting a moment, I'll get dressed and meet you outside."

Within minutes, Tristen joined the young man in the passageway. They walked side-by-side without saying a word.

I sure hope this doesn't have anything to do with my boys or Solana,

*but if it does concern anyone in my family, then I want it to be good news.
I need to calm myself and get centered. Breathe. That's what I need to do:
calm myself and just breathe.*

The fortress was so large that it took the two of them almost fifteen
minutes to get to the council chambers. The separate outbuilding
was a miniature castle with its own moat and drawbridge within
the castle fortress. Tristen felt reluctant to cross over and enter. He
quit walking as he gently reached out and grabbed the page's arm
and stopped him.

"Did the council tell you why I've been summoned?" Tristen
asked.

"No, sir, I was only told to collect you and to bring you here."

Tristen's face lit up when he saw Mac exiting the council
chambers doors.

"Ah, perfect timing. Lord Gordon has arrived to bring you
into the council chambers, and he should be able to answer your
questions, sir," the page said.

Mac called out to Tristen, "Good morning. Thank you for
coming on such short notice. We have a lot to discuss with you. I
hope you're ready for an intense, but what I hope will be a rewarding
conversation with us."

"Is everything okay?" asked Tristen. "Are the boys okay? Have you
learned of anything new concerning Solana and her whereabouts?"

"Tristen, I'd like to say you have nothing to be concerned about,
but that wouldn't be fair to you. However, I can confirm that the
boys are fine at this moment, but here is not the place for us to talk
about such matters. I think it best if we discuss such matters within
the confines of the council chambers, but first I need to get you
through our security," replied Mac, motioning to Tristen to come
across the drawbridge.

Having lived in the open and free Precaveros tribal lands his
entire life, Tristen found it hard to embrace all the security measures
and rules the Gordons seemed to hold so dear.

"Mac, I mean you no disrespect, but I'm curious about something. Why is all of this necessary? Either you trust the people in this fortress or not, and if not, why are they here?"

"Tristen, you've been living among us within these castle walls for years, and only until recently have we ascertained that you are indeed someone worthy of our trust. We now agree that we want you to join our ranks, but we wouldn't have left you sleeping in the streets until we made that assessment. This separation of areas within the fortress affords us the security necessary for us to conduct business while accommodating guests, such as yourself."

Mac motioned to Tristen to come forward as he fingerprinted him, took his picture, took a scan of his retina and had Tristen read a simple sentence for voice recognition.

Once his information had been uploaded into the security system, Tristen was checked in, and he and Mac entered the impressive Gordon Chivalran council chambers. The large oval room could seat what looked to be over 200 occupants in luxury and comfort. Tristen noticed that there wasn't a bad seat in the house and, as was typical, there was a wonderful array of food and assorted drinks being enjoyed by those assembled.

"Mac, I guess they're taking a break, awaiting my arrival?" whispered Tristen.

"They'd be at break now anyway, and we thought it a prudent time to ask you to join us. Come, let's get a bite to eat and something to drink before the meeting resumes," offered Mac.

Within minutes of Tristen getting a sizeable blueberry muffin and a double espresso, the meeting was called to order and everyone took their seats.

"Tristen, if you would please come and take the seat next to me," offered Lord Brian Michael Gordon, motioning to Tristen to take the seat to his right.

After all the niceties were completed and Tristen was welcomed to the meeting, the discussion that Tristen was hoping for finally began.

"Tristen Robert Gordon, due to recent events and final conduct of the extensive investigation of you and your associates, we have all agreed that it's time for you to join the Gordon leadership and the Gordon Chivalran regiment as a member of the council. You were voted in by consensus. Are you willing to join us and to partake in our official ceremony scheduled to take place two weeks from today? There you will be asked to take vows and be formally sworn in as a member of the Gordon Chivalran and gifted the title of Lord." asked Brian Michael.

"Yes, I am honored to be asked to join the ranks of the Gordons of the Scottish highlands."

"Before you're sworn in, we'll need to get you educated on the rich history of both the Gordon dynasty and the Gordon Chivalran, and how we fit into the global Chivalran regiments at large. You'll be kept very busy the next two weeks focused solely on this endeavor. You can trust me when I say that you'll wish that you had more time. As part of the ceremony, we'll expect to receive a commitment from you in word and in blood. These rites will afford you membership in both of these prestigious brotherhoods. These oaths should not be taken lightly, and once given are irreversibly binding. You will be pledged to us for as long as you shall live. The oaths will be given to me, Lord Brian Michael Gordon, the Gordon dynasty clan chieftain *and* the Gordon Chivalran high chair. Do you understand?"

"Yes, I do," confirmed Tristen.

"Good. In the meantime, nothing said or seen here will ever be discussed with anyone who is not currently present in this room, unless you are given express permission to do so by me or Lord MacAllister. We must also have your pledge that you will agree to abide by any and all decisions and or proposed plans of action deemed necessary by this council," stated Brian Michael.

"I do. That is as long as it will bring no harm to my wife and my sons," said Tristen.

"There can be no caveats. It's a *yes* or a *no*, warned Brian Michael.

"You are family, and the safety and welfare of your children are why we are here today."

"I believe you, so . . . I guess it's a *yes*. I do," relinquished Tristen.

"Thank you," said Brian Michael. He then methodically covered all that had transpired relative to their investigation of him, ending the discussion by focusing primarily on what they had learned about Bradley and Quentin over the past few weeks. Brian Michael didn't leave out any information, and for the sake of thoroughness he ended his recap with an introduction.

"Tristen, I don't think you have met another of your cousins who also happens to be a Gordon Chivalran recruit, Justin John "Jay" Gordon. Jay was sent to investigate a signal anomaly that we detected emanating in the Celtston area. He has just returned and is here to share his findings with us, to include some interesting fallout from *that* event, and all that has transpired since that fateful day."

Jay stood and walked to Tristen and shook his hand.

"Jay, please take the speaker's seat."

"We need to figure out our next steps," said Brian Michael. "I think we would all benefit from Jay's personal experience with the boys, the people of Celtston, Seth MacLeod and the situation overall. Jay, could you please tell us what you *believe* to be the most prudent action or actions we should consider pursuing."

At that very moment, the meeting was interrupted by a courier unceremoniously entering the chambers to deliver an urgent message. All eyes were on the courier as he made his way over to Jay, not Brian Michael, as one would have thought would be the case.

"Sir, I was told to find you and make sure you received this package in support of this meeting," the courier said, handing Jay the message.

"Jay, please read it," Brian Michael said. He then politely dismissed the courier, telling him to wait outside the chambers.

Jay fought to open the tightly wrapped piece of correspondence.

"Sir, this letter is from Michael Robert Sidlau, and it isn't good news.

"Jay, please read it aloud," said Brian Michael.

"Yes, sir." He turned to the gathering at large and began reading.

"Jay, to allay any immediate concerns that you might be entertaining, I can tell you that Bradley and Quentin are alive and well. However, our confidence that we are able to keep them safe and free from harm is waning. We think it best the boys are secreted away from here as soon as possible, before another incident occurs like the one that transpired earlier this afternoon. Today would not be soon enough for you to retrieve them. We're standing by awaiting your reply and plan of action, with my utmost respect and sincerity, Michael Robert Sidlau."

"What I just heard was that the boys are in danger, but to what extent we do not know. The boys are in need of greater protection than can be provided by the small complement of elders of an isolated island in the north Atlantic, and we need to retrieve the two of them now," said Brian Michael.

"Sir, that's my take. *Something* pretty serious must have happened for Michael to send this letter. We need to move out now, or I fear that Seth, and by extension Rosen, may do the boys harm, or kidnap them before we're able to take the needed actions to ensure their safety," warned Jay.

"Mac, it's a good thing I always listen to your instinctual warnings. Our preplanning will once again prove to be of great value," said Brian Michael, turning to Tristen and winking.

"Tristen, our team is prepositioned and ready to pick your boys up early tomorrow morning. We should be able to secret the boys out from under Seth's nose before sunrise, with a little help from Michael. Do you trust us to take care of this for you?"

"I trust you have my boys' best interest at heart, but I can't say that I feel good about what's going on right now. I should've brought them here with me. They'd have been better off under your protection," responded Tristen.

"Tristen, it wouldn't have been wise to bring the boys here before all that has transpired had played out, but it is now. You'll learn why in your studies over the next two weeks. I do apologize, but we're going to ask that you please go with the page who is waiting outside of these chambers to take you back to your accommodation. I'll meet up with you later to provide you with an update."

"Thank you . . . thanks to all of you," said Tristen.

He reluctantly departed the council chambers, leaving the other Gordons to develop and execute a master plan that would hopefully rescue his sons from imminent danger.

CHAPTER TWENTY-ONE

THE PURSUIT

As soon as the boys left the Celtston elder's meeting room, they headed off in different directions, unaccompanied. Quentin went to meet up with Nicole, whose turn it was to pick up the weekly groceries, and Bradley couldn't wait to find Skeeter to tell him all that had transpired.

While on his way to Skeeter's house, as he was nearing the last building at the edge of town, Bradley noticed that there was a shadow of a person walking behind him at a distance. Being somewhat paranoid after the discussion with the Celtston elders, Bradley found himself wondering, *Are they following me? They're so far away and I can't tell who it is.*

As a precaution, Bradley decided to make a few evasive maneuvers to see if he was indeed being followed or was just being paranoid. Much to his dismay, he noticed that the person was taking each of the nonsensical turns that he had, even though they were heading way out of the township proper.

The pursuer closed in, giving Bradley a clear look at his face. It was Seth MacLeod.

I've got to get out of here, thought Bradley, feeling slightly panicked and quickening his pace. He turned and saw that Seth was carrying something close to his side. At first Bradley thought it to be a thick pipe of some kind, but then realized that it wasn't a pipe.

Oh my God . . . he's got a rifle.

I've got to get help, thought Bradley, taking an unplanned left-angled jaunt towards Michael's house, the closest and safest refuge he could think of, since the stranger had essentially blocked his access back to town. Bradley found himself running without even realizing it.

Upon Bradley's arrival at Michael's house, he jumped the porch stairs in one grand leap. As soon as he reached the front door, he started to pound on it with his fists in the hopes Michael would be home. To his great disappointment, no one came to the door.

He must still be in town. I've got to hide somewhere—the caves. He won't be able to find me there.

Bradley vaulted over the side porch railing, nimbly landing on the thick grass with the intent of running so fast to the labyrinth entrance that he'd leave the stranger far behind. Once Bradley was out in the middle of the open field and totally exposed, he could see that he hadn't lost Seth. As soon as Seth arrived at the top of the hill, he lifted his rifle to his eye.

Feeling helpless, the memory of a similar scenario occurred to Bradley. It was that awful day when his mother had vanished, and Bradley and his brother hid in their imaginary cave from their pursuers. Bradley imagined the cave, just as his mother had taught him, and within seconds he vanished.

Unbeknownst to Bradley, Seth caught his disappearing act on a video-camera integrated into the gun sight.

"I *got* you," said Seth under his breath.

"Come out, Bradley. I won't hurt you. I just want to talk. I've been sent here to bring you to meet others with similar special abilities as your own. I want to bring you to a place where you no longer have to hide your talents. We can help you *and* Quentin to reach your full potential. I promise to not keep anything from you like the others have. You're an adult now, and I promise you'll be afforded the respect you deserve," promised Seth.

No response.

"Bradley, we know all about your mother and father. There's so much more for me to tell you. What will it hurt if you come out and talk with me?"

There's no way I'm coming out to talk to you, was all that Bradley could think.

"Don't you want to know what really happened the day your mother disappeared? It's not fair to keep you in the dark any longer. How could anyone who actually cared about you do something like that to you? Who do you think really has your mother? *We* don't . . . so *they* must. Do you really think that your father would have left you here for so many years if he cared about you? Think about it. Who's kidding who?"

Bradley had been feeling like the adults had all been lying to him. Seth's questions were the same ones he'd been entertaining for all of these years. It was still hard for him not to, but he wasn't willing to trust this stranger, even though he was asking legitimate questions. But contrary to his offer of goodness, this guy was carrying a gun, so Bradley didn't move a muscle.

Seth had been slowly inching in Bradley's direction the entire time he was talking to him until he finally arrived at the spot where he witnessed Bradley disappear. He started feeling around in a methodical back and forth motion as he continually stepped forward after completing each sweep of the area with his arms outstretched, but he felt nothing—just air.

Bradley didn't just disappear, he vanished. That's why he isn't responding to me. He isn't here in the clearing any more.

Seth clumsily pulled out his phone and quickly dialed Rosen, who answered after only one ring.

"Hello, Seth. This time I'm certain you have something good to report."

"You're not going to believe what happened. The boy disappeared in front of my eyes. He vanished, and I have it all on video. He's gone from here, and I don't know where he went," exclaimed Seth.

"Magnificent! You've done well. This changes the exit strategy we've planned for you tomorrow. I need for you to grab the boys and secret them away with you when you depart the island. I'm glad I thought to send you some company just in case such an opportunity presented itself. I've sent some of your best tactical team members on my yacht that should arrive in your area no later than zero-five-thirty. They'll be contacting you via your secure radio soon thereafter, about an hour before sunrise. This should provide you with more than enough time to go over the extraction plan with them. In the meantime, I'll let the team know about the plus two travelers," beamed Rosen.

"I'll be standing by and doing what needs to be done to prep for the exfil. The way things have been working out for me, I could really use the assist," admitted Seth.

"I know I don't need to tell you that this is a game changer. You've obtained exactly what we needed to solidify our position. You have evidence that will cast doubt on the integrity of Chief Solano *and* the traitorous son of Lord Robert Clifton Gordon. I don't know how I'll ever repay you, but I will."

"I'll report out once we're on the boat and on the way home," said Seth, feeling quite pleased with himself, hanging up his cell, doing an about face, and heading back into town.

Bradley couldn't believe what he heard Seth say, and there was *no* telling what the other guy was saying on the other end. So, to be sure he was out of harm's way, Bradley didn't move a muscle, waiting for some time before he felt the looming danger had passed.

What am I supposed to do now? Where the heck is Michael? I need to hide in a better place until he gets back here. I'm going into the hillside tunnels, decided Bradley, stealthily moving towards his secret hiding place on the landside of the cliff.

The hidden cave entrance was so small and concealed that no one who hadn't been told or shown that it existed would likely ever find it. Once inside, Bradley felt he was safe for the moment. He slid down the cave wall into a sitting position, stretched out his legs and closed his eyes in an attempt to calm himself so he could absorb all that had just occurred. He was exhausted. Hiding for that length of time appeared to have drained all the energy out of him, and once he allowed himself the luxury of breathing slowly, he helplessly fell into a deep sleep.

CHAPTER TWENTY-TWO

PETER

Bradley suddenly awoke but was reluctant to open his eyes after having experienced a very vivid dream whereby his mother was talking to him about his present predicament. She reminded him of his duty to care for Quentin. The dream seemed so real that Bradley felt like she was in the room.

I know that she's not really here, but I sure wish she was. It never fails, she always tells me some good stuff that I can actually use, but it's never enough to help me to figure out exactly what to do . . .

Bradley felt compelled to open his eyes, only to discover that he wasn't at home in his room.

Oh no, I'm still in the cave. There's no telling what time it is. I have to get out of here.

He jumped up and made a move towards the cave opening, stopping in his tracks when he heard a sound emanating deep within one of the tunnels. He thought he heard footsteps, and he hoped that it was Michael looking for him, so he called out.

"Michael . . . is that you?"

It was eerily quiet.

It was probably nothing . . . but I really thought I heard something back there . . .

When all of the sudden he saw what appeared to be a shadow of someone or something coming from inside the middle tunnel—a tall something.

Oh no, did Seth follow me? Has he come to finish me off?

Bradley stood perfectly still, breathing lightly.

"Bradley, please don't be afraid. I'm not here to harm you, and the time has come for us to meet one another," said the figure, exuding a profound sense of serenity.

"Who are you? You're too tall to be Seth. Are you with Seth?" whispered Bradley.

"No Bradley, I was sent here to give you a message from your mother, Solana," said the figure.

"From my mother . . . she's alive?" exclaimed Bradley. "How would *you* know anything about my mother?"

"Solana *is* alive, and I've seen her recently, so I know this to be true. My name is Peter van der Pouw, but you may call me Peter. I have been sent to give you a message, but I need for you to come with me so I can deliver the message in a more safe and secure location."

"You must be the person who left me the document in the tunnel, aren't you?"

"Yes, I am, and had you been alone I would have talked with you then," replied Peter.

"You mean you were in the submerged cavern with us? How did you get in here from back there?"

"I was in the tunnel system with you. I was making sure that you would survive the precarious situation you got yourselves into," responded Peter. "Bradley, follow me."

"How do I know you're not with Seth, and that you're not here to hurt me?" asked Bradley.

"If I wanted to hurt you, I could have done so while you were napping, but here you are, safe and sound. Come now, we don't have much time, but I have much to tell you," said Peter.

Bradley let go of his defensive stance and threw caution to the wind, as he decided to follow the stranger deeper into the tunnel. There seemed to be light ahead even though they were going further underground, or so he thought.

"I've been in this tunnel a number of times and I don't recall seeing this entrance back in here," said Bradley, not really expecting a response.

When the lighting was such that Bradley could finally see, he got a better look at the shadowy figure. He was a bit taller than the average-sized man, with light brown hair.

He looks to be pretty slim and fit, but I think I could take him, thought Bradley, continuing to follow the man further into the tunnel, witnessing him walking into what looked to be a solid rock wall.

How could I have passed by this entrance so many times when I was down here with the guys, and never have seen this entrance before?

Subtle lighting masked the entrance.

This is kind of cool, cogitated Bradley, as he headed down the steep-sloped tunnel passage. *Maybe I should turn around. Maybe I should go and get Kyle, or Michael?*

Right when he thought to turn around, he spied a light in the tunnel ahead. He wondered where the light was coming from.

It has to be man-made. I have to find out the light source.

Against his better judgment, he proceeded onward

I need to know who's doing all of this and why. I need to know if Michael has anything to do with all that's been going on. Does he know this guy? Is he the friend I thought him to be? It's hard for me to believe he doesn't know this tunnel system exists.

Then the stranger disappeared once again into what at first looked to be another solid wall. As Bradley reached it there was yet another hidden doorway that he followed the stranger through. Once inside he couldn't believe what he was seeing. He had entered into a vast, open cavern. The place looked other-worldly. How could such a place exist underneath Michael's house? The ceiling, over one hundred-feet high, was flush with all manner and size of stalactites. They looked to be held up by gigantic prehistoric bird-sized truncated legs, with talons the size of a Volkswagen Beetle. The far wall had a massive, thick glass window located on what Bradley figured to be the ocean-facing side of the cavern.

"You can see the Atlantic Ocean from in here, but how? This vast room looks to be the size of three jumbo airplane hangars. Where does that massive opening lead? What else is in here? If I didn't know any better, I'd think the uneven stripes of gold, blue, green, lavender, and other colored striations that are running throughout those massive stalactites up there are made of real gold, sapphires, emeralds, amethyst, and other such valuable stones. But I know that can't be the case. There's way too much of it for any of it to be actual gemstones. If those riches existed, someone would've mined them by now . . . I sure wish I had my video camera, or at least my sketch pad and pencil to capture what I'm seeing here. No one is going to believe me when I tell them what's down here."

When Bradley took a moment to catch his breath, Peter responded.

"Those are real gemstones and pure veins of gold and other valued elements. Where I come from, they are plentiful and we use the materials for decoration and to add color to our living environments. They're what we use for building structures and our *enclaves*, what you would call a township or city."

"What about this floor? It looks to be made of one massive, solid piece of polished gray, black, and pink granite? What are the streaks of minerals and elements running throughout it?" asked Bradley, starting to walk about and pointing at the various materials. "That's turquoise and I believe that one over there is hematite . . . oh, oh and over here this must be rose quartz, but I'm not sure what this white, metallic, translucent one is? What makes it glow like that? It's emitting light . . . that's *so cool* . . ."

"The translucent, white, *glowing* material is what we refer to as Americium, but this is a yet-to-be discovered isotope by the scientists that live in the world that you inhabit today. It is abundant deeper within the earth. It has a half-life of over a million years, because it is not exposed to the surface air impurities and the solar impacts that the crustal regions are exposed to. As of today, this material hasn't been captured in the chemical periodic tables that you have studied in school. For ease of our discussions we'll refer to it as AM 250. AM 250 is an alpha ray emitter we use for illumination or to light our living spaces. It provides ample lighting for us to see in tunnels. It's a natural, non-toxic light source used by Arcanians. *I* am an Arcanian," announced Peter, pointing to his chest. "I am from Arcania."

Bradley had been totally distracted by the wonders of the voluminous cavern. He had forgotten that he was being lured into an unexplored tunnel system by a complete stranger. A stranger who was describing a subterranean wonderland filled with untold riches and as-yet undiscovered miraculous elements. Bradley's head was spinning.

"What are you talking about? This place can't be underneath Michael's house. There's no way you could've kept this place hidden for so long from the Celtston elders or his family," exclaimed Bradley. "Where have you taken me? You moved me to a different location when I passed out in the cave without my knowing it. Where are we?" demanded Bradley.

"Bradley, look around. Where do you think you are?" said Peter still standing in the shadows of the enclosure.

Peter finally stepped into the light and Bradley was able to get a really good look at him. He was a handsome man who looked much younger than he sounded. Bradley figured that he was probably around forty years old. Peter was wearing a muted yet shiny, dark cloth jumpsuit with no zippers, and pull-on shoes. It was hard to tell what materials were used to make up his outfit, but it was nothing like he'd ever seen before, and it was way too dressy for spelunking in the lava tubes, that was for sure.

Surprisingly, Peter looked at Bradley with a calmness about him that conveyed no ill will. Bradley no longer felt threatened.

"I'm pretty sure that leads to the Atlantic Ocean, and I can understand why no one has found this place from the ocean side of the island. There are way too many steep and jagged rock outcroppings, and the waves breaking against them are massive. It would be much too dangerous to attempt entry, even with a smaller craft like a skiff or a kayak. Judging by the direction and distance you've taken me, I'm pretty sure that we're somewhere beneath Michael Sidlau's house—somewhere in the lava tubes."

"Yes and no," said Peter. "Yes, we're in the lava tube system, but no, we're not underneath Celtston island. If you look close enough out of the window, you'll see that those waves are breaking underwater where the Atlantic Ocean slams into the base of this offshore atoll. These underwater outcroppings are five degrees northwest of the island and are part of the clump of offshore atolls that lay barren and uninhabited due to the harsh environment surrounding them. We're three hundred and five feet below the surface."

Bradley looked at Peter with disbelief. He quickly walked over to the window with an outstretched hand that came in contact with the window's vitreous surface, to confirm that he could actually touch it. It was a physical window and not an opening to the sea from the upper cliffs. Upon further inspection, when looking beyond the breaking waves he could see large fish schooling just beyond where the waves were crashing against the cliff face.

"We *are* underwater, and by the size of those fish we're pretty far down. What's going on here?" probed Bradley.

"The window is made up of a thick, homogenous sheet of a colorless, transparent layer of zirconia that separates this outpost from the open ocean waters. It's a very strong material that is similar to zircon on the surface," explained Peter.

"I'm not talking about the window, Peter. Where am I? *Who* are you?" fretted Bradley.

"Bradley, please come over and have a seat, so we can talk and I can give you some answers. I have much to tell you, and I have less than an hour to do so. Our time together is running short,"

He motioned to Bradley to sit at a table with four high-backed chairs, all made of the same material as the floor.

"Where did those chairs and that table come from? They look like they were cut right out of the granite that the floor is made of, but how?"

Peter gently put his hand on Bradley's arm, walked him over to a chair, and helped him to sit. Peter took a seat in the chair to his right, allowing both of them a view of the ocean. There was a crystal-clear decanter full of a light, pulpy, pink substance and two crystal glasses. Peter did the honors of serving them a drink, being careful not to spill a drop of the precious fluid. Peter handed Bradley a glass of the liquid, and the two of them sat back in their surprisingly comfortable chairs whose stone shapes seemed to be a perfect fit for their bodies. They both took a long, slow drink. The liquid tasted like Bradley's favorite drink of all time—freshly squeezed passion fruit. He hadn't had a drink of it since he'd left Precaveros. He savored every drop of the liquid. Peter, seeing that his thirst had not been quenched, poured Bradley another glass.

Bradley noticed almost immediately that the electrolytic property of the drink was helping him to feel much better, more like himself, as he listened to Peter's remarkable account.

"There is much that you need to know and when the time is right you will be approached by individuals who will enlighten you, but now is not the time. I live here, just beyond that entrance over there," said Peter, pointing to the large opening. "I am the sentinel of this outpost that insulates the entry to my homeland, Arcania, from the outside world—the surface world, your world."

"Your mother was allowed to enter Arcania via a similar outpost near the Precaveros tribal lands when she was being pursued. She is there now, and she is safe and sound. She cannot return to you because once you enter the inner workings of Arcania, you are not allowed to leave, and you can no longer interact with the surface dwellers. That is, unless you are accepted into an elite group within our society, *the Untethered*, that you will learn more about later.

"Your mother is now one of us. She is an *Arcanian,* because she possesses the abilities that are needed to be part of our world. She also has the unique attributes that the Untethered possess, and in time she might be accepted into this illustrious assemblage. But she has much to do to prove herself. Even after she has been unconditionally accepted by the Arcanians, there is no guarantee that she will ever qualify to enter their ranks. Therefore, unless you agree to become an Arcanian when and if you are called upon to do so, you may never see your mother in person again during your lifetime. For now, I hope it's enough for you to know that she is alive and well."

"You're telling me that you know my mother and that you've talked to her. You've *seen* her and she's alive?"

"Yes, and she wanted me to give you a message. She told me to tell you to follow the clues given to you, and you will obtain the solace you seek," said Peter.

"*Right* . . . you've been talking to my mother?" mocked Bradley.

"Yes, I have, and as I have said, she is alive and well. But the only way you will ever be able to see her is if you enter Arcania, and we're not ready for you to do that yet. There is much you must do here on the surface before that day comes. Your mother does talk to you in your dreams. She told me to tell you that the dreams are real."

"You're telling me that all of the dreams I've had where my mother comes and talks to me are real conversations that I've been having with her?"

"I can't confirm *all* of your dreams fall into that category, but if you think about the dreams in which you were aided in coming to the right decision or to take the correct actions, those are the dreams where your mother spoke to you. I suspect that the rest are just dreams. The dreams that you awaken from that are fear-based are from your psyche, or they could be from another source other than your mother; another discussion for another day," replied Peter.

"I'll take your word for it, because I want it to be true, but I still don't get why she isn't allowed to come and see me. You're here. Why can't she come? If I see her in person, I'll know for sure that what you're telling me is true."

"I'm only here with you today to relay a matter of some urgency. It's been deemed essential that I make sure that you and your brother Quentin take your leave of Celtston as soon as possible. My being allowed to contact you, a surface dweller, is a very rare circumstance. I've been tasked with the responsibility of getting you to a safe haven in the Scottish highlands, to your father's family's fortress—the Gordon castle. There are those who care for you a great deal who are working with your father at this very moment to execute a plan that'll take you off the island first thing tomorrow morning, before sunrise. How this will happen will be told to you this evening by your Uncle Richard and Michael Robert Sidlau, so I won't spend the precious time I have with you to discuss the details of your departure."

"I'm to leave right away?" asked Bradley.

"Yes. Michael will be the one helping you and Quentin to get off of the island in the morning without Seth MacLeod being privy to your departure. In this way, we'll be thwarting Seth's plan to kidnap you and Quentin, which he will attempt to do shortly after sunrise tomorrow, when the two of you would normally be walking to school."

"You know Michael?"

"I do not know him personally, but I do know *of* him. He is a distant relative of yours who truly cares about you. He thinks of you like a son, so he can be trusted. My only problem with him thus far has been his desire to have you by his side. This emotion allowed him to let his guard down and he got sloppy. He should've foreseen the danger that Seth poses to you, but none of that matters now. You'll be leaving the island and you will be meeting up with your father forthwith," said Peter.

"My father, but never my mother? This is all so confusing. Why am I so important to you?"

"Let's start with a brief history of who you are and why we care enough about you to reveal ourselves to you. The best way to describe who you are is to tell you who you are not. You're not a fictional character that is the offspring of a god or a deity referred to as a demigod, and you're not a child of a witch or warlock with magical powers. You're a *real* child living in the *real* world who has naturally tapped abilities that any Arcanian is capable of expressing. We all have at least two of these special talents, but you and your brother appear to have more than two abilities, and there are good reasons for that.

"I was sent here to help you understand your place in the world in which we live, both on top of and within this earth. I want to give you an idea, not a comprehensive rendering. Today, I need to tell you a brief synopsis of a world that up until now, you didn't know existed. This subsurface paradise is called Arcania and is the place of the first advanced inhabitants of this planet. We came to *be* before the surface of the earth was habitable, when it was literally *hell* on the earth's surface.

Arcania runs throughout the interior of the planet and is connected via the continuous global alluvial transport that is deep within the earth, at depths of eight miles below. Our alluvial transport is only accessible from the surface via specific lava tube labyrinth entrance points, and only by those with the abilities needed to access them—innate Arcanian talents. There is nothing supernatural about them. All Arcanians have telepathic abilities that are second nature to us and are the primary method of communication. Our abilities are very rare on the surface and very few surface dwellers possess even one of them. Those that do usually never master the ability to the level of even the least-capable Arcanian. There are too many distractions in the surface environment that preclude them from being proficient. The majority of surface dwellers that fully possess any of these talents are culled from your population ideally before they reach their fifth birthday. The Chivalran and the Veneré keep track of these individuals, and when their prowess is proven, the high chair of the Veneré presents these individuals to us. If we find them worthy, they are allowed to enter Arcania and live out their lives in a peaceful and loving existence . . . the true *Heaven in Earth*."

"If these are natural abilities, why can't you teach everyone how to use them?" asked Bradley.

"That's a good question. As the surface cooled so very long ago, a small cadre of Arcanians felt the need to explore and began living on the surface, but there were consequences. They were exposed to impurities in the air and water, solar bombardments, and viruses and bacteria that mutated their DNA and their genetics. Over time, they and their offspring no longer possessed the needed abilities to remain Arcanians. They lost their telepathic and intuitive abilities that are essential Arcanian societal attributes. As the years passed and the ancient post-Arcanians that had become surface dwellers died off, the *idea* of a wonderland called Arcania past into myth and legend. You now hear of it as the lost city of Atlantis or the true Panacea or some such nomenclature, but these memories are merely the remnants of the Arcanian surface dwellers. Many urban legends are sourced from Arcania as well; such as the reputed *elixir of life*, only thought to exist because we are blessed with much longer lives than a surface dweller could believe possible."

"I'm having trouble believing anything that you're telling me," said Bradley.

"Your mother is one of the few adults ever allowed to enter Arcania and live. She was only allowed to enter that fateful day because if she had been found, she could have exposed you and your brother, and we weren't ready for that to happen yet. You and Quentin possess more abilities than you have yet realized, but over time will become apparent to you."

"We've always felt so out of place. I guess this is why," posed Bradley.

"The three of you were purposefully allowed to remain on the surface, even though we knew you possessed the essential Arcanian attributes, because your arrival was foretold to us. As was prophesized, your abilities are exceptional, making you an Arcanum. You are thought to not only be *an* Arcanum, but *the* Arcanum, the one that we reverently refer to as the long-awaited Millenarian. The, *we,* I speak of includes the Chivalran, the Veneré and the Arcanians. If you are he, then when you have been able to express all of your talents fully, you'll be able to know everything that is and is yet to be. A thousand years is a long time, even for an Arcanian. We live to be around four hundred years old. There is no living Arcanian who was alive when the last Millenarian came to be. For some reason, our records are sketchy as to what all transpired during that time, but we know prosperity and peace ensued for years after their coming.

The Veneré thought your mother to be the next Millenarian in error, and this is the reason they attempted to kidnap her. Her aggressors were not far from the truth. Your mother is an exceptional human being due to her blood lines. Her abilities are strong, but while she is not the Millenarian, it would take someone extraordinary to give birth to such a being."

"I don't understand how anyone could draw that conclusion. I mean, you're right about the telepathic ability, but Quentin and I both have that and so do other people. But as far as anything else, you're mistaken. I don't have any more than that to show you."

"Bradley, you're a very talented young man. You've been blessed with many wondrous gifts. We suspect that you are endowed with all of the natural abilities that Arcanians can possess, save one. Your family is missing the blood line of the Keats. But even so, if our assumptions are correct, you may very well be the next Millenarian," explained Peter.

"How come I don't know what these *talents* are?" asked Bradley.

"Once we get you to Scotland, we'll be able to help you lay out a plan that will allow you to realize your full potential, and we'll teach you to be proficient in each of your abilities. It won't be easy, and you'll struggle at first, but with time and effort you'll eventually reach a heightened state of awareness. What you learn will certainly fly in the face of many things that you've come to believe about yourself and the world around you. You'll come to understand that your current beliefs based on the conventional wisdom of surface dwellers, are inaccurate at best, and in many cases erroneous. They will prove to be barriers to your success if not discarded."

"Why don't the Arcanians and the surface dwellers live together? Why don't you teach us what you know or help us to be better?" pressed Bradley.

"These are tough questions and they deserve answers, but for now, suffice to say that there are good reasons why the two worlds don't interact. The surface dwellers are mutations of the Arcanians who underwent devolution, and they do not possess the needed abilities to survive in Arcania," replied Peter.

"It sounds like you have total disdain for the human race. I don't like how you're talking about us."

"Bradley, I'd like to ask your forgiveness if I have somehow offended you. That was certainly not my intention. My characterization of the world you live in is in no way meant to demean or insult you," beseeched Peter.

"I know you meant me no disrespect, but you make me feel like I need to defend the entire human race by the way you talk about them—about *us*."

"There's so much you need to learn about your own personal history, that of the Arcanians and the surface dwellers. When you do, I fully anticipate that you'll better appreciate what I'm telling you, but alas our time here has now come to an end, and I do not want to leave you with the wrong impression."

"I'm fine," said Bradley.

"There exists an intricate link between Arcania and the Surface. What one does often affects the other. Throughout history we've been able to minimize the impacts to Arcania resulting from the misdeeds of surface dwellers, but there now exist forces and people on the surface that have stepped over boundaries that could result in dire consequences for Arcania that we can no longer ignore. What they're doing *will* impact us all."

"Thank you for being honest with me, but like all of the adults in my life, you've told me only a smidgen of what's actually going on while you expect me to dutifully follow along. You want me to leave the only place in which I feel some sense of belonging and go to a new place that I know nothing about. You've chosen only to tell me what *you* want me to know versus what I would like to know. I'm really tired of being treated like this. What if I just say *no*? I won't leave Celtston. I won't be your puppet in a show I want no part of. What would happen then?"

"We both know you want to be with your father, so I wouldn't say that you don't want to go to the Scotland, and at this moment you have no better choice. If you don't leave with your early morning transport, you *will* be kidnapped and taken to the Veneré. It's up to you to determine which of these paths make more sense for you and your brother. You want to be treated like an adult, yet you seem challenged in thinking logically versus emotionally. You have to get your emotions in check so you can think and act appropriately. Your unchecked emotions will only hinder you from achieving your maximum potential," stated Peter.

"You can't leave now. I have way too many questions for you."

"We'll be contacting you again in Scotland. I must get going, but before I do, I need to know that you'll keep what I've shared with you a secret . . . even from Quentin . . . for now. He's too young to handle the enormity of this situation."

"No one would believe me anyway, but you should know that I can't promise to keep this from Quentin. We're mentally linked and he knows what I'm thinking. So why ask me to keep it secret from him? I promised him that I'd never hide anything from him, and I won't start now. He's capable of handling way more than you think, and he doesn't talk to anyone but me about anything."

"Then Quentin can be told if he asks you about it; otherwise, no one else is to be made aware of any of this. Is that understood?"

"Yeah . . . okay."

"Bradley, this last item is hard to discuss because part of it is conceptual and part of it usually has to be experienced for a person to gain a real appreciation for it. Please stop me if I say something that you don't understand or if you require any clarification." implored Peter.

"I'm listening," said Bradley.

"You've been protected your entire life in both the Precaveros tribal lands and now here in Celtston from exposure to too many people at once. You and Quentin, like myself, have strong empathic abilities and it's my understanding that Quentin possesses heightened empathic abilities that have, from time to time, caused him great discomfort. Do you know what it means to be empathic?"

"No, not really," said Bradley, starting to lose patience with Peter for talking about something other than what he wanted to discuss.

"Bradley, an empath can identify with *and* understand another person's situation. They can *feel* what another person is feeling and *glean* what another person's motives are. When you add in your telepathic abilities you can pick up a lot of information from other people, and when you have hundreds, thousands, and in some cities, millions of people, an empath can easily become overwhelmed and debilitated if they're not properly trained to handle the overload of feelings and information. Many highly empathic people become overly depressed, paranoid, and in many instances, suicidal before others around them become aware of their abilities, and in most cases, it is likely that they never will. These people are called crazy and deemed to be mental cases, because they're misunderstood and not trained to handle the onslaught of what they perceive as negative information."

"Is that what has been happening to Quentin?" asked Bradley.

"Quentin has received no training in how to properly handle his abilities—they overwhelm him. That's why he seems so aggressive with other people and is so eager to find places where there are *no* people around. He's like a human antenna that can't shut itself off. Once he's far enough away from the others, he is finally able to *literally* get them out of his head."

"That makes *so much* sense. I never knew that was why, and I couldn't figure out how to help him," exclaimed Bradley. "But why don't I have the same problem with all of this? From what you're telling me, we're both empathic and we're both telepathic."

"Solana told us that she taught you how to handle mental intrusions that you experience, but she never referred to it as the handling of an empathic ability. She started training you when you were a toddler. You were taught how to ignore the thoughts and feelings of others. You learned that other people felt things differently than you, and you've naturally turned that ability off. There was no time to afford Quentin the same training. It's obvious that you are proficient in discerning between the two. As we age, this discernment becomes more difficult. People are so much easier to train at an early age. This is the very reason that surface dwellers who are allowed to become Arcanians are brought to join us before age five, or as soon as possible thereafter."

"It has been so long, but I know what you're saying is true," admitted Bradley.

"You have gained the capacity to effectively deal with empathic intrusions through instruction, whereby you find it much easier to be around other people, but if you're honest with yourself you'll have to admit that you feel exhausted after these encounters."

Bradley nodded. "You're right."

"Unfortunately for Quentin, your mother left before he was old enough to receive the same level of training. No one here in Celtston, including your Aunt Benitita, has any empathic abilities of note and therefore can't recognize Quentin's *issues* as such. The sad thing is that they keep trying to get him to engage in team sports and other activities with children his age which is the exact opposite of what he needs without the proper coping skills. You've helped your brother adjust to this environment by your example more than you know, but you will both require some personalized training if you ever hope to engage with the society at large and not be overwhelmed by the encounters. I firmly believe that you will come to master your abilities."

"Why did you wait so long to tell me all of this? Quentin and I have had to fend for ourselves all this time and you just watched! You allowed us to be separated from our home, our parents, our family, and friends. You've kept us in the dark about our mother's fate until this moment. I don't understand why you did that."

"There is still so much that you must learn, but all concerned parties were attempting to let the two of you grow up, and to have some semblance of a normal childhood, and for the most part you have. You have friends. You've had an outstanding education, and you have learned useful skills that only experience can provide, skills that lay the foundation for what is to come."

"*Normal* . . . our lives are anything but normal," countered Bradley.

"You have a loving mother and father, and relatives on both sides of your family, some of whom you have yet to meet, that love and care for you very much. You have two Chivalran regiments sworn to protect you, as well as the Arcanians themselves watching over you. In time, we hope to amend the hardships you've been forced to endure, but that time *isn't* now. Right now, we need to discuss what you can expect to encounter when you leave the safe haven of Celtston."

"It's funny, I've wanted to escape from Celtston and search for my father for as long as I can remember, but now that I'm actually leaving, I don't want to go."

"The Gordon fortress will be your new haven. The only difference is that the people, to include the Veneré, the Chivalran, the Gordons and the Misticatos, believe what they hold as *their* truth. To them it's their reality, so they ignorantly fight to maintain the status quo. They will do anything they deem appropriate to save and preserve it, but they are often misguided. You're about to enter into the heart of the surface dwellers, and up until now you've been protected. You've been allowed to live a simple life with genuine people, who truly care for one another, and share common goals. You have never been exposed to the volume and diversity of hearts and minds that you'll soon be encountering. With so many of them surrounding you, it's going to be hard for you to discern the difference between what is right and what is wrong. All of these humans will have their own agendas, both personal and as part of the organizations they represent. Each of these comes with their own belief systems, cultures, societal norms, and prejudices. Until now, you have been free of this underdeveloped, but highly influential side of humanity."

"This all sounds so horrible," said Bradley.

"You know what you believe. You have sound morals. You're humble, intelligent, kind, caring, and nonjudgmental. You are a good person in every sense of the word. You'll have to work hard to ensure that you don't allow yourself to be manipulated, coerced, or by other means forced to take inappropriate actions for the wrong reasons. You cannot allow these people to think for you. Listen to them but keep your mind free to draw your own conclusions. Demand to be presented all of the facts of any situation. Make sure that those with whom you choose to interact are worthy of your trust and loyalty," stated Peter.

"I thought not getting chosen for the boats was the worst thing that could ever happen to me, after the disappearance of my mother, but I was wrong. This is definitely worse, and there's nothing I can do to stop it from happening, is there?"

"I wish there were," responded Peter, standing up and motioning to Bradley to join him as he headed toward the outpost exit.

Bradley stood up and started walking with Peter without saying a word. But just as they came to the tunnel entrance, Bradley stopped and yelled out, "Why can't I stay here? Why can't I go and get Quentin, and we move to Arcania? I'm so tired and I'd like to know what it feels like to not be worried and afraid all of the time. Would you *please* take me with you?" pleaded Bradley.

"The time has not yet come for you to enter into Arcania, but that time will come. The surface dwellers are on a path to destruction that none of us can survive, and you must play your part in the divergence of this path. Otherwise, there will be nowhere for anyone to go above or below the Earth's surface."

Peter, finally recognizing Bradley had stopped, turned around and walked back to him, placing both of his hands on Bradley's shoulders as he looked him in the eyes.

"Bradley, I know this is a *hard* thing to ask of you, but you are not alone. There are resources for you to access all around the world. Once you arrive in Scotland you'll be engaged by another Arcanian outpost that is located near your homeland. They'll find you once you've had a chance to get settled. Everything is going to be okay. You're going to be okay. Come along now. We have to hurry. You've got a lot to do before sunrise."

And on that note, Peter turned and headed into the tunnel as Bradley slowly followed, stopping to take one last, longing look at the dazzling outpost.

CHAPTER TWENTY-THREE

FOREGONE CONCLUSION

B radley peeked out from the cave to look around the area before he decided it was safe for him to run over to Michael's. He was relieved to see Michael sitting in his big rocking chair on the porch. Michael was drinking his evening ginger tea as though he didn't have a care in the world. As soon as Michael caught a glimpse of Bradley coming from the cliff-side of his house, he was up on his feet, waving and shouting.

"It's about time you showed up! Where have you been?"

"You're not going to believe what happened to me. I still don't believe it," exclaimed Bradley.

"Seth chased me with a rifle. He kept aiming at me, but he never got the chance to fire because I kept moving and was finally able to slip away from him—it was insane!"

"I hid in the secret cave until I was sure that he'd quit chasing me. Since it was nearing sunset, I figured you'd be home by now—so here I am."

"Bradley, slow down. Take it easy. First of all, I'm glad you're safe and sound, but as much as I want to hear what you have to say, why don't you wait until your Uncle Richard and Quentin get here. Please . . . take a seat," said Michael, motioning to Bradley to sit in the rocking chair next to him.

"You're right," said Bradley who sat down and poured himself a cup of delicious, freshly made ginger tea.

"I'm really glad to see that you're okay. We were starting to worry about you. You shouldn't have gone off on your own. Remember what Captain Nopar said about the buddy system? Why'd you head off by yourselves? You're in danger from Seth and possibly others. From what you've already told me, we had good reason to worry."

"I was on my way over to Skeeter's; he was going to be my buddy, and Quentin went to meet up with Nicole," said Bradley.

"Well, none of that matters now. I'll tell you why when Quentin and your Uncle Richard get here," said Michael.

Minutes later they saw the tops of their heads breaching the top of the hill.

"Good, it looks like they remembered to bring your bare essentials. You two are going to be spending the night with me. I'll be able to keep you safe here."

"I was hoping that we'd be staying with you tonight," said Bradley.

"I received a secret communique from your family in Scotland, your Uncle Jay Gordon, to be exact. Your Uncle Richard and I need to talk to you about it," said Michael.

"After all that's happened to us, I would be worried if we hadn't received any word from the Gordons. Celtston is no longer safe for Quentin and me. The time has come for us to leave for Scotland to join up with our father."

At that moment, Quentin ran up the steps and embraced his big brother.

"I'm so glad you're okay. Something happened to you, didn't it?"

"Why don't we move inside to a more comfortable and private setting so we can get caught up on today's happenings?" proposed Michael.

They all settled into the cozy kitchen nook while the boys munched on the freshly made, saucer-sized chocolate chunk oatmeal cookies and sipped tea.

"Richard, you were right. Seth did make a move on Bradley this afternoon," Michael said. "Bradley, could you please tell us what happened to you, starting from when you and Quentin mistakenly parted ways after our meeting?"

Bradley told his story, being careful not to dwell on some of the details that he didn't fully understand himself. He kept quiet about his meeting with Peter van der Pouw. The remainder of what he had to say was enough to outrage them all, but Uncle Richard seemed almost temporarily insane upon hearing the news.

"How dare he aim a rifle at you? He's finally stepped way over any line!" raged Uncle Richard.

"Uncle Richard, he could have shot me, but he didn't. All he did was give someone a call to tell them that he couldn't find me. He had no idea where I was hiding. He looked around for a bit, and then he pulled out a big phone and called someone named *Rosend* or *Rosse* . . . something like that," said Bradley.

"*Rosen* is the name. He called Rosen," said Michael.

"Oh, is he the guy you told us about earlier today?" asked Bradley.

"Yes."

"What did Seth say to him?" asked Uncle Richard.

"He told the guy that he finally got me on video exhibiting a special ability. He kept saying he caught me vanishing, because he couldn't see where I was hiding. He was really happy about it, and the guy on the other end of the phone must have been pretty happy too, because Seth seemed to like what he was hearing," Bradley said.

"Seth told him that he'd be ready and standing by, but I couldn't hear for what. I got the impression that he was sending someone to Celtston to pick him up, and soon. The last thing he said to the man was *got it—plan for plus two.* I have no idea what that meant."

"It's not important anymore. I'll tell you why in a minute, but could you please finish your story? There has to be more, because you've been missing for hours. What happened next?" probed Uncle Richard.

Bradley didn't respond, squirming uncomfortably.

"Bradley, the only reason we hadn't sent someone to find you sooner is that Seth was seen calmly eating dinner at the B&B. We figured you were probably okay, and there was no need for us to overreact. After all, it wouldn't have been the first time that you've snuck off for some private time and were late getting home."

"I guess I was more tired than I thought, because when I finally entered the hidden cave and I realized that Seth couldn't find me, I sat down, leaned against the wall to wait him out and I fell asleep. When I woke up it was getting dark, and after I made sure Seth had left the area, I ran over here."

"We're just glad that you're safe. Now comes the hard part," Uncle Richard said. "You'll be leaving Celtston, and I can't be here when that happens,"

"Bradley and Quentin, while I know at times you might have thought that I didn't love you two as my own, I want you to know that I always have. You are family. I don't want you to leave Celtston, but I know that we don't have adequate resources to fight someone as powerful as Rosen. So, there you have it, the bad side of things. But there is a good side as well. You're finally going to be reunited with your father, where you should be."

The boys stood to give Uncle Richard a proper goodbye.

"I love you both," said Uncle Richard, as he gave each of them a big polar bear hug. "Your Aunt Benitita will be so unhappy to learn of your departure, and so mad at me for letting you go before she returned home. She would've wanted the opportunity to give you a proper sendoff, but here we are."

"Thank you for everything you've done for us. We'll never forget you," promised Bradley.

Quentin gave Uncle Richard one more hug and looked down to hide the tears streaming down his cheeks, embarrassed by the fact that he couldn't act more grown up. He wiped his tears, stood up straight and looked at Uncle Richard as he gave his parting words.

"Boys, I'll be taking my leave now to allow for Michael to go over the plans for your departure with you. You'll be leaving early tomorrow morning. He's the only one on this island that is privy to the details of your exit strategy. You take care of yourselves and each other. We'll be seeing one another soon enough," said Uncle Richard as he turned to leave, stopping at the door to get one last look at the two boys. He smiled, waved and winked as he turned and left the house, careful not to slam the screen door behind him.

Michael jumped right into the details of their escape plan.

"Bradley and Quentin, come back over here and take a seat, if you would please," motioning to the bench across from him. He started their briefing before they even had a chance to sit back down.

"I've prepared two rooms for you upstairs. We need to get you to bed right away, since we're heading out very early in the morning. I'll be waking you up at three, and you'll be off the island before sunrise. We're hoping to get you suited up, and in the water no later than four-thirty."

"In the water?" said Bradley.

"Yep, you'll be night diving out to a submersible that is about two-thirds of a mile off the northeast coast of Celtston. Jay and another Gordon Chivalran have been sent to retrieve you and will rendezvous with us down in the sanctuary's main cavern. You'll be leaving via a tunnel that will take you out beyond the smashing waves and rock outcroppings."

"I've never done a night dive, *or* dove in the open ocean," reminded Quentin.

"Quentin, the two guys that are coming to retrieve you are expert divers. You'll both be partnered with one of them whose purpose is to care for you, and to ensure you safely reach the submarine. You have *absolutely* nothing to worry about. When I get you up in the morning, we'll go over the plan in detail so that you're comfortable before your dive. You did really well when we took you on the discovery shallow coastal water dives, and you handled yourself well when we dove the external caverns and tunnels. All you had with you was a tank light and a handheld light to illuminate your way, and you did just fine. Do you think you can handle it okay?" asked Michael.

"I'll do my best," replied Quentin, feebly.

"That's all I can ask of you. Trust me, you'll be fine," said Michael.

"Michael, after all that you've done for us, I hate to be the one to ask, but before we go to bed would it be possible for us to eat something more than cookies? I'm *starved*," said Bradley.

"Me too," said Quentin."

"Well, I might have a *little* something for dinner," said Michael, going over to the warm oven and pulling out a tray with three large overflowing fried shrimp hoagies. He then retrieved a bowl of coleslaw from the refrigerator that he placed on the table with a big wooden spoon. It would be their last meal together in Michael's home.

CHAPTER TWENTY-FOUR

NIGHT DIVE

The dreaded three a.m. wakeup call came when Michael gently tugged on Bradley's arm, then Quentin's. They needed to awaken so that they could prepare themselves for their predawn adventure.

Quentin's mental and emotional state was in overdrive. *No telling what will be out there and how big it will be*, was all he could think.

It took Michael and Bradley several minutes to calm him down enough to where he was able to put on his dive gear with their assistance.

As soon as the boys had been fully outfitted and had the needed equipment assembled, they began their dive buddy safety checks to ensure their gear was properly assembled and working.

"The two divers are ready for departure," Michael said as he saluted them. He then led them over to the stone steps leading down to the water's edge.

Bradley and Quentin, walking side-by-side, slowly descended the steps down to the water as Jay and the other Gordon Chivalran emerged on the surface of the water within the cavern. The two men were holding onto large diver propulsion vehicles, which they referred to as DPVs.

"I see you brought your own motorcycles?" beamed Michael.

"Yeah, I like having my own compact, underwater hand-held motorcycle of sorts. The only downside to this one is that it's too quiet and doesn't have a cool seat or handle bars, but it will make our dive much easier, and it will save us from having to swim over twelve hundred yards in the dark," said Jay, laughing.

"Jay, I'm sure glad to see you two," said Michael.

"Michael, all kidding aside, we have to get out of here right away. There's an unknown vessel with no running lights sitting approximately a half mile northwest of the port, not too far from where the sub is situated. Our intel is that it belongs to Rosen's spec ops team. Are the boys ready to depart?"

"Yes, they're good to go," responded Michael.

"Okay then," said Jay.

"I taught Bradley and Quentin to scuba dive and they're both good divers, but there's one thing I need to let you know. While Quentin knows how to dive, and he knows how to execute the most basic rescue diver scenarios, he's never had the opportunity to dive at night out in the open ocean. He has expressed some concerns about this dive, but I'm sure he'll be fine," said Michael, looking over at Quentin, hoping to see confirmation.

"Quentin, are you ready to go?" asked Jay, "I think you'll make a great dive buddy if you'll have me?"

"Yeah, I'd like to be your dive buddy and I'm okay now," said Quentin, feeling embarrassed by the special attention.

"Good morning, Bradley, I'd like to introduce you to my good friend Wilson Cropp. Wilson's your new dive buddy," Jay said.

Bradley turned to Michael to say farewell, but before he could speak, Michael cleared his throat, trying not to get too emotional.

"Bradley you're the son I never had. If you need *anything, anytime, anywhere* in the world, don't hesitate to call me. Jay knows how to get in touch with me. We'll get together again when this is all over, and in the meantime, I'll be keeping track of you. You have the marine radio information to call me if you ever need to."

"You know I will . . . *Thank you* for everything you've done for me and for being here for me—*for us*. The hardest thing about leaving Celtston is leaving you," said Bradley.

"I hate to break the two of you up, but we need to go sooner rather than later," said Jay. "I think it's time for our pre-dive brief. If everyone could please look my way so we can discuss what we're about to do."

Both boys plopped into the water so that they could move closer to Jay.

"We're going to do this dive differently than how you have been taught. While you have tank lights and handheld lights as your primary and your backup lights, we will be turning them off once we exit the tunnel and enter the open ocean waters, because of the vessel sitting offshore. We don't want to be picked up by their spotters. But don't let that worry you; we'll be making our way to the ship on our DPVs, which have their own low-level lighting on the dashboards. The dashboard lights will allow us to see our navigation equipment. The DPVs are self-propelled with a state-of-the-art navigation system that'll be doing the work for us. All we have to do is to hold on to these handlebars," said Jay, gripping the DPV handlebars. "The DPVs will take us to the submarine. She's lying in wait approximately twelve hundred yards northeast of Celtston."

Both boys listened intently.

"Now, you might have noticed that there are only two DPVs. This is because the two of us are wearing body harnesses with tandem straps. They will allow each of you to ride with each of us. All we need for you to do is to hold on tightly to each of these straps with your hands during the transit."

Jay pulled on the two straps located on back of Wilson's harness to show the boys how it was done.

"All you need to do is enjoy the ride," said Jay, leaning forward over Wilson's left shoulder and giving the boys a thumbs up. "You'll be able to look over our shoulders and see what we see on the dashboard. When we reach open water, we'll descend to sixty feet to complete transit—understand?"

Both boys gave the okay sign.

"There is one caveat; our emergency protocol should any of us get separated from the group. The person who finds themselves lost *does not* go to the surface, like you've been taught. We can't risk any of us being spotted by the mystery vessel topside. The person who finds himself separated from the group should remain calm, hover at fifty feet, and flash their primary light once every three seconds. You turn it on for a second, then off, then count to three."

Jay put his fingers up for each number he counted.

"One, two, three. Then the individual will repeat the sequence until such time as they are found and be assured that *we will find you*. The *only* reason that we would turn our lights on is if there is an emergency—understand?"

"Yes, sir," the boys responded.

"If any issue or concern arises during our transit, we need for you to tap your dive buddy on the left side of his cheek, like this, to get his attention," said Jay, touching his face two times. "This will let your dive buddy know that *we*," as Jay pointed to all four of them, "need to stop and address the issue or concern. Do you have any questions? . . . Any concerns? . . . Please, let's talk about them now. We want the two of you to feel comfortable with this maneuver," said Jay.

"Okay. I think it's safe to say that we're good-to-go," said Jay, looking up to Michael.

"Michael, thank you for prepping the boys for us. You've made *this* part of our job easy. See you soon."

"You take care of them for me," said Michael.

"You know I will."

Wilson led the team out of the cavern, accompanied by Bradley. Jay asked Wilson to lead so that Quentin could see his big brother, with the hope that it would help to keep Quentin calm during the transit. Jay remained in the wake of Wilson's fins so that they wouldn't lose one another in the darkness. The DPV's dashboards provided enough low-level red lighting so that when within eight feet of one another, they could see the outline of the other divers, but that was all—pitch blackness enshrouded them. In spite of the ominous surroundings, the dive was going well, and Quentin seemed relaxed enough that Jay no longer felt concerned that he'd panic and head to the surface.

Ten minutes into the dive, they reached open ocean and descended to sixty feet. They had made it over halfway to the sub when out of nowhere, all four divers saw something big moving towards them. Whatever it was passed over Jay's back, slightly bumping into Quentin, causing him to almost lose his grasp on the tandem straps. The encounter totally freaked Quentin out, so much so that Jay, Wilson, and Bradley heard Quentin scream through his regulator.

Quentin held on and remembered how to get his dive buddy's attention. He started to smash his finger into Jay's left cheek over and over again, frantically indicating he had an issue. Whatever it was that had just committed the *hit-and-run* really scared Quentin, and he was having trouble remaining calm.

Jay signaled over to Wilson, who responded immediately. He was at his side within seconds, bringing Bradley close enough to engage his brother, hoping that seeing Bradley would pacify Quentin. Wilson, ever the pragmatist, was concerned that unless Quentin calmed down, his erratic flailing would garner the attention of some large nocturnal predator, ever vigilant on its quest for vulnerable prey.

Once Bradley was close enough, he grabbed his brother and made eye contact, sending a mental message.

"*Quentin, please calm down. I need for you to relax. Remember: stop, think, and breathe. Calmly assess the situation.*" When Bradley could see that he had Quentin's attention, he gave Quentin the okay sign, but instead of Quentin acquiescing, he kept shaking his head, "*No . . . no, it's not okay. That thing is still here. We just can't see him. It's over there in the darkness, just hanging out and watching us.*" Quentin pointed in the direction where he knew it lay waiting.

Bradley turned but couldn't see anything. Bradley gently pulled Quentin's face towards him to regain his eye contact. "*Relax little brother. We'll be fine.*"

Bradley turned quickly to see if he could see what Quentin was referring to, but he couldn't see anything. His quick movements caused Wilson and Jay to look in the same direction expecting to see something barreling towards them, but there was nothing to be seen.

Quentin remained staring into the darkness, and Bradley took the opportunity to check him out. No leaks or tears or any equipment damage was obvious, so he once again engaged Quentin. Bradley gently pulled Quentin's face toward him to regain his eye contact, and gave him the okay sign, but his time Quentin returned the signal. For some reason he seemed to have relaxed, so Bradley signaled to Wilson and Jay that everything was okay.

Jay then signaled for a modification to their dive configuration, altering it from leader-follower to side-along diving as he aligned himself with Wilson. Diving side-by-side allowed them to more readily communicate when necessary and would hopefully make them appear to be a larger, more formidable specimen—less likely to be attacked.

They continued on their underwater journey, having to head into the direction that Quentin indicated to be the creature's location. Initially, there was no sign of the monster giving the divers a false sense of hope, when to everyone's dismay they saw it hanging out to the right of them, close enough for them to see with the low level

DPV lighting. It appeared to be a large, gray Greenland shark nearly twenty feet long. Wilson had seen the impressive beasts before. This one had to weigh a ton, he surmised, and was probably more than 500 years old, because this type of shark only grows about one centimeter per year. It was an ugly shark, with a bizarre, long, thick gray body, a small head with a bulbous snout and ghostly eyes that looked like they were covered with parasites and cataracts. It had a gaping mouth that exposed teeth that looked like miniature reciprocating saws.

The strange thing was that, as scary as it looked, it didn't give any indication that it was hunting the divers. It appeared to be *accompanying* them, like a dog on a walk with its owner. Miraculously, the Greenland shark kept its distance, but stayed abreast of them the entire journey, almost as if it was an escort. Once they reached the submarine, the shark started to swim in a long wide elliptical pattern around the sub making the divers think that it was going to make its move and attack, but instead it stayed the course, acting as if it were more like a guard on duty.

The divers entered the exterior hatch, with Jay going last to ensure the safety of his entourage. Once inside, the hatch was flushed of water and the divers were able to remove their regulators and speak. Wilson finally uttered his first words since they had all been introduced.

"I've never seen a Greenland shark act that way; that was *crazy*. They're known as *corkscrew killers*. They literally twist a seal until their skin breaks open in a corkscrew pattern the full length of their bodies, and then they *eat* them. I didn't know they came this far down from Greenland. I know the waters are cold here, but I didn't think they were cold enough."

"He was guarding us," said Quentin.

"*Guarding us*? Maybe he was pacing us hoping we would tire out," said Jay.

"No, Quentin's right, he was making sure we made it to safety," said Bradley.

"So that's why you calmed down, Quentin? You actually thought he was there to protect us?" marveled Jay.

"Well, whatever it took to get you to feel okay out there was fine by me, but I hope to never *ever* be in that situation again. Thanks to you two I have a great fish story to tell. Mind you, *no one* will believe me, but I do have a story to tell," said Wilson, as he winked and started to help Bradley get out of his gear. Jay did the same with Quentin.

CHAPTER TWENTY-FIVE

THWARTED

While the quartet was undergoing their night dive escape, Seth was executing his plan to kidnap the boys. He had worked tirelessly through the wee hours of the morning with Rosen's spec ops team leaders, Chris Cassara and Blake Regalos, to finalize their mission plan. They had found a great spot to hide their gear for the kidnapping—a large outcropping of granite that was located almost two miles northwest of the Celtston harbor. They were hiding the boat to make sure their return transportation would still be available once they conducted the easy snatch-and-grab of their two targets.

"Should I go ahead and throw my stuff in the boat now, or do you want me to wait until we're done?" asked Seth.

"Now is good. We might not have the luxury of time later, if you know what I mean," said Chris.

Seth walked over to the boat and carefully pulled off just enough of the debris to allow him to place his pack under the seat closest to the bow. He then replaced the camouflage materials to conceal the boat. Once that was taken care of, he returned to observe Chris and Blake completing the removal of the dive gear that they had been wearing since they arrived.

"Since I didn't hear your boat motor, I wasn't sure you'd arrived yet," said Seth.

"That's because we scuba-dived with the RIB in tow on the surface for the last nine-hundred yards to prevent anyone from hearing us coming ashore," said Chris, shouldering his rifle, and making sure he was prepped and ready to go.

"The boys will be heading to school forty minutes before dawn. We need to get going if we want to be in position before they walk by the retrieval site. It will take us a good five minutes to get there. Follow me," said Seth.

"Why are these kids going to school so early in the morning?" questioned Blake.

"Because they have chores to do," responded Seth.

"You couldn't have gotten me to go to school before daylight," said Blake.

"No kid I know would get up this early," agreed Chris.

"We're almost there, so no more talking," said Seth.

"Roger that," said Chris as the three of them walked to the footpath where they knew Quentin and Bradley would soon be.

As they reached their hiding spot, the three of them took their positions on either side of the narrow pathway and assumed their concealed postures.

The boys never showed up. At twelve minutes passed their anticipated arrival time, Chris broke their silence.

"I don't think they're coming this way and we can't afford to wait much longer. Sunrise is in thirteen minutes. We need to leave or risk exposing ourselves."

"Wait. I hear someone talking . . . look over there . . . someone's coming," whispered Seth.

"Yeah, but there's three of them, and two of them aren't tall enough to be either of our targets," whispered Blake. "One of them is a female. See the skirt?"

Then Chris placed his index finger on his lips so Seth and Blake knew to stop the chatter.

They watched the trio approach, the female among them talking.

"I still can't believe Father didn't at least let us say goodbye to Bradley and Quentin. I understand why he couldn't tell us exactly *how* and *when* they were leaving for their safety, but now there is no telling when or if we'll *ever* see them again," complained Nicole.

"Get real. They've only gone to Scotland, not to Australia. They'll only be a few days boat ride away. We can visit them any time, once we are no longer required to keep their whereabouts a secret," said Chance.

"Yeah Nicole, you heard father, they had to leave under the cover of darkness because some really bad men are after them. It's the only way he could ensure their safety," said Spencer.

"I know . . . I know . . . but still, I would've liked to have said goodbye," pouted Nicole.

As soon as the kids were out of sight, Seth was the first to speak.

"Did you hear that? I can't believe it. After all of our careful planning we've been thwarted. They've trumped us. These simple people were able to make chumps out of us . . ."

"They didn't act alone," said Blake.

"I *hate* these Gordons. They've caused the only two blemishes on my otherwise spotless record. Both debacles happened on my watch. I can't let Rosen know I failed him again," said Chris.

"Chris, this isn't your fault. I was the point person on location, and I misjudged the situation," countered Seth.

"Both of you stop it. We don't have time for this. Let's get out of here. We only have seven minutes before dawn," said Blake.

The submarine was surprisingly plush, with décor similar to an elegant but windowless cabin cruiser, or so the boys thought until they reached the bridge area. From there they could see outside through a panoramic viewing port.

"This is great! You can see everything out there," exclaimed Quentin.

Upon hearing the excited voices of his guests, the boat's captain turned and said, "You must be Quentin Gordon, the younger of our two travelers. I'm Steve McGowan, but you can call me Captain Steve. It's nice to make your acquaintance. I have to tell you that I'm glad to have you safely onboard," said Captain Steve, sticking out his hand to shake hands with Quentin.

"And you must be Bradley. The Gordon family resemblance is uncanny," said Captain Steve, shaking Bradley's hand. "I knew your grandfather, Lord Robert Gordon, a good man."

"We're glad to be here," said Bradley. "Thank-you for having us . . . I mean, for *saving* us."

"It was touch and go for a few minutes there, because at the very time you were scheduled to return to the boat, the unlit vessel launched a RIB with two guys that we suspect to be spec op dudes on board. It looked to be heading your way. We thought we'd have to intervene, when much to our astonishment they modified their heading and aimed towards the northern port region—*phew*," said Captain Steve, pretending to wipe his brow. "We dodged a bullet."

"Well if you dodged a bullet, then we dodged a cannon ball," said Jay, as he retold their harrowing adventure with the Greenland shark, their unwelcome chaperone. Wilson animatedly contributed by recapping their narrow escape from the beast, everyone on the bridge chuckling.

"Sir, are we underway yet?" Bradley asked the captain.

"Not yet, son. We want to see what our kindred souls on the unlit vessel are doing out there before we leave the area," said Captain Steve.

And before Bradley could ask his next question, the boat's first mate called out, "Captain, the RIB is on its way back to the unlit vessel plus one, and when they left the shore, they didn't bother to execute any stealth maneuvers."

"Judging by what Jay and Wilson just told us, I suspect they're light two passengers—thanks to you two. Boy would I like to be a fly on the wall when they tell their boss," said Captain Steve. "Set course to Gordon Manor."

"Aye aye, Captain. Ahead full, one hundred and three degrees to port, destination Gordon Manor."

Once on board the unlit vessel, the *Uño*, Seth made the dreaded call via secure video conferencing.

"Hello, Rosen," said Seth, letting out a long sigh. "We have some bad news."

"I figured as much, since you waited until the appointed time to call me. What happened?"

"The boys are gone. They must have left port last night," said Seth.

"No, they didn't. We were monitoring the area and no boats came in or out from the island the entire night," reported Chris.

"No *surface* boats," said Rosen. "But since we're talking about the Gordons, they could've arrived and departed via submarine, one with stealth technologies. It would've been easy for them to take the boys off island right under your noses."

"Rosen, we'll go and get them. We'll send a team to the highlands as soon as possible. They won't be expecting us to be so bold," proffered Chris.

"What makes you so sure that they're heading here?" asked Rosen.

"The only *good* thing that happened was that we overheard the target's cousins complaining that they hadn't been able to give a proper sendoff to the boys before they left for Scotland," said Seth.

"Actually . . . while it would've made our lives much easier at first glance if you had been successful, your failed mission might turn out to be more of a blessing than a curse. *Yes*, I think it a prudent move for us," said Rosen, "yes indeed."

"How can this be a *good* thing?" Seth asked.

"Think about it. The Gordons will be full of themselves, believing they pulled one over on us, and that they now have the boys tucked away in a secret hiding place. They would be wrong on both counts. First of all, we know where their father is and where they're likely to hide them, and secondly, they're now located where we can readily access them without the interference of the magnetic anomalies of the Precaveros tribal lands and those of Celtston. These locations have hindered our abilities to effectively deal with this situation."

"*So*, even though the mission didn't go as planned, we still have some modicum of success to claim?" said Chris.

"Yes. As of today, we have tangible evidence that allows us to label Lord Robert Clifton Gordon's grandsons *Elusives*. Like father, like sons. They are openly defying the Veneré rules of engagement," proclaimed Rosen. Good day gentlemen and thank you for your service. You've done the *world* a great service."

ACKNOWLEDGMENTS

The Arcanum would not have been possible without The Bard of Machipongo, Ken Sutton, a noteworthy and accomplished poet and novelist who generously shared his extraordinary proficiencies with the subtleties of the American-English language during many coaching sessions while enjoying Fog Cutter coffee and an extra-toasted and buttered sesame seed bagel.

GLOSSARY OF TERMS

Arcania: A closed society located within the earth; the true Heaven.

Arcanians: The inhabitants of the center of the earth, they predate humans and are blessed with profound abilities, including living 400-plus Earth years.

Arcanums: Rare and exceptional humans who possess Arcanian level special abilities

Chivalran: A knighthood with principles and qualities of idealized bravery, courtesy, honor, and devotion. Tasked to protect the weak from those thought to be against the continuous progress of mankind's pursuit of improvement (or at least the improvement allowed by the Veneré). They are the defenders, champions, and zealous upholders of the Veneré beliefs.

Elusives: Arcanums hiding from the Veneré and eluding capture. Their abilities are undefined until they undergo the Kupellation. They are not considered a problem until proven otherwise, and then could be re-designated.

Enclave: Denotes Arcanum gatherings within Arcania that lie wholly within the boundaries of the interior of the earth, aka Heaven in Earth.

Humans: Also known as surface dwellers, they are de-evolved and mutated Arcanians inhabiting Earth's toxic surface environment.

Kupellation: The test that separates the precious from the mundane.

Surface of the Earth: Known as *Hell on Earth,* inhabited by humans.

Veneré: Honored above all, they are worthy of reverence by virtue of dignity, character, and position. They created a relationship of protection and partial control over humanity worldwide by their exceptional talents. They are charged with the melioration of mankind, the belief that society has an innate tendency toward improvement. The Veneré guard against all who would hinder this improvement and other menaces to human society.

Untethered: Elite Arcanians who interface with surface dwellers.

CPSIA information can be obtained
at www.ICGtesting.com
Printed in the USA
BVHW030331150820
586468BV00005B/19